Praise for *A Friend of the Family*

"Stunning . . . An unqualified success . . . Grodstein's sentences are finely made and precisely fitted to one another and her story . . . She has written a novel that will leave her reader sitting up, sifting the evidence in the dead of night."

—*The Boston Globe*

"A gripping novel . . . Told with great understanding and sensitivity, gripping readers so that they will find the book hard to put down."   —*Chicago Tribune*

"Horrifyingly plausible and deeply poignant . . . Will leave you shaken and chastened—and grateful for the warning."

—*The Washington Post Book World*

"What a wonderful and compelling read. This book is full of insights and honesty; you will have a hard time putting it down . . . Grodstein's skills at storytelling are unwavering."

—Elizabeth Strout, author of *Olive Kitteridge*

"A persuasive indictment of a certain kind of privileged narrow-mindedness . . . In the best tradition of parenting gone catastrophically awry."   —*O: The Oprah Magazine*

"Involving at every level: character, plot, language. One of the more complicated portraits of a father's love for his son we've ever read . . . Highly recommended."   —*McSweeney's*

"Suspense worthy of Hitchcock . . . This is less a novel about one imperfect citizen than a sharp account of the status-driven suburban culture that turned him into a monster of conformity." —*The New York Times Book Review*

"Grodstein's harsh, honest prose makes this haunting tale worthwhile." —*People*

"Spot-on in its depiction of affection and jealousy among longtime friends; boozy suburban bashes; unrequited love; and adjusting to middle age." —*USA Today*

"A gripping portrayal of a suburban family in free-fall . . . The structure of compromise and principle supporting a happy family is precariously perched to begin with, and in Grodstein's skilled hands love is an unstable element." —*Minneapolis Star Tribune*

"In her wonderful second novel, Grodstein traces a suburban crisis and gives especially perceptive attention to the father-son bond . . . An astute dissector of male aspiration, Grodstein brings great insight into a father's protective urge for his son in this gripping portrait of an American family in crisis." —*San Francisco Examiner*

THE EXPLANATION FOR EVERYTHING

WITHDRAWN

also by LAUREN GRODSTEIN

The Best of Animals

Reproduction Is the Flaw of Love

A Friend of the Family

The

EXPLANATION

for

EVERYTHING

a novel

LAUREN GRODSTEIN

ALGONQUIN BOOKS OF CHAPEL HILL 2013

Published by
ALGONQUIN BOOKS OF CHAPEL HILL
Post Office Box 2225
Chapel Hill, North Carolina 27515-2225

a division of
WORKMAN PUBLISHING
225 Varick Street
New York, New York 10014

This is a work of fiction. While, as in all fiction, the literary
perceptions and insights are based on experience, all names,
characters, places, and incidents either are products of the
author's imagination or are used fictitiously.

LIBRARY OF CONGRESS CATALOGING-IN-PUBLICATION DATA
Grodstein, Lauren.
The explanation for everything : a novel /
Lauren Grodstein.—First edition.
pages cm
ISBN 978-1-61620-112-8
I. Title.
PS3607.R63E97 2013
813'.6—dc23   2013014957

10 9 8 7 6 5 4 3 2 1
First Edition

For Ben and Natey,
again and always

THE EXPLANATION FOR EVERYTHING

ONE

The first time Andy met Louisa, she was covered in blood. He was a bit bloodied himself, having just suffered a minor bicycle accident where Nassau intersects with Mercer and nobody can see himself coming or going. It was a Sunday morning in 1994, and Andy was wearing the ridiculous clothing he'd let himself get talked into by the cute salesgirl at Kopp's, purple spandex shorts — "junk-huggers!" Rosenblum hooted — and a black and silver nylon shirt. Anyway, he'd been daydreaming, yes, but he was reflexively careful at that intersection. And then an Audi out of nowhere, some cursing, an unnecessary ambulance, and now here he was, cradling what was almost certainly a broken wrist and thinking about his dissertation and the way the Mercer County emergency room smelled like urine and paint. The orange plastic chair was hard under his butt; his bicycle-friendly spandex shorts offered no padding whatsoever.

Then, as CNN began to rotate through yet another story on O.J. Simpson, this girl sat down next to him, hair trailing down her shoulders and around her face, the most magnificent sample of human hair he'd ever seen. Brown and gold streaks and some blond in there too, curls and waves, like in a magazine. The face wasn't bad either, as far as he could tell from profile: a nice curve of the cheek, a slightly oversized, bumpy nose, a full mouth. But it was that hair he couldn't stop looking at. He had the absurd compulsion to stick his hands in it, and was grateful to his probably broken wrist for stopping what would have otherwise been a sure breach of etiquette.

She was not looking at him. Her left hand was wrapped in red-stained gauze, and she had blood on her white T-shirt, and blood on her jeans.

"What are you here for?" he asked. The question was absurd, but he felt that if he talked to her, he would almost certainly not stick his good hand in her hair, or, if he did, conversation would offer him an opportunity to first ask permission.

She turned her head. The face was prettier straight on than it was in profile, nice eyes, the shape of almonds, and irises the color of almonds too, and the bumps in the nose receded as a matter of perspective. She had small, shell-like ears, each one rimmed with stud earrings. She smiled. "I cut myself."

"Right," he said. She smiled at him again, and for the first time since the Audi, he didn't think, even obliquely, about his wrist. "How so?"

"Opening a can of caviar. Isn't that ridiculous? I think I cut a cephalic vein. The shit will *not* stop bleeding." She looked down at her bandaged arm, sighed heavily.

"A cephalic vein, huh?" he said. "Interesting." Here Andy was thinking of the Latin word *cephalicus* and trying to show off. "Isn't that a vein in your head?"

"Your arm," she said, holding out hers. It was a thin, freckled arm, finely covered with reddish gold hairs, except for the part that was wrapped in reddening gauze.

"But cephalization is the formation of neural structures in the head." He knew this from his biology training. "So that doesn't make any sense, that it would be in your arm."

"And yet it is."

"But that doesn't make sense." Why was he fighting with her? "Are you a biologist?"

She shook her head. "I'm actually a nurse," she said. "In Philly. Which is too bad, because if I were in Philly I'd probably get some kind of professional courtesy. But of course I have to cut myself in Princeton, where nobody knows me. And so," she said, grandly, "I wait."

"Was it really a can of caviar?"

"Who would make that up?"

"Does it hurt?"

"No worse than your wrist," she said, looking at the wrist he was cradling. Her gaze was pointed; his wrist was in his lap. Andy crossed his legs. Oh, these ridiculous bicycle shorts!

"How long do you think I'm going to wait, anyway?" she asked, raising her almond-colored eyes.

"I've been here since eight thirty."

"Christ," she said. "It's almost noon."

"Is it?" Could he say to her that time stopped the second he first caught sight of her and her hair? She leaned back against the chair, closed her eyes. She had long black lashes, thick like a paintbrush. She breathed in and out deeply, as though she were a person preparing to sleep. Andy hadn't spent time with a woman with anything like regularity in months. Most of his friends in the department were male, and Rosenblum, of course, and even the plurality of his students. How nice it was, he thought, to talk to a woman! To this beautiful woman!

"What are you doing in Princeton?" he asked, even though she gave no indication she wanted to keep talking.

"Boyfriend," she said, her eyes still closed.

"Oh," Andy said. He did not feel dejected, because he had never considered himself an actual candidate to become this woman's boyfriend; the fact that she already had one couldn't be a deterrent from a position he had never considered occupying. How could he ever be this woman's boyfriend? The women Andy dated were severe, prone to nervous breakdowns over their studies. When they cut themselves, it was usually on purpose. "Where is he now?"

"He had to study. He's got his math orals coming up."

"So he just dropped you here?"

"I know, right?" She opened her eyes. "It's probably time to get a new boyfriend."

But before Andy could follow that tantalizing lead—what kind of new boyfriend and where would you go looking for this new boyfriend?—a woman with a clipboard appeared in the doorway to the examining room. "Waite? Andrew Waite?"

He stood.

"Is she telling you to wait?" the woman said. Lou. Lou asked him this. She was sitting up again, and the gauze around her wrist looked ever darker with blood, and he wanted to pick her up and carry her off to a better place or, at the very least, give her his place in line.

Instead, he said, "That's my last name. Waite."

"Oh," she said.

"Do you want my turn?"

She smiled at him again, gently, as though he were a fool.

"You look like you're in worse shape than I am," he said in a rush. "Seriously. I'll be fine. You should take my turn, you're bleeding to death."

She shook her head and a curl of that hair fell into her face. "That's nice," she said. "Thank you, that's really nice, but you should go ahead. I'm not going to die."

Andy felt himself heartened by this. This girl wasn't going to die. Louisa—he did not yet know she was Louisa—said she wasn't going to die. And he did not yet know that he shouldn't believe her.

"Okay," he said, and followed the beckoning of the woman with the clipboard, and when he turned to look at her one more time, she winked at him, and he was fairly certain he blushed back. He wished once more that he was wearing a different pair of shorts.

HANK ROSENBLUM, ANDY'S friend, mentor, and guide to all things masculine, who had been divorced four times yet paradoxically considered himself an expert on women, said that she had just been looking to flirt. In Rosenblum's opinion, women who said, "I probably need a new boyfriend" to the goobers breathing down their necks in emergency rooms were almost certainly just looking for a little affirmation, but still, he said, there was no reason Andy couldn't keep an eye out. In fact, Rosenblum said, if she had a boyfriend in the math department, he'd be happy to do a little spying on Andy's behalf. Although Rosenblum himself was a member of Princeton's biology department, he had a few friends in math he liked to hit up for statistical models every so often. Further, the mathematicians enjoyed a garden behind their building where a man could smoke a pipeful of tobacco in peace. Rosenblum liked to spend time there, identifying flowers with a pipe in his mouth. He fancied himself a gentleman horticulturist.

"So?" Rosenblum said, as Andy delivered a stack of graded papers—papers he'd graded painstakingly with his uninjured left hand. "You want me to find her for you?"

"I don't know," he said. "She's got a boyfriend."

"So that's it? You let her go?" Rosenblum was sitting amid the educated squalor of his office, files everywhere like the aftermath of a ticker tape parade, books on every surface, dead plants, a dead terrarium, an empty aquarium, an empty ashtray, and the detritus of his life as a celebrity: T-shirts, posters, and pins emblazoned with his face over the title of his most recent bestseller, *Religion's Dangerous Lie*.

Andy leaned back against Rosenblum's doorframe. He was already itching under his cast, and the thing was supposed to stay on for six more weeks. "I don't think I ever had her, Hank. I don't see how I can let her go."

Rosenblum raised his crazed eyebrows. "Well, for chrissakes, Andrew, sit down. Didn't your mother ever teach you it's rude to stand in people's doorways? Or don't people know that in Ohio?"

This was part of Rosenblum's cosmology—that Andy was a fatherless rube from the sticks (greater Cleveland) who needed a sophisticate like Rosenblum (who hailed from the most Jewish precincts of Brooklyn) to show him the ways of the world. Andy was one in a line of students to whom Rosenblum had taken a liking, cooked dinner for ("You ever try ahi tuna? No, idiot, it doesn't come from a can"), poured wine for, tried to train not only as a biologist but as a certain kind of bon vivant, one attuned to the pleasures of the world as much as the wonders of the microscope. Andy had proven himself a keen student—Rosenblum's major requirement, in a mentee, was that he be both bright and a touch sycophantic—and the fact that he was from Ohio, of all places, made Rosenblum that much more interested in Andy's transformation. "Ohio!" he would hoot, apropos of little. "Is there any state more depressingly nowhere than *Ohio*? Has anything great ever happened in Ohio? To anyone from Ohio? In the whole history of Ohio?"

"Paul Newman?" Andy would offer. "Neil Armstrong?"

"Hollywood!" Rosenblum would counter, self-righteous. "The moon!"

Rosenblum liked to take Andy out to eat on occasion at the finest restaurants in central New Jersey ("Which of course is like swimming on the finest beach in Siberia, but what can we do?") and took him to J. Press for a decent suit to wear to the Gene and Genome convention in Chicago ("We'll charge it to the department," Rosenblum said, rakishly, although Andy suspected he'd paid for it himself).

And of course, amid all this Pygmalion bustle, Rosenblum oversaw Andy's biology training. Andy was interested in gene theory, and Rosenblum, one of the premier American evolutionary biologists of his generation, guided Andy's research through generations of mice and endlessly revised papers. It was with Rosenblum that Andy published his first research, and it was under Rosenblum's careful supervision that Andy devised his dissertation thesis around the relationship between specific brain structures and specific degenerative conditions.

And it was under Rosenblum that Andy became an avowed and devoted atheist, seeking out, like his mentor, the superstitious gaze of the Believer wherever it roamed and staring it down in an unlosable game of chicken.

"Listen, my young friend," Rosenblum said, flicking something invisible from his cuff before turning his attention back to Andy's pathetic figure slumping into the seat opposite him. "Don't be a schmuck. This beautiful girl gives you an opening, you can't just let her go."

"It really wasn't such a great opening. And anyway, when I left the ER she was gone."

"So? You can't get a nurse to give you her records? Find out her address?"

"Hank, come on."

"You said she's a nurse in Philly. Did she tell you where?"

"Obviously if she had I would know where to look for her."

"Then we're going to have to go through the boyfriend," Rosenblum sighed. He'd put on weight in the years since Andy had met him, sat like a half-bald Buddha behind his rosewood desk. "This boyfriend's in math, you said? Okay, we'll start with math."

"We?"

Rosenblum couldn't help himself—so loving, so pushy. "I can see who's administering the bastard's orals. Maybe we can fail him. You want me to fail him? A few people in math owe me favors."

"Jesus, Hank." Rosenblum was like that too—sneaky and morally unhinged. "I can ask around myself."

"Fine," he said. "Be that way." He shifted the stack of papers Andy had delivered, the ones he would never read. "But don't let her go, Andrew. How old are you, twenty-four? I had been married twice by the time I was twenty-four."

"That's not true."

"I was a father several times over."

"That's not true either."

"Get out of here," Rosenblum said. "I'm sick of you. Men like you, sensitive men. Really, you make me sick." But Rosenblum was smiling.

"Thanks, Hank. That's good of you."

"I mean it," said Rosenblum. "Get out of here. Go find your girl."

Which turned out to be much easier than snooping around the math department, not that Andy didn't snoop around the math department and its rose bushes, or dream up ways of stealing her ER records, or imagine combing Princeton's colonial avenues in search, Rapunzel-like, of a flash of that beautiful hair.

But none of this was necessary, because two weeks after first crossing her emergent path, there she was, in front of the Record Exchange, bending down to tie a shoe. He realized that since he'd been expecting to see her everywhere, he wasn't surprised when he finally did. She was wearing a jacket but a bandage peeked out from under it, enclosing her left hand. His own wrist itched madly. There she was, his girl, a fellow veteran from an imaginary war.

"Hey!" he said. "Hey!" He tried to tone down his grin but it was impossible, he was too happy, she was too lovely—and standing right there.

"Mr. Waite," she said. "Hello." She remembered his name! And she was smiling too. She gathered her hair back in her good hand and pushed it off her shoulders, but it immediately breezed back around her face. "I was wondering if I'd bump into you again."

"Visiting your boyfriend?"

"Walking to the train."

"You're going to walk?"

She sighed, kicked one of the bags at her feet. "He failed his orals. He's moving to New Mexico. I'm not going with him." She looked embarrassed. "So I think," she said, "that's the end of that. And therefore," grandly, "I walk."

"Ah," Andy said. He wanted to take this in but again that lunatic desire to plunge his hands into the depths of her hair (and this time, now, to cradle her face, to kiss her pillow-soft lips. Man, he was itchy). Had Rosenblum fixed this for him? The boyfriend's failure? He'd send him a box of cigars. "I'm sorry."

"Thanks," she said. She had a huge duffel bag and a roller suitcase. A lot of stuff. "It's probably fine. I mean, I think we'll both end up fine. And I need to spend more time in Philly anyway. Not that there's anything so great about Philly. But it is, you know, where I'm supposed to be working."

"I like Philly," he said. They grinned at each other again, stupidly. "What's your name, anyway?"

"I'm Louisa," she said.

"That's pretty."

"It is," she said. "But you should call me Lou."

AND FROM THERE, it was easy. He felt, in fact, that the ease was his reward for everything that had been so hard from the beginning: escaping Ohio, finding a place at Princeton, finding a few friends, finding Rosenblum. Putting together a life for himself, learning to cook and clean and look after himself and live like a grown-up with no one but Rosenblum to show him the way, to help him figure out what mattered. He walked Lou to the train, hefting her duffel bag with his good hand down the bumpy side street to the jitney.

"How do I find you again? If you're not coming back to Princeton?"

"You call me," she said, making it sound like an instruction. He called her. She called him back. That easy. They were married at the Princeton Faculty Club in front of forty people a year later, her parents from Arizona, his mother from Ohio. Rosenblum did the officiating, which was a service he provided to all comers so that no man would be forced to interact with clergy in order to participate in a state institution, like marriage.

Lou promised she would nurture him. Andy promised he would take care of her for the rest of her days. They honeymooned in Paris, he wrote his dissertation in their tiny studio in Philadelphia, and once he was officially Dr. Waite, they moved to Miami for his postdoc. There, she worked twelve-hour shifts in the NICU of Kendall Regional. He performed EEGs on rats. At night, in the air-conditioned haven of their moderately priced apartment in Quail Run ("Whence the quail?" she would ask. "Where do they run?") they would lie together in their bed and imagine their future children.

TWO

Twelve years later: two children, a tenure-track job at a small liberal arts college in southern New Jersey, an office with a geriatric computer and a parking-lot view. A basement lab. Three dozen mice. No Lou.

He had never grown used to her absence, but he had learned to endure it, and to ignore her ghost, who was often waiting for him around the corner, or behind him in the office when he thought he was alone. He used to talk to her; during his first several years in New Jersey he talked to her several times a day. She would smirk or nod or roll her eyes, as expressive in death as she had been in life. When he said something to her she didn't believe, she would laugh silently. But when he told her, "I like it here, Lou, and I'm doing okay," she didn't laugh, even though he was lying. When he told her, "I guess I'll stay here for the rest of my life," and looked up to meet her eyes, he found her looking away, and then disappearing, a magic trick.

Would he stay here for the rest of his life? He supposed he would, if he got tenure. And this was where he thought about what Rosenblum often told him about tenure: it's like a prison in all the bad ways—you know where you'll be stuck for the rest of your life—but in the good ways too, since you'll always know where your next meal's coming from. He had filed his paperwork just before he took off for the summer. It had felt, in some small way, like resignation.

Still, he did enjoy his reputation as a campus provocateur. On the first day of the fall 2011 semester, a September-ish breeze blowing in his hair, Jackson Browne on the radio ("Doctor My Eyes"), it was pleasant to imagine himself a seasoned academic off to raise undergraduate hackles at the dawn of a bright new school year. Sure, yes, everything would be all right. There was a crease in his Dockers, a glimmer in his eye as he drove his girls to school. "You're teaching There Is No God, huh?" Rachel asked when he dropped them off.

"How did you know?"

"You're whistling."

His morning class, colloquially called There Is No God (Special Topics in Evolutionary Biology: Ethics and Debate, Course B:413), was one he taught every third semester, subject to demand. It was a distillation of a similar course Hank Rosenblum had originated at Princeton, but whereas the Princeton course drew consternation, even controversy, the Exton Reed version was delivered to students who were happy to swallow whatever they were fed. Which, in this case, was a big bowl of Darwinian theory spiced with a few contemporary major thinkers: Dawkins; Dennett; Rosenblum, of course (who, despite his downfall, was still considered a player in the evolution game). The students were generally seniors, most of whom had no particular feeling for or against Darwin. The hard-core religious types, the Campus Crusaders for Christ, tended to stay away, although occasionally a few of them would infiltrate for purposes of either changing Andy's mind or reminding their classmates that fellowship and pizza were available in the campus center Thursday evenings from seven to nine.

At a larger school, a research-oriented biologist like Andy almost certainly wouldn't be allowed to teach a course like this; it would be given to a social scientist or an evolutionary theorist. But at Exton Reed, eleven hundred students and forty-two acres of crumbling quad hidden in the ass end of New Jersey, there was nobody else even interested in teaching There Is No God, much less capable of it. The other members of his department included a seventy-year-old microbiologist, a politically rowdy ornithologist, a grumpy botanist, and a fashionable ecologist who taught the department's global warming seminar with appropriate hysteria. The five of them rotated through the teaching of biology's academic cornerstones: the 101, 102, 201 rotation required to get kids into med school or master's programs. They hired adjuncts to oversee labs. They kept boxes of dead frogs and fetal pigs in the cafeteria's deep freezer. They rarely socialized.

At 8:17, Andy pulled into the faculty parking lot, collected his briefcase, straightened his tie. He was still whistling. He was glad to be getting on with things. He had forced himself, this summer, to try to relax—his tenure paperwork was in, after all, and he knew his file looked good: three conference papers, two published articles, a mini-grant from the New Jersey Institute of Research Science. Possible important progress with his mice. So now all he could do was wait until April for the board's final decree. Yet although he'd planned to spend his summer reading historical biographies and camping with his girls, he found himself, by July, prone to long bouts of desolation. He worried constantly about what he'd do without tenure, tried to come up with Plan Bs. He could teach at a high school (even though the thought of high school students made him fearful and exhausted). He could work in someone else's lab (but whose?). He could use the hours the girls were at school to obsessively clean the house.

But now, as the campus shifted into new-semester gear, Andy found himself crossing its weedy gravel pathways with optimism, almost delight. He stopped in the campus center for a cup of coffee and became immersed in unusually nimble chitchat with the barista, the janitor, a student who looked familiar but whose name he couldn't place. By the time he opened the door to his fourth-floor office in Scientific Hall, he felt almost—yes, there it was—he felt cheerful.

Louisa's ghost nodded her greeting to him as he opened the

door. He had expected to see her, but he said nothing to her, and soon enough she shimmered away.

EXTON REED WAS small, but also perversely over-crowded; as a result, there was nowhere to teach There Is No God but the tiny seminar room on the top floor, the fifth floor, of Scientific Hall, searingly hot and serenaded by the whoosh of the building's plumbing, as a network of drainpipes ran across the ceiling. Scientific Hall, like most of Exton Reed's buildings, dated from the 1950s, when the smell of GI profits convinced the trustees of the Exton Ladies' Institute of Reed Township to transform their small, underfunded finishing school into a small, underfunded liberal arts college. Scientific Hall went up in the northeast corner of the quad, where it stood opposite the campus center and freshman dorms; in the adjacent corner hulked Carruthers, the humanities building, named for Exton Reed's major donor, the Carruthers family of Carruthers Cranberry. In the middle of the quad stood an oversized statue of Henrietta Exton, who founded the Exton Ladies' Institute at the end of the eighteen hundreds. Inscribed on the statue's pedestal were several inspirational themes and quotations translated into Latin, including the campus's motto, ABOVE ALL, RHETORIC, which only Andy seemed to find amusing.

The campus itself was ringed by parking lots and the bait-and-tackles and convenience stores of Reed Township, whose Main Street offered, for entertainment purposes, a single-screen movie theater and a bar called the Library. Anyone who wanted something better could drive to Philadelphia, forty-five minutes away, but most kids simply skipped town on the weekends to visit their boyfriends or do their laundry back home.

Already parched and overheated in the far reaches of Scientific Hall, Andy hung his blazer on the back of his chair and wrote his introductory statements on the blackboard.

1: Evolution is the explanation for everything

2: Darwin is right

3: And people who don't believe Darwin are wrong

Then he wiped the dust off his hands (Christ, was it too much to ask for a PowerPoint setup?) and sat down to wait for his students. A few minutes before nine, they started to trickle in, already bored-looking, some wearing clothing they had probably slept in. Andy didn't begrudge them. Twenty years ago, during his own undergraduate days at Ohio State, he once went two weeks without changing clothes on a tendollar dare.

A few of them nodded at him as they took their seats; others, eager to show how little they cared, took out their iPhones and started fiddling. Eight women, four men (on par with the campus 2:1 ratio) and then, in a last-minute dash through the door, Lionel Shell, in a Rick Santorum sweater-vest and the kind of glasses whose lenses turned dark when you stood in the sun.

"Professor," Lionel Shell said, crisply. He was a skinny devout Christian from rural Delaware who had taken the course three semesters ago as a sophomore, and who had spent those fourteen weeks alternately glowering at Andy and raising his hand with a passion that dragged him halfway across his desk.

"I got special permission from the registrar to take this again for credit," Lionel said. "Before you give me any grief."

"On what grounds?"

"On the grounds that I'm writing a response paper to this course that will change the university's position on letting you teach atheism every other year."

"Are you now?" Andy said, outwardly civil, inwardly delighted. When Rosenblum taught this course at Princeton, he had jackoffs like Lionel every other seminar (Andy, who served as his reader/grader, remembered them all). He had always found it a little disappointing that his own course engendered such mild protest, so much acquiescence. "Well, that's great. I look forward to hearing what you come up with."

"And when I'm done, I'll be sending it to the Board of Trustees."

"Are you threatening me?" Andy suppressed a smile.

Lionel took off his glasses, cleaned them primly, slid them back on his face. "I just think this is an issue that deserves broader attention on campus. It's not personal."

"Well, I agree with you, Lionel, that issues of scientific ethics deserve broader airing on campus, and across the country."

"Indeed," said indomitable Lionel, refusing to fall for Andy's condescension. "Still, I think I'll be keeping an eye on you."

"I would expect nothing less," Andy said. He stood, eyed his students (the sloppy, the angsty, the covert nose-pickers) and launched into his spiel.

"Are you guys aware that of the eight major Republican candidates who ran for this year's nomination, six said publicly that they didn't believe in evolution?" He waited for gasps, and a few students, to their credit, did look faintly surprised.

"Did you know that 71 percent of Americans say that science is a matter of opinion, not fact? And 64 percent believe that God has a place in the scientific curriculum?"

They opened their notebooks, unsure whether or not class had already started. "Friends, I view this set of statistics as a national emergency (calling students "friends"—that was another move from the Rosenblum playbook). And by the way, Lionel, if you want to help me draw attention to these issues, I would welcome the help entirely. Believe me."

Lionel arranged his face into its glower.

"Now guys, before I hand out your syllabus, I'd like you all to take a moment to read the three statements I've written on the board." He gave them their moment. "Anybody have any questions? Objections?"

Predictable silence. "So who are you people, anyway?"

The thirteen went around the room clockwise, introducing themselves by name and major (seven biology, two English, three chemistry, and Lionel: an independently designed major in Public and Religious Discourse). As always, Andy attempted to link each name to a defining feature, a mole or a haircut; this was a memory-enhancing technique he kept trying but was never quite able to master. These students had all been born in the early nineties, a generation of Maxes and Hunters and Kaylas and Ariels. This particular group was an indistinct mix of Haleys and Jordans, and Andy forgot each name the minute a student said it. But he nodded at each of them and smiled, and most of them smiled back.

"So, as you all know, this is Special Topics in Evolutionary Biology: Ethics and Debate." Andy, per his shtick, let his introductory smile dissolve into a pissy little frown. "But listen, guys, I have to say, I'm rather interested in the fact that none of you seem to want to debate. Interested, and maybe even a little disappointed."

The students looked worried. They had already disappointed the professor. One of the Haleys put down her pen; another started frantically taking notes.

Andy walked the perimeter of the room. "I asked you if everybody would agree to the statement that people who don't agree with Darwin are wrong."

The class eyed one another, knowing they were being set up and resenting it already.

"Nobody said they would disagree with Darwin, and ordinarily this would make me happy. However, there are thirteen of you in this classroom, and twelve of you seem to agree with what I wrote on the board. But it is statistically radically unlikely that thirteen Americans in the year 2011—even twelve college students, even twelve thoughtful young people like yourselves—it is statistically very unlikely that each one of you accepts Darwinian evolution as the fundamental explanation for everything in the universe, from the way life expanded to fill every niche of habitable space on the planet to perhaps, as physicists are now proving, the universe itself."

A few of the students resumed note taking. A few others just looked annoyed. "Guys, Darwinian evolution explains everything about us," Andy said. "Everything."

He took a second to let this sink in.

"So what that means, of course, is that we do not need a supernatural explanation for life. We don't need God, or gods, or four turtles carrying the planet on their shells. We don't need the myths of religion. Americans, as a rule, don't appreciate this line of thinking. And your accents and presentation tell me that all of you are Americans. And yet each one of you agrees with this fundamental truth—that natural selection, not God, is responsible for the diversity of life on the planet. At least, that seems to be what you're telling me."

Now the students checked one another out to see who would crack first. After twenty seconds, nobody did.

"But I would imagine that deep down," Andy said, "at least some of you think that although maybe God didn't separate the land from the waters, specifically, he probably got this whole ball rolling, somehow, in a sort of deist sense. Or maybe you hold some kind of Bible-as-metaphor opinion that God might have taken more than seven days to do it, but still he had some hand in fashioning the lion, the lamb, etcetera. Am I right?"

A few of the students nodded. Lionel, of course, was already panting from the exertion of raising his hand.

"And some of you probably have some other ideas. Lionel, for instance."

"I believe that God created the universe in seven days," Lionel said, the words tumbling out. "I believe that God created man and woman, good and evil, and that the Bible is his living document, and that Genesis tells us the true story of creation, and without God there is no purpose or pleasure in our lives, but with him watching over us, we all have the opportunity to live lives that matter. Not just to ourselves, but to everyone. And I believe that—"

Andy cut him off with a hand. "Anybody agree with Lionel over here?"

A few Haleys, a Jordan, a Max or two tentatively nodded his head.

"Well," Andy said, distributing his syllabus, "I look forward to changing your minds."

LUNCH WAS COLD leftovers under the shade of a dogwood by the parking lot, then back to his office to hand his first-day-of-the-semester paperwork over to Rosemary, the department secretary.

"Going home? If you leave now, you'll be early for soccer." Rosemary knew him and his priorities.

"Just as soon," Andy said, "as I check on my friends downstairs."

In August, before he and the girls made their annual pilgrimage to Ohio, Andy had run a half-dozen spectrophotometer scans to confirm his thinking on the neuropeptide receptivity of certain members of his population. He needed a few more numbers to bulk up his grant application to the National Science Foundation (his very first such application: almost half a million dollars for new equipment, new animals, and perhaps a few postdocs of his own). At the previous year's Academic Biology conference he'd spoken to a few NSF reps, in vague but optimistic terms, of his research; they in turn encouraged him to apply for a midcareer grant, agreeing that his hypothesis seemed sound. "Of course," said one, "you'll need some solid numbers to get your hands on our money."

"Of course," Andy said. "I've got solid numbers."

"You do?"

"Very solid." And at this, everyone in the group chuckled as if at a familiar punch line, leaving Andy to look down at his loafers, embarrassed and unsure why.

The grant wasn't due until early spring, however, and if Andy had been perhaps overstating his results, inflating the solidity of his numbers for the NSF reps' appreciation, he should have enough time to run the data again and straighten out his hypothesis. The problem was that a significant number of his mice weren't necessarily behaving the way their brain scans predicted. Some mice who had been bred to drink until their neurons seized were, for mysterious reasons, drinking in moderation, while other mice, mice who should have always chosen water over wine, were sucking down ethanol like junkies. Maybe he had ordered the wrong mice, or screwed up his records? He'd start over with another batch as soon as it was delivered—but the concerns persisted. Mice with brain chemistries that suggested one way of acting were stubbornly acting another way, and for a few delirious moments Andy wondered if they were playing a practical joke on him.

Still his mood remained surprisingly buoyant until, on the third floor of the staircase, he was waylaid by a tubby undergraduate in an Exton Reed sweatshirt.

"Professor? Are you Professor Waite?"

Andy fought the urge to deny it. "Can I help you?"

"I need to talk to you about a project."

"You do?"

The girl nodded. She had wide eyes and wheat-colored hair, a poof of inexpertly cut bangs above a broad face.

"Well, listen, I have to head down to my lab right now, I don't have a lot of time. If you'd like to make an appointment—"

"I can walk with you."

Andy took a half step back. "Of course." So silently they

made their way down the concrete-block stairwell to the basement labs, and silently the girl waited while Andy fumbled with his keys, turned on the lights, and was greeted by the cheery squeak of various *Mus musculus* and the chemical funk of paraformaldehyde. The girl stood in the corner of the pale green lab and watched as Andy made his rounds from one cage to another, making sure none of his animals were seizing, making sure his hard-core alkies had enough ethanol in their bottles that they weren't going to start frothing from delirium tremens, assuming they acted like they were supposed to act.

"Professor?" said the girl in the corner.

Jamie, his tech, had taken good care of the mice since he'd last seen them, keeping their shavings fresh, their water bottles full, but still they seemed (Jesus, what was happening to him?) glad he was back. They squeaked amiably at his attentions.

"Professor Waite?"

Andy murmured to them softly as was his way, because by certain lights they were his closest colleagues, and sometimes it was hard not to get attached.

"Professor?" the girl said for the third time, softly, like a plea.

"I'm sorry," Andy said. "Yes, here we go." He tipped a dropperful of ethanol into a C56BL/6's cage, then made his way back to the front of the room, the tall black lab table, his stacks of notebooks of mouse pedigrees. "So how can I be of service?"

"I'm looking to do an important project," the girl said. "My name is Melissa Potter, and I'm a transfer student here, I just got my associate's degree. I'm really interested in doing this research, and then this guy I know, Lionel Shell, said you'd be the one to talk to, so—"

"Lionel said you should talk to me?"

"He said you were really nice."

"Did he now?" Andy said.

The girl looked at the floor; he'd embarrassed her. "He did."

Andy let the silence fester.

"Well anyway, he said you'd probably help me, and I'm really anxious to get this done, I need to take a lot of credits at once since I can't really afford to spend too many semesters here, so I . . . so . . ." Andy was flipping through his notebooks, marking down the dose of ethanol he had just doled out.

"So I was hoping . . ."

"You were hoping . . .?" He pivoted to look at her. She was fingering a gold cross she wore around her neck.

She stood up taller. "I was hoping you'd sponsor me for an independent study."

An independent study: a nightmare in all ways, especially bureaucratic. He ambled to a cage in the front of the room, peeked in, six mice dreaming happily of whatever mice dream of. "What would you like to design a study in, Melissa?"

The eyes back on the ground. She sucked on her cross for just a moment, then let it drop from her mouth. She said, "Intelligent design."

Andy stopped ambling.

Lionel had set him up.

Then again, without really thinking about it, Andy had been waiting for someone to mention intelligent design for years. But all he said to Melissa Potter was, "Excuse me?"

"I really wouldn't make it too much work for you to sponsor me, Professor Waite. I would do all the background research and find the textbooks and the scholarship," she said, quickly, for someone (he?) had already taught this young lady that not taking too much of a professor's time was paramount in getting one to agree to anything. "I just need someone in the sciences to sign the paperwork and help oversee my project."

"Melissa, I wish I could help you—" he said.

"Great."

"—But you should know that I'm a Darwinian. I teach a class some people call There Is No God. I'm not sure why Lionel would suggest that I—"

"He said you were smart," Melissa said. "Tough and smart. That you'd challenge me."

Flattery. Jesus. "Look, Melissa, intelligent design isn't a scientifically proven theory. You know that, right? Not only is it not proven, but it's not provable."

"Well, nothing is totally provable."

"Actually, some things," he said. "Some things are." He watched her heavy face crumple, then rearrange itself in an expression of fierce determination.

"But Darwinism is unprovable too, right?" she said. "It's

just a theory too—I mean they call it the theory of evolution, don't they?"

Ah, this old chestnut. "But when scientists use the word *theory*, they don't mean something that can't be explained. They call it the 'theory of gravity,' for instance, but the force of gravity isn't open to debate."

"So maybe there's another explanation for life on earth," Melissa said. "A better one than just natural selection or whatever kind of crap that is."

Natural selection or whatever kind of crap. Andy sighed: American education.

"I was thinking," she continued, "what you're doing in this lab is experimental. I mean your whole career is based on things that are experimental, isn't it? Isn't that what science professors do? So couldn't you help me design some kind of experimental system, some kind of curriculum, to help me prove that there was an intelligent force behind the creation of the planet? Just, like, an experiment? And then if it doesn't work then, whatever, at least we tried."

Andy sighed, ran a hand through his hair. He had spent the past five years at Exton Reed just, like, experimenting, trying to prove that the genetics of alcoholism lead to immutable behavior patterns. Something as basic as this—genes lead to behaviors—felt, at this moment, impossible to prove, felt like trying to prove that the Beatles were better than the Rolling Stones. Who could say for sure? Weren't there outlying examples? He had, for the past four years, overseen a small laboratory and a vivarium which stocked, at the moment, forty-two mice in varying shades of drunk. He clocked more hours with these mice than he did with almost anyone else in the world. And yet even they remained essentially mysterious to him, even after he cut them open and looked inside their brains. Four years and hundreds of mice and thousands of dollars and simple questions of behavior could not be solved, so how on earth did this girl want to solve the origins of life?

Or, to put it another way: how to explain to a girl like this the difference between that which could be quantified and that which could be taken only on faith?

Andy looked down at the glossy black lab table, saw his face reflected back. He was forty for a few more months, and looked exactly forty, exactly average, except for what might be thicker-than-average sandy-colored hair. He had blurry bags under his eyes. He no longer slept very well. He was haunted by a ghost.

"Melissa, I'm an advocate of student inquiry, I really am," he said, hearing himself retreat to pedantry, irritating even himself. "And if you'd like to inquire into the nature of God, I'm sure you can find a religion professor—"

"I don't want to inquire into the nature of God. That's what I do at church, not at school."

"Exactly."

"I want to study the origin of life, and that's something you study in the biology department."

"I suppose so," Andy said. "But I think it depends on the way you undertake the study."

"So you're saying you won't support my research," the girl said. Her voice was matter-of-fact, but she was slumping.

"Melissa," Andy said, "the thing about intelligent design is that there's no way to put the theory through the scientific method, so there's no way to say whether or not it's right or wrong. I can't support your research because there's no real research that can be performed on the subject. No way to apply the scientific method toward questions of intentionality in the design of the planet."

"So you won't sponsor me?"

The black-rimmed clock above his lab table clicked loudly toward 3:55. It would take him thirty minutes minimum to get to Rachel's practice, and he still had a few papers to file upstairs. Still, the look on this girl's face, disappointed, maybe even disgusted. Well. It was the first day of the semester. Would it kill him to try to be a little generous? To try to recapture just a bit of the optimism with which he'd arrived this morning?

"Let's brainstorm for a minute, Melissa. I bet we could come up with something else. Something we could try out in the lab—maybe we could even do a little experiment with the mice. Would that work for you?"

"No," she said.

Andy forced himself not to sigh. The clock ticked again, as was its irregular habit.

"Intelligent design," said the girl, "or nothing," and first Andy wanted to punch her, but then, regarding her stubborn expression, felt curiously and briefly cheered. A determined student! Well, good on her. Also he thought, fuck this, he had to get out of there, he needed to prep for tomorrow's undergraduate onslaught, and he wanted to see his daughter's practice, but Melissa looked so grim, so enormous with steely grimness, that despite himself he pulled out the stool from behind his lab table and with a chivalrous hand gesture invited her to sit down.

"There are so many issues concerning evolution that scientists haven't even begun to fathom, Melissa. I feel certain there's something you'd find interesting if you just agreed to look."

She shook her potato-shaped head. "I have a question for you, Professor Waite."

He noted that her eyes were surprisingly light, a greenish gray.

"There are two ways to see the world, right?" she said. "I mean, there are probably many more than two ways, but what I'm asking you here is to imagine two ways of looking at the world."

"Two ways," Andy said, neither frustrated nor hurried. "Fine."

"There's *your* way," she said, "where everything is accidental, where the fact that the earth tilts on an axis, the fact that it has a moon to control the tides, the fact that it is just the exact distance from the sun to keep us warm without boiling us alive—and even more than that, the fact that we're here, the fact that we love each other and protect each other, is all an accident of timing and chemicals."

"That's my way?"

"Yes," Melissa said. "That is your way, because that is the way of Darwin, which says that we are no more important, no more intentional, than the dust on your desk. We might as well be like your caged mice for all the agency we have in the grand scheme of things."

"All right," Andy said, neither aggravated nor impatient.

"But here's your other option. A world in which life has purpose," Melissa said. "God put us here for a reason, and that reason is out in the world for us to discover. There's a reason we can see stars in the sky. There's a reason we can dig into the crust of the earth and find out what came before us. There's a reason we were given the kinds of brains that would further your . . . scientific inquiry. There's a reason for life. There's a design behind it."

Andy did not look at the clock. "I see what you're saying, Melissa, but that's not a binary I'm comfortable with."

"Your world is the world of coincidence, of meaninglessness. You choose the world that would have us as specks of dust, as mice in a cage. Is that the kind of world you want to live in, Professor Waite?"

Andy took a breath.

"Professor?"

He hated these rushes of memory, these forces that sucked him in like dark matter at the least convenient times, shattering him. But there he was, out of the shabby lab in the basement of Scientific Hall and instead in Miami, the apartment in Miami, four lushly carpeted and heavily air-conditioned rooms. It was night, and Lou, hugely pregnant with Belle, was lying down next to Rachel in her big-girl bed. Reading *Richard Scarry's Best Word Book Ever.* Giggling together. Louisa's belly rising up and down.

Specks of dust, dust to dust. Andy blinked his eyes, hard. He came back to where he was.

"Professor?" Melissa tried again. "Is that what you want?"

"It's not," Andy said. "But I've realized over the years that what I want doesn't really matter either way."

"But that's not true," Melissa said. "You get to decide what you want and you get to decide what really matters."

The chill from the air-conditioning had made the hair on his arms stand up. For a moment, he lost his head. "Melissa, if you can come up with a reading list I approve of, I'll do your independent study."

"I can do that," she said, cheerfully. "That's no problem."

"But you should know I'm going to include some scientists I believe in. Henry Rosenblum, you heard of him?"

"You want me to read Henry Rosenblum?"

"Lots of him," Andy said. "Dawkins too. Those are my conditions."

Why he was bothering with conditions at all he wasn't entirely sure, but if he was going to jump through hoops for her, then he would make her do the same for him.

Melissa sighed. "Do you think there's anyone else in the bio department who will take my project on?"

"I'd be shocked," Andy said. "In fact, I'd be shocked if there was anyone else in the department who would ever let you finish a sentence about intelligent design." She fingered her cross. "So are you willing?"

"I guess I have no choice," Melissa said.

"Not if you're serious about this study."

"Okay," Melissa said. She hoisted her backpack over her shoulders and galumphed out of his basement laboratory. Andy watched her go, listened to her heavy footsteps. She didn't even have the courtesy to say thanks.

He returned to his drunken mice, dreaming their placid, inebriated dreams. He reached in and scratched one on the nose; like a bum, or one of his daughters, it seemed to snort before it rolled over. Poor mice. They were the only animals whose alcoholism he was able to forgive—he knew the genetics behind it, after all—and he often found himself envying them their single-minded devotion to drinking, and their peace.

. . .

EVERY YEAR, ANDY took his girls out for ice cream on the first day of the semester, because the first day of the semester usually coincided with the last day of the season at Curley's, the custard stand at the end of Deborah Boulevard. The girls had been planning their ice cream orders all week, and refined them as they cut across the park to Curley's.

"I'm having a caramel–peanut butter sundae with M&M's," said Belle, who was eight and prone to overkill. "Or maybe banana fudge with M&M's. Dad, if I get banana fudge will you get caramel?"

"What you're getting is type 2 diabetes," said ten-year-old Rachel. She tossed her long hair. "I'm getting a frozen banana. You should too, Tubs."

"Don't call your sister Tubs," Andy said, even though Tubs had been Belle's nickname until just this past year.

"Whatever. Eat a banana. I'm getting a sundae." In unison, the three hopped over a marshy puddle at the edge of Memorial Park.

A small crowd had gathered under Curley's flashing neon sign, gravely licking their cones. Andy recognized most of the faces: kids from his girls' classes, Joe who ran the pizza place down the block, and his neighbor, Sheila Humphreys, who was probably his closest friend in this town, even though they rarely spent more than an hour or two together at a time. Sheila was a single mother whose son was in Belle's class, and who invited him over for dinner sometimes, or who joined them for pizza at Joe's. Sometimes he changed her oil for her; sometimes she watched his girls on the weekends.

"You guys still coming over tomorrow night?" Sheila asked, in lieu of hello. She popped the last of a cone into her mouth. She had a spot of something greenish on her chin.

"Sure," Andy said, even though it took him a moment to remember what she was talking about. Oh, sure—a few weeks ago she had invited him over for a "celebration," which was both kind and perplexing. What were they celebrating? "Oh, you know," Sheila had said. "The start of a new semester. New school years for the kids. Jeez, Andy, can't a woman just celebrate every so often?"

Andy had acquiesced, even though the idea made him antsy; he worried that after dinner was over he'd owe her something, more energy or kindness.

"Dad! C'mon, Dad, it's our turn to order," said Belle, pulling on his sleeve.

"How was your first day of school?" Sheila asked.

"It was . . . adequate. The mice behaved."

"Did they miss you while you were gone?"

"I think one of them might have had a seizure."

"Ah," Sheila chuckled. "That's how you know it's love."

"I'm sorry?"

"When someone has a seizure," Sheila said. "That's how you know he really loves you."

She laughed, so Andy did too, even though he wasn't entirely sure he understood the joke. "So what should I bring tomorrow?"

"Bring? Bring yourselves," Sheila said. "Your girls. I'm making seafood stew. Will everyone eat that?"

"Dad!"

"Sounds great," Andy said, even though he had no idea whether his girls would eat seafood stew. "We'll be there."

"It's been so long since I've had a real dinner party!" Sheila said. Her son, Jeremy, was working intently on his chocolate soft-serve, forming concentric circles in its surface with his spoon. "I'm excited."

"So are we."

"Oh my God, Dad, you're holding up the line!"

"I'll let you go," Sheila said. "I'll see you tomorrow." And then she put a hand on Jeremy's back and led him toward the boulevard, away from Curley's. The boy was still staring into his ice cream. And Andy felt an odd sense of wanting to start that conversation over again, even though he had no idea what he'd say differently. He paid for the girls' ice cream and banana, and then stood where Sheila had just been standing over a few dribblings of green, looking out into the darkness where she'd disappeared.

THREE

He wrote his letters at five thirty in the morning, a habit generated from fury. Five thirty in the morning was an angry time to
be awake, always dark, always punishing; Andy would always
rather be doing something else. What would a normal man
do at this spiteful hour? Sleep, he supposed, but if sleep were
impossible then maybe the normal man would jog or read or
make a big pot of coffee or have sex with his wife. In Andy's
old life he might have done any of these things. Instead, he
was up at five thirty on a perfectly good Friday, a day when he
could have slept until seven.

He made coffee, turned on the radio, turned off the radio,
listened to the blackbirds sing outside.

A letter a day. Andy told himself he could stop whenever
he wanted to—it was just that so far he had never wanted to
stop.

Dear Mr McGee:

The semester started yesterday and with it came the usual dread: I wasn't prepared, my students wouldn't like me, I wouldn't like my students. I've been teaching for twelve years and much about the job has become worse, but sometimes I wonder if it's the students who are worse or if it's me. Not that the students of twelve years ago were demonstrably more intelligent than today's but there's a kind of focus, I think, that's gone missing. Twelve years ago a student couldn't download porn during class time. (In my current students' defense, however, twelve years ago their counterparts still had a future to prepare for. Now they move back to their parents' houses with their heads held high.)

Anyway, as both you and I have learned, McGee, time insists on marching on, so regardless of how I would prefer to spend the next several months I will spend the bulk of them on campus, droning at students who will try to tune in and eventually tune out, shifting piles of paper, counting the stink bugs that have gathered in my office since we went to Ohio this past August. The tech took decent care of the mice while I was away, but still I'm going to have to start doing scans again this week if I want to get my grant in on time.

(Incidentally, McGee, I know I mentioned this to you in a previous letter, but it bears repeating that my drunks have a detectably lower level of neuropeptide Y in their brains, which has, I believe, increased their tendency toward alcoholism. Perhaps this neuropeptide factor will be manipulated medically one day to some pharma's great profit. Unfortunately that day will be too late for you, McGee, and of course too late for me.)

The girls are still asleep, thank goodness—lately Belle's been having nightmares and insisting I sleep next to her, or, worse, climbing into Rachel's bed and then both of them are groggy and annoyed the next day. As I've mentioned to you many times, it's not easy being a single father, but the task seems infinitely harder when the girls are sniping at each other over issues of purloined sweatshirts and ugly hairdos, which is what they do when they're overtired. Belle seems unable tell me what her nightmares are about. She is usually very articulate and so naturally this has me worried, as do the nightmares.

But they remain asleep for the moment, and I can hear the crickets going outside. It still stuns me that this is where I live and that Lou has never seen this house.

A neighbor told me she spied a black bear rooting through her garbage the other day, which made me think I better start buying tighter lids for our garbage cans, maybe even one of those steel cages. This was another thing I never had to worry about in Florida. But it's almost autumn again, and that's when the animals get hungry. What would I do if I saw a bear, McGee? Would I have the guts to shoot?

(McGee, rest easy: I don't even own a gun).

Another way I can measure how time passes—seven years already—is that Rachel has started looking so much like Lou did in her twenties. Her hair is getting a little darker, like Lou's was, and sometimes she makes these faces—when she's confused, she narrows her eyes just like her mother did. I've been looking at pictures, just to see. I have some pictures where Rachel could be Lou's little sister. It's creepy, or perhaps it's just genetics.

Anyway, right now I need some coffee, and then I suppose I should start prepping next week's classes. I have dry cleaning to pick up. And your parole hearing is this January. I haven't booked my tickets, but my mother has agreed to come watch the girls while I'm away, which is a start.

In the meantime, I remain,

Your faithful correspondent,
Andy Waite

Later that afternoon, Sheila's. On the way home from work he bought three sunflowers at a farm stand, gave them to Belle to hand to Sheila. "These are lovely!" she said, standing at the doorway to welcome them. "Thank you, Belle."

"It was my father's idea," Belle said, then followed Rachel who followed Jeremy to the rec room, where the PlayStation was.

"Thank you, Andy," Sheila said, giving him what he recognized as her flirtiest smile. She led him into the kitchen, where the late afternoon sun lasered through the windows, yet Andy's fingers—his whole body—felt cold.

"Hey, could you do me a favor?" she asked, reaching across the stained linoleum countertop for a paper bag. She held it out to him as though it contained a child's lunch or shoes to go in for repair. "They've got to be boiled alive."

"What has to be boiled alive?"

She held the bag open for a moment so Andy could peek inside: two lobsters, alive and kicking, furious about their predicament.

"It's silly, but it's hard for me," she said, wiping her hands on her stained canvas apron. "I was hoping you could."

Andy took a half step backward, listening to the scrabble-scrabble-scrabble of the bagged lobsters, and to the sound, in the distant living room, of his daughters playing something violent on her son's PlayStation. Sheila pushed her heat-frizzled bangs off her face. Again, her flirty smile.

Here it was, he thought. Obligation. "Ah," he said. "Well."

Sheila's house was beautiful, the nicest one on the block, a Victorian whose upkeep she couldn't quite manage. An overgrown lawn, a loose board in the front porch, that sort of thing. But her kitchen, despite the disarray, was haphazardly inviting, potted herbs on the windowsill by the sink, a worn-out block of knives. In general, Andy liked being there. When she invited his family for dinner he was usually at least halfway grateful. But now, with the heat, and the scrabbling lobsters—and he was almost certain his daughters were playing a game where they mowed each other down with machine gun—he felt dizzy and uncharacteristically out of words.

"It just takes a second," she said, forcing the bag into his hands. "Come on, Andy, pour 'em in the water. I still have to finish the stew."

Well. The thing had to be done—there was no way around it, and regardless of his objections (the heat, the sweat, the moral question, his older daughter shooting his younger's avatar in the head) it would be unmanly for him to refuse. The lobsters would go into the boiling water and scrabble for perhaps thirty seconds more, and then the scrabbling would turn into a faint scratching at the merciless stainless steel sides of the pot. And then, after another minute or so, the noise would disappear. Life, such as it was, would be extinguished.

Sheila would remove the lobsters from the stockpot with tongs, perhaps holding them up for a moment to let the water bead off them, to admire how rosy they'd turned when boiled. Then she'd decapitate and deshell them to the benefit of the seafood stew she was making him and his daughters to celebrate the beginning of the new school year.

"Go on then," Sheila said. "They might break through the bag if you don't get them in there soon."

What was his problem? "Right," he said. "Okay." He dumped the desperate beasts into the stockpot, and merciless

Sheila clapped her hands. He looked out her window, at the overgrown maples with the menacing roots.

The scrabbling inside the pot grew manic.

"Stew is a great way to stretch lobster meat," Sheila said, turning her attention to a bowl full of potatoes. "It's still an indulgence, of course, but buying two is a whole lot cheaper than buying four."

She blew a stream of air upward into her frizzy bangs. She was not just a murderer; she was a parsimonious murderer.

But oh, how could he be churlish about this celebration? She didn't have to do anything for him at all, much less buy him lobsters, much less carefully prepare them for ungrateful him and his ungrateful daughters. As they sat at the table together, Sheila's dark wooden table, under the cracked plaster ceiling of her dining room, Andy watched both his girls gaze longingly at Jeremy's chicken nuggets. The stew in their bowls was milky. Potatoes and translucent pieces of fish bobbed around the surface.

"I'd like to propose a toast," Sheila said, raising her glass of iced tea. She had been in AA for five years, and was very open about her alcoholism and related troubles; perversely, this was one of the first things he had liked about her. "To Professor Waite," she said. "On the occasion of a new semester at Exton Reed. And to you kids too. Fifth grade and third grade!"

"Ugh, don't remind me," said Rachel, who just this past month had begun affecting an attitude of disenchantment.

Was this normal preteen posturing? Or if something were really wrong, would she tell him?

"And Andy, aren't you up for tenure at the end of the year?" said Sheila, who remembered everything.

"Ugh," he said. "Don't remind me."

"Come on," said Sheila. "You're a shoo-in."

"With tenure there's no such thing as a shoo-in. Even at Exton Reed."

"But you said your experiments were going so well!"

"Circumstances change," he said, mildly. He didn't want his daughters to know what he worried about. "We'll have to wait and see."

"Girls," said mock-exasperated Sheila, "why can't your father ever be optimistic?"

"Because then we wouldn't recognize him," Rachel said.

"It's not his fault," said Belle, an expert in fault. "He's had a lot of bad luck."

"But good luck too," said Sheila.

"Good luck too," Andy repeated, to prove he could fake cheer. "I mean, here I am with you guys! If that's not good luck, I don't know what is." Then, to avoid their worried faces, Andy ducked his head into his underseasoned stew.

THEY LIVED FOUR houses down from Sheila and Jeremy on twisty, underlit Stanwick Street, settled among the hunting clubs and fishing holes and cranberry bogs of Mount

Deborah Township, centrally located in the New Jersey Pine Barrens. The house suited him: it was small and middle-aged, with a yard too crowded with evergreens for anybody to expect him to mow. His daughters shared a room in the back, and he occupied the drafty bedroom in the front, and to the side of the house, unexpected and graceful, was a diminutive oval swimming pool. He put a pair of rocking chairs on the porch, and every November he watched the crab apples splat on the front lawn.

"Girls," he said, as they cut across their next-door neighbor's lawn, "watch out for the pool." They were both of an age to roll their eyes at him, but, as far as he could tell, neither did. Rachel, three steps ahead of him, cut a graceful figure in the gloaming. Belle almost tripped on a felled branch but caught herself in time.

Almost autumn but the house was stuffy. Andy opened windows, pulled the strings on the overhead fans. He was the second widower in a row to own this house; the previous one had died right there in the wood-paneled den, on the couch, in front of the Sunday morning news shows. The widower's daughter had knocked the price almost in half to get the house off her hands, and now Andy's own couch sat in the grooves on the carpet the old man had left.

Belle fell asleep on Rachel's bottom bunk; rather than take the top, Rachel squeezed in next to her and fell asleep smushed between her sister and the wall. At eleven o'clock, the Pine

Barren frogs chorusing outside, Andy turned off their night-light and kissed them each on their smooth sweaty foreheads. They often slept curled together this way, and Andy wondered when they might stop, and what would stop them—puberty, he guessed. Which Rachel would be facing down any moment, if she wasn't already.

"Dad?"

"I'm here, honey." But Rachel was only talking in her sleep. He stood at their doorway for another minute in case she said anything else, then backed away.

Andy was scheduled for nine o'clock classes this semester, which he preferred: sleepy students were docile students, and he'd get off campus early enough, most days, to make it to Rachel's soccer practices. Every year he thought about offering to help coach, but every year he remembered he didn't know anything about soccer, and could well do more harm than good. So he stood on the sidelines and watched Rachel race up and down the fields, mud splattering her shin guards. She played halfback and she was good, and even though they both knew he didn't have to watch her practice, she never told him to stay away.

What had his mother told him after Louisa died? Just an hour at a time. Just get through one hour, and then the next, and before you know it, it's a whole new day.

He sat down on the couch, fiddled with one of the cigars he kept in the box next to the DVD player. He was limiting himself to two a week, but he'd deliberately forgotten when he started counting new weeks. Did a week start on Sunday? Monday? Had he already smoked two in the past seven days?

Screw it. A rustle of leaves outside the open window as a predator swished through the night to pick off a vole or a kitten. He stood up with his cigar, his cutter, and the Zippo that Lou bought him a decade ago in Miami. He would smoke and keep an eye out for cats.

"Knock knock?"

Sheila was standing in his doorway. She had changed her shirt, was wearing a thin cotton T-shirt cut low.

"I was just going outside," he said. "You want to smoke?"

They were tentative with each other but for this one aberrant intimacy: occasionally, when their kids were asleep, they would share a cigar on his porch. Sheila kept a walkie-talkie tucked into the belt loop of her jeans to listen for Jeremy.

She said, "I thought you'd never ask."

They sat together in silence as Andy cut and lit the cigar. He handed it over to Sheila, who put it briefly to her mouth—did she even really like smoking cigars?—then looked at the thing as it burned in her hand. She had pulled up her bangs with a tortoiseshell barrette, her no-nonsense glasses, jeans belted at the waist—they had never so much as kissed. Perhaps the moment for kissing had passed, but maybe that moment never quite passed. But it never came, either. Sheila had a thin-lipped smile so sincere and so chapped he could feel it scratch at his heart.

"Here you go," she said, passing back the cigar.

"Thank you." Andy let the tobacco tickle his mouth, the smoke stream through pursed lips. "Dinner was really nice, by the way."

"I'm sorry about the lobsters."

"Why are you sorry?"

"You looked like you were going to faint," she said. "For some reason I thought it wouldn't bother you. I don't know. I could have done it myself, I guess."

"Are you apologizing?" Andy asked.

She didn't answer.

"Don't apologize. That was one of the nicest things anyone has done for me in a long time. I love lobster."

Sheila waved a hand in front of her face. The smoke? The false gratitude?

"You know, I was thinking—I don't even know when your birthday is," she said. "We've never celebrated anything before."

"November," he said.

"So you're a Scorpio."

He had probably never mentioned that he didn't believe in astrology—that in fact he took a principled stand against it. "Sagittarius."

"I'm a Cancer," she said. "July."

More silence, then another rustle through the trees. Another animal. Even though he had completed his graduate studies at Princeton, fifty miles to the north, Andy had never been aware of the Pine Barrens, the greatest expanse of virgin pine forest in the country, until he'd found himself teaching biology at Exton Reed. This part of New Jersey was all sandy soil over an aquifer so pure you could dig a hole and drink right out of it, and stunted trees that would go down in forest fires every few summers to be reborn, again, come spring. It was the only place in New Jersey where it was truly possible to live off the grid. He knew of families in the immediate area who generated their own electricity and pumped that crystalline water from wells and shot their own deer and could name every owl species from a distance of twenty yards. His daughters went to school with kids from these families; they called them "pineys" and wouldn't invite them to their birthday parties, which was fine with Andy.

"And you'll be thirty-six, right?"

"I'm sorry?" he said.

"In November."

"Forty-one."

"Really? I always thought you were younger than that."

Andy shrugged, puffed on the cigar. Sheila was leaning back against the cheap green all-weather cushions of his rocking chair, closing her eyes. She slapped her hand lazily when a mosquito approached.

"I turned forty a few years ago," she said. "What surprised me was how useless I suddenly felt. I remember my mother describing that feeling when she was sixty or so, how she felt like she was just being greedy at this point—that anything she was going to do from sixty on was just marking time."

Andy looked at Sheila, curious. Her conversation was usually cheerful and practical; she wanted to know if she could pick up the girls, if he needed anything at the Pathmark. If he could replace the lightbulb she couldn't quite reach.

"I feel like that all the time," he said.

"You do?"

"I felt like that even before Lou died—but then it was mostly my biology background getting in the way of basic human happiness."

She smiled at him through closed eyes. He could tell that she liked it when he talked about biology. "Because you'd had your kids."

"Right," he said. "We'd had our kids, and I knew it would be my job to help feed and look out for them for a while, but the truth is, genetically, once I had my girls there wasn't much use for me anymore. I'd done my part. And also my back started hurting around my thirty-third birthday, and I remember thinking, well, this is it. The beginning of the end."

"Because your back hurt?" Sheila laughed. "Honestly, Andy, you're worse than I am."

The smoke plumed around them. His clothes would stink and Rachel would give him grief about it unless he did the laundry tonight. What time was it? The moon glowed overhead, enormous.

"I was never depressed until John," she said. "Never. Not a day." John was Sheila's ex-husband, who'd had an affair with her best friend when Jeremy was a toddler. John and the best friend now lived on the other side of town, which was only a few blocks away, really. Sheila was civil to them whenever she saw them, which was another thing Andy admired about her. Sheila was civil, and when she spoke about what happened, she was generally neither vindictive nor pathetic. "But of course when John left, that was when it became clear I had to keep living. Just when I didn't want to anymore."

"Same with me and Lou."

"I know," she said.

After John left, Sheila started drinking, which she did with increasing fervor and recklessness until her mother threatened to call social services to take Jeremy away. Sheila, chastened, went to rehab, while Jeremy went to Disney World with his grandmother, and now most mornings, after she dropped him off at school but before she went to her job as a dental hygienist, Sheila attended the AA meeting in the rec room at Our Lady of Lourdes. She had invited Andy to attend the meetings for his research a few times, but he had never gone. He didn't do that kind of sociological work, for one thing, and for another he couldn't abide setting foot in a room full of drunks. Or in a church.

"Look at that," she said, gesturing to his lawn. Tiptoeing

close to them, suddenly visible under the porch lights, a pale yellow kitten. "That thing's hardly older than a few weeks."

Behind it, another kitten, then another, and then a larger cat, a feral tabby.

"You think they want food?"

"They were probably planning to attack my garbage."

"Poor babies," she said. She stood, and he did too, stubbing out the cigar in the ashtray he kept on the small side table. Sheila was standing closer to him than she usually did, and he could smell the smoke in her hair, and the faint remains of the tarragon and parsley she'd used in the stew.

A rustle behind them, and a fast, surprising breeze.

"What the—"

When they looked again, the cats had disappeared. That old shiver went through Andy. There were predators all around. Without meaning to, exactly—or without thinking too hard about it—he touched Sheila's face. Her skin was soft and slightly slick, a comfort. She leaned upward. As he kissed her, a mosquito buzzed near his ear. She smacked it for him, and they laughed, which made it easier to kiss again.

In ten minutes, they were in his bedroom. "Is this okay?" he whispered. He was taking off her clothes as he asked. Her underwear was exactly what he would have expected: sturdy and beige. Silvery stretch marks glinted in the dim light. He kissed her neck. The meal, the tobacco buzz, the heat, the moonlight,

Sheila's peppery skin—he kissed her neck harder, then down to her collarbone. He licked the space between her clavicles. Should he be doing this? With anyone? With Sheila? She was one of his few real friends, even though he wasn't such a good friend to her, or as good as he should have been. He buried his mouth in the side of her neck.

"It's so okay," she said, leaning her head back.

"Are you sure?"

"Of course," she said. "Are you?"

He murmured nothing specific. He worried that he didn't have any condoms, but she didn't ask about them. Funny, he thought, that he had never before had sex with a woman in her forties.

Once they got started, moving quietly, easily, Andy kept thinking that all this was inevitable, and that he should have known it was inevitable: this house, this heat, Lou's death, Sheila above him, her body larger than he would have guessed, and pale like the moon. Her breasts were small and loose; he put one in his mouth and she moaned. It felt rehearsed, but pleasant. A song whose words they'd forgotten but whose tune they could still hum.

"Well," he said when they were done. She had allowed herself a few minutes in his arms on the sweaty blue sheets.

"Well," she said. Now she was tugging on her jeans, and suddenly he felt overwhelmed with panic—what if, having done this, they would no longer be friends? Andy didn't want close friends but he didn't want to be friendless, either.

"Was that okay?" he asked.

"It was better than okay," she said. "It was really great. It had been a while." She leaned over and kissed him. He was sitting up on the bed, the sheets arranged around him for modesty. He was still wearing the T-shirt he'd worn all day. "I better get home, though," she said.

"Okay."

She fastened her bra. "Were you wondering when we would finally get around to that?" she asked.

"I guess so," he said.

"I was," she said. Through the darkness, she looked at herself in his mirror, clipped her bangs back up off her forehead. Why did she bother? "It was really nice," she said, then sat down on the bed next to him. "Do you think we . . ."

He waited for her to finish, but she didn't. "Do you think we what?"

"Do you think we'll see more of each other now?" she asked, after another second in the dark.

"Well," Andy said, "the semester's starting . . ."

Sheila paused. "Right, but—"

"But of course we'll see each other. Don't we always?"

"I guess so," she said. She touched his knee, then stood. "We always do." She walked to the door.

"Wait," he said, then kissed her briefly on the cheek, one last time. "Thank you," he said.

"You're welcome," she said. That felt like the right place to leave it, as though she was the one who had done him a favor.

She let herself out, and he waited to hear the door close. On the floor, he saw her walkie-talkie. It must have slipped out of her jeans when he pulled them off. He could chase after her, return it, or wait until the morning, or—or if he never gave it back, maybe that would mean she'd never come over at night-time again. He could cut the line right there. Return things to their uncomplicated past.

Andy stood, pulled on his pants, collected his laundry. On his way out the door, he looked at his denuded bed, and smelled the repellent fumes of cigars and sweat. How had this happened? Why tonight of all nights had he let down his guard? The full moon, he supposed. The lobsters. The fact that he couldn't think of a good reason not to anymore.

Andy turned on the hall light. Lou's ghost stood in the doorway of the kitchen, where she usually stood. Passing through the kitchen toward the basement laundry room, not acknowledging Lou or her silence, he placed Sheila's walkie-talkie gently in the trash, then went down the stairs to start the spin cycle. The stairs, wooden planks as old as the house, creaked as he walked. The whole cement basement was lit like a haunted house by a single lightbulb. Over the ancient Whirl-pool a small spider moved across a filigreed web. He poured the detergent, started the water. That old pain in his back. The spider stopped moving, then plunged, by a single thread, behind the washing machine and out of sight.

The stairs creaked again as he made his way back up.

"Dad?" he thought he heard from inside his daughters' bed-room, and his heart lightened.

"Yes?" he said, standing outside their door.

"Go to sleep," said one of them. "You're making the floors creak."

"Right," he said, mortified. "Sorry."

How odd this mixture of loneliness and longing to be left alone. He poked his face in their room because he couldn't resist, but they were already asleep again, facing opposite directions, strands of long blondish brownish hair, just like their mother's, intertwined.

FOUR

Andy stood at the sideline, watching Rachel race up and down the field in her muddy cleats and shin guards, her body skinny and angular in blue rayon shorts and the yellow T-shirt with the penguins on it she'd brought home from a field trip to the Camden aquarium. Her ponytail achieved liftoff as she chased after the ball, until she was whooshed out of the way by another girl, bigger, faster, with less-aerodynamic hair. They were running drills. The coach called out praise for the other girl, and Rachel looked down at her feet; Andy felt crushed for her even as she picked herself up again and began a new sprint down the field.

The only other parents who came to practice seemed to come for the sideline gossip as much as they did to watch their ten-year-olds drill. Big-boned farm ladies who'd recently taken up jobs at the Target in Marlton—some of them still wore their smocks—or worked at the liquor store in Glassboro or the souvenir shop in Chatsworth, they drove thirty miles back and forth to their jobs, early morning hours, and by the time they got to the soccer fields their feet were aching and so were their hearts for a little companionship, a little chitchat. He heard them bellow in riotous laughter. They wore stiff dark jeans, dyed their hair.

If Lou were still alive they wouldn't live in Mount Deborah. If Lou were still alive they would have picked one of the fancier towns. She would have inspired him to make enough money to make it work. Or maybe they would have picked a house by the sea.

At the playground by the far end of the soccer field, Belle sat on top of the jungle gym and surveyed the landscape. She was the master of all her eye could see. A few kids, their mothers, wandered beneath her: her subjects. She shouted, "Hey, Daddy!"

"Hey, Belle!"

"Is Rachel done yet?"

"Almost!"

"I'm sick of always waiting for Rachel!"

"What?" She was almost too far away to hear clearly.

"I'm sick of it!"

"Sick of what?"

He sat down on the bleachers, away from the clique of Mount Deborah moms, the cold wetness of the aluminum cutting through his pants. September and the very first leaves were considering change, the birch trees scattered among the pines. Above the briny soccer field flew Vs of Canada geese, then a thicket of sparrows. Sheila never made it to practice; she worked until six most days. But sometimes Andy saw her ex-husband in the stands, watching Jeremy with an intensity that worried him.

"Wow! Rachel's doing well today!" said Janet Goldsmith.

"She's been kicking balls in the backyard."

"You can tell," said Janet. "She's really improved. I bet she makes the traveling team this year."

"Dad!" Belle came running to him from the jungle gym. She had scratches on her legs, mosquito bites on her arms—her beautiful round face blighted by little red marks. "Can I go have pizza with Madeline's family? Madeline's mom said I should ask you." From the playground, Madeline's mother raised a hand in greeting, a semaphored "is that okay?"

"Here, let me give you some money." He handed Belle a five and off she ran, back toward the playground, to Madeline and Madeline's mother. His girls had friends in Mount Deborah. They had soccer teams, people to eat pizza with, a school they seemed to like. A swimming pool of their very own. By the end of their two weeks in Ohio, Belle was starting to get anxious, antsy. "I want to go back to *our* house," she said. "I don't like it here anymore."

"Why not?"

She looked at him like it should be obvious. "I miss New Jersey."

Occasionally, when he was feeling maudlin, he asked Rachel if she could remember Miami. "A little," she would say. "It was hot," or "we lived in an apartment," or "we went to Disney World that one time." She didn't say, "I remember how Mama used to sing me to sleep, Woody Guthrie songs." She didn't say, "I remember the way my mama's hair fell in curls down her face." She didn't say, "I remember how much she loved me." But oh how much she had loved those girls.

Rachel was three and Belle was one and she had left the house that night to pick up some McDonald's, because neither Andy nor Lou liked to cook back then and it was too late to scrounge up anything better than a couple of Big Macs and fries. Andy's chronic worries about their money would slip in moments like this: obviously, it was cheaper to just boil some macaroni (a box of macaroni at Publix was forty-nine cents on special; they had stocked up over the weekend and now macaroni was spilling out of the cabinet they used as a pantry) but he'd been working so hard at the lab, and putting together job applications, and the idea of a McDonald's burger and some beers . . .

Belle was asleep in the small room the girls shared overlooking the pool in their complex. Rachel was playing. The apartment was pastel and Florida-bright and they always kept the air-conditioning on too high and this was another way that Andy should have been more vigilant about their finances but he hated to come home and be hot, he really did.

Their last conversation: "I'll go."

"No, you've been drinking." And that was true, he had been drinking, but just a little: three and a half bottles of Heineken in the two hours since he'd been home, during which he'd watched *Dora the Explorer* with Rachel while Lou nursed the baby, bathed the baby, teased him for singing the "I'm the Map" song, and put the baby down. It was easy to go through beers while watching *Dora the Explorer*. It was easy to drink too much in the air-conditioned escape from the Florida heat.

"You sure?"

"It'll be good to get out of the house a little," she said. She'd stopped working in the NICU once Belle was born, and now she taught yoga on Saturdays at the Gold Fitness on Palmetto (forty dollars per class and that was their AC bill right there) but spent most of her weekdays at the Publix, at the library, at the playground, at the pool. Lou always said that what surprised her the most about the girls was how physical the labor was: so much carrying, so much moisture. Little children were always damp. But then, when they slept: Belle in her crib, Rachel in the little bed they'd bought her off craigslist, shaped like a pink Corvette—their eyelashes so long and black against their white skin it was like they'd been painted on, their cheeks so rosy in their sleep, their chests moving up and down in unison. Nothing was sweeter.

Andy gave her a five from his wallet—neither one of them ever carried much cash—and went to check on the girls, one of his greatest pleasures. He imagined, in the next few years, he'd find a job somewhere—he was hoping Ohio, to be close to his mother, or maybe California. Lou looked like she belonged in California. They would buy a small house. They would have at least one more kid, probably a girl (he had a sneaking suspicion he could only make girls) but maybe, fingers crossed, he'd have a son.

He'd get tenure, they'd buy a bigger house, in Ohio, in Wisconsin, in California. There were jobs that year at Kenyon, Claremont McKenna, the University of Cincinnati. He'd also applied to schools in New Jersey, Maine, and Connecticut, because the job market was so tough and he wanted to hedge his bets.

Lou had left her cell phone on the kitchen counter. In the bedroom, Belle slept like an angel.

When she didn't come home after a half hour he started to worry and when she didn't come home in an hour he called the police but nobody could give him any real information although yes, there had been an accident on Eighty-seventh, yes, a Mazda, and that's when he banged on the door next door, that nice old Jewish couple who sometimes invited Rachel over to light Shabbat candles, and Rona Katz told him to calm down, not to worry, but it was too late, she was in his living room and he was out the door speeding speeding toward the intersection of Eighty-seventh and Manor by the entrance to Route 1.

There were orange cones, flare lights, traffic. He pulled the car into the parking lot at Blockbuster, got out, ran ran ran ran ran out of breath kept running to the accident, the McDonald's across from the Steak 'n Shake, yes, he knew what he was going to see, and there it was: the ambulance, Oliver McGee, the drunk kid from the complex, on a stretcher, their Mazda crushed like a can, his wife still in that crushed Mazda since the doors were accordioned shut and there was no way she'd have been able to get out. There was no way anyone could get her out. He raced to the door. Her head slammed against the windshield. The cops pulled him away. On the seat, blood and brain.

BUT IN HIS dreams, both erotic and scientific, she was perfect. She was whole. It was Lou's body that came to him even more than her voice, which was surprising: in life, although her appearance had been the first draw, soon enough it was her conversation that kept him interested, generous and mordantly funny. She liked dirty jokes. Before the girls were born she'd read long-winded fantasy novels featuring magic dwarves and big-breasted sorceresses. She was impatient with everybody, especially in Florida, where people talked too slow, and usually in check-out lines. When he was pressed into servitude as a teaching assistant in Human Anatomy, she came with him to the cadaver lab, looked at the splayed-open bodies with an appraising eye, remembered fondly her own days in nursing school, and said, "Catch!" pretending to throw him a human eyeball. She wasn't even wearing gloves.

She'd had such a beautiful body. It worked so beautifully, the choreography of her limbs, the delicate threading of her arteries and veins, the miracle of her vision, iris through lens through retina through optic nerve to the visual cortex in her pulsing splattered brain. And deep inside her smooth freckled belly—if he peered there, put his head against her soft warmth—he could almost see the uterus, the fallopian tubes, the ova, their children.

The night of the accident, an ambulance took Lou's body away to the morgue, and Andy returned home to his children. Rona Katz was sitting in his kitchen, playing Go Fish with Rachel, who was still awake.

"Daddy? What took you so long? Where's Mommy?"

Rona Katz looked at him, and her face seemed to turn gray. She returned to the deck of cards, began straightening them.

"Rachel," he said. "I love you very much."

Rona bent her head at his kitchen table.

"Your mother is not coming home," he said. The story of the rest of his life.

ANDY SAT AT this new kitchen table, this new house, and tried to draft his statement to the parole board. Oliver McGee had been sentenced to eight to twelve years; he would have gotten more except that Lou hadn't yet clicked on her seat belt. Otherwise he might have gotten twenty.

As it was, this was Oliver's third arrest for drunk driving (and after the trial everyone told Andy—and what was he supposed to do with this information, exactly?—everyone told him it had just been a matter of time). Only eight to twelve and already it had been six and already he was up for parole for the third time. As he had the first two times, Andy spent hours drafting the right kinds of words to the parole board, not hysterical, not vindictive, but rather the calmly plaintive words of a man who had lost his beloved wife to Oliver McGee's driving and couldn't bear the thought of the same thing happening to anyone else.

He'd expected these statements would get easier to write, but in fact this time it was harder. He'd already used his best material the first two times. This current iteration was taking him hours; the simplicity of his object kept slipping away from him. Frustratingly, these were hours he should have spent preparing his tests, or reading his journals, or even sleeping. He would have been sleeping, maybe, if it weren't for the recent spate of troubling dreams. But instead, it was midnight, and here he was, the letter, the purposeful nature of the letter, slipping away again and again in a steaming pile of words. And tomorrow it would be five thirty, and here he'd be again.

Oliver McGee had been his neighbor in the Quail Run apartment complex. Nineteen, living with his mother and grandmother in one of the end-unit town houses, supposedly finishing high school but Andy saw him all the time on weekday mornings, sprawled out on one of the benches by the swimming pool, snoring a drunken snore. Complaints were made to management but what could they do? They ushered him off the benches. They let him get drunk, quietly, inside his own town house. His mom and grandma both worked but the television was on all day, every day; Andy heard it as he walked to his apartment. Sometimes, at night, Oliver would speed out of the parking lot, flying over speed bumps like Evel Knievel.

"That kid's going to kill himself one day," Andy said, watching Oliver from his kitchen window, spinning out into the night.

"If he's lucky," Lou said. "If he's not he'll kill somebody else."

During the trial, the mother and the grandmother were heartbroken not only for Andy and the girls but also, of course, for Oliver, who in the way of these things had once been a pretty nice kid. He used to like to skateboard, evidently. He used to be a pretty good artist. The character witnesses included his former high school art teacher but even the teacher had to admit that Oliver's performance started to suffer once he began drinking vodka out of Poland Spring bottles in class.

After the accident, Andy decided to turn his research away from degenerative disease and instead toward the mechanisms of alcoholism. He applied for and received a new postdoc with a biologist who was decoding brain waves in rats. Every day, at the lab, he would scrutinize the electroencephelograms of rats who had been dosed with varying amounts of ethanol, rats with different levels of different neuropeptides coursing through their brains. The goal of the research was to measure the way the different genetic makeups protected rats against intoxication. One of the sponsors of the research was a drug manufacturer who was trying to find the holy grail, medication that could ward off the effects of drink.

What would the royalties look like on that patent? A pill you could take before you left the bar, diminishing the effect of whatever you'd just imbibed, refocusing your mind so you could take the wheel. A pill that would let you get crazy on the dance floor, then go to work the next day clear-eyed and levelheaded. Andy and his colleagues called it the Margaritapill. Other labs were making some headway on this — dihydromyricetin looked promising — and the drug company gave his lab millions to try to catch up. Not that Andy himself was fueled by imagined riches. His fuel came from somewhere murkier — to understand, to know what to blame.

He was hired a year later at Exton Reed, a college he'd never heard of, on the strength of his coauthored papers, and his research was the object of some fascination during his interview. "So tell me, Andy," said Linda Schoenmeyer, an ornithologist who'd never had anything to do with rodents. "How exactly do you give an EEG to a rat? Do you have, like, tiny little sensors? Do you have to shave their little heads?"

How to explain? "We, you know, we insert receptors into their brains. While they're under general anesthesia," he said.

"And then we hook the receptors up to an EEG reader. The rats don't even notice." This wasn't exactly true—the rats awoke from anesthesia groggy and pissed off, with little white plugs sticking out of their bloodied heads, but there was no reason to get into the nitty-gritty on his interview.

"You stick receptors?" Linda asked. "Into their brains?"

"That is how they do it," Marty Reuben, the botanist, said. "I've read about this sort of thing."

The biologists seemed much too dismayed for what was, in the annals of animal research, actually fairly benign intervention, but they didn't judge him unkindly for it. They just seemed chastened by their ignorance, and apologized, when he accepted the job, that they really didn't have the resources to conduct brain surgery on rats but perhaps they could support him in simpler research, if he was so inclined?

A simple house, a simple life, a simple job, simple research: he was so inclined.

"Laurence and I would love to have you and your wife to dinner once you get settled," said Nina Graff.

He hadn't wanted to explain it to them in the interview. "Louisa was killed in a car accident last winter," Andy said. "But thank you for your invitation."

FIVE

Members of the Florida Prison Parole Board:

It is with great sadness that I write, once again, my victim impact statement regarding parole for Oliver McGee, prisoner N24633. Mr. McGee killed my wife, Louisa Waite, in a motor vehicle accident in August 2004. As you undoubtedly know, Mr. McGee's blood alcohol content the night he drove his car into my wife's was almost four times the legal limit; that he was able to drive the car at all seems like the darkest sort of miracle, since someone that drunk shouldn't be able to fit a key into the ignition, much less put a car into drive. Yet there he was, nineteen years old, swerving back and forth on Eighty-seventh Street before slamming, for no reason except the perverse misfiring of the drunken brain, into the Mazda my wife was driving to McDonald's to bring back dinner for me. Our daughters were then one and almost four.

In previous letters I have prevailed upon you to keep Mr.

McGee locked up as a preventive measure, a way to keep
a killer behind bars for the protection of society, the logic
being (logic that's been borne out by my own professional
studies into alcoholism) that once a drunk always a drunk — or,
to be more politic about it, the logic being that alcoholism is
a genetic state, not a curable disease, and therefore Oliver
McGee will almost certainly drink again, and if he does, there
is a chance he will kill again. He has shown neither the ability
to stay sober nor the conviction that he should, if he must
drink, at least turn in his keys.

I believe that he might kill again. But this is not why I want
him to stay in jail, as he has already inflicted his damage upon
me and I am not generous enough anymore to give a shit
about who else he hurts. This time I am writing my letter with
a different set of justifications, a different set of reasons I
want Oliver McGee to rot in jail. Expressly:

Have I ever mentioned to you, esteemed members of
the parole board, that my wife, Lou, was a NICU nurse for
eleven years? Do you know, parole board members, what a
NICU nurse does? Let me explain the work for you here: A
NICU nurse warms and soothes and feeds with a dropperlike
feeder the palm-sized babies who were born at twenty-five,
twenty-six weeks' gestation. These are babies who by all
means should not be alive, but by some miracle (that word
again, and again so dark) they *are* alive, and they will grow
and thrive, except for the ones who won't. The ones who

won't, with the translucent skin threaded by desperate veins, and the tangerine-sized heads in knit caps, and the eyes covered by strips of gauze because the undeveloped corneas will be damaged by the light—these babies with the brain damage and the breathing trouble and the spastic limbs and the chickenlike cries, some of these babies will teeter on the brink of death, and the parents will look at the NICU nurse with their hearts in one place and their heads somewhere else and they will say to that nurse, "What do we do?"

The nurse will hold their hands. She will tend to their babies. She will, if they want her to, pray for them.

And the parents and the doctors will go back and forth and back and forth—proceed with one intervention after another, keep this squawking chicken baby alive another hour, another day, the hope of a normal future coming in and out of focus like a lens splashed with rain. Or maybe merciful providence will perform the intervention and the baby, who has only known in its short, pathetic life the heat of the incubator and the dropperful of liquid—if providence is merciful, this baby will be allowed to pass into the hereafter.

Despite the mercy of the thing, however, when one of these infants would give up its sad struggle, my wife, Lou, would come home from work and cry and cry. She would sit there on the couch—I can see her sitting there—with her beautiful hair streaming down her back and her shoulders shaking and I would rub her shoulders and she would cry it out, letting out whatever she could not reveal in front of the grieving parents. In front of the parents, she was warm and reassuring and invincible. At home, she was a puddle.

It has occurred to me so many times, members of the parole board, that these NICU babies have the great privilege of time and love and interventions and, when the time comes, if the time does come, they are allowed appropriate, stricken good-byes. They have whole bodies to bury in family plots. And who are these babies? Who are they? They have been on the planet for *twenty-six weeks*. They are the barest minimum of what it means to be a person. They are skin and skittish hearts and squawks and blind eyes and clogged lungs and nothing. And yet these babies are so often saved. Yes! Saved by my wife! And the ones who die at least get a proper good-bye, and when she was alive my wife came home and mourned each one of them.

Of course you do not need me to elaborate on the obvious, members of the parole board, that these NICU babies, these barely viable blobs of nothing—most of them live. Parts of my wife's skull, on the other hand, were found on the curb in front of a fast-food restaurant.

Andy stopped typing. His fingers ached. He felt sweaty. This was the part where he always felt sweaty. And someone was breathing behind him.

"Are you working on your grant stuff, Dad?"

"I thought you were asleep."

"I was thirsty." Belle was standing on her tiptoes, searching through the cabinets for the cup she liked, the oversized purple one. She was wearing one of his old T-shirts to sleep in, which hung down to her knees and rode low across her shoulders. He didn't know whether she wore the shirt because she liked it or because he'd neglected to buy her pajamas. He often didn't know what he was supposed to buy them until they'd gone without for too long.

"You shouldn't drink too much before you go to bed," he said mildly, watching Belle fill her cup with milk.

"I know," she said. She sat down at the table across from him, pushed her cup across the table. "You want some?"

"Sure."

Belle too was starting to change—she still had that tubby belly but she was starting to show the collarbones of an older girl, thin and sharp. "Who's Mr. McGee?" she said.

"What?"

"On your computer," she said. Jesus Christ, her eyes were good. And she could read! Of course she could read, she was eight years old. She read all the time. She had stacks of books in her room.

"Is he a friend of yours?"

"Yes," Andy said.

"Why do you call him Mr. McGee if he's your friend?"

"I don't know his first name," Andy lied.

"You don't know it?"

Andy had never told his daughters the real reason he went, alone, to Okeechobee every few years. He told them it was a conference. He didn't want them to think of their mother's death, or her killer, or that, perhaps most frightening, that their father felt vengeful often to the point of derangement. "Why don't you know your friend's name?"

He stood, opened the refrigerator, poured her some more milk.

"Is it Oliver?" Belle asked.

"Yes," Andy sighed.

"He's the one who killed my mom?"

"Yes," Andy said. The chill of the refrigerator air on his arms.

"What are you saying about him?"

"I'm writing to the jail," he said. He closed the refrigerator door. "They want to let him out."

"Will they?"

"I hope not," he said.

"Why not?

"I don't know, Belle." What should he say? "I hope they don't, but I actually don't know. But even if they do, you know—even if they do, he can never hurt us again."

"Thank you," said Belle, taking the milk from his hands. Andy waited for the warmth to return to his hands. Oliver McGee was sitting in a jail cell just outside Okeechobee. His wife was cremated and sprinkled into the Atlantic. But he and Belle and Rachel were here, in this kitchen, in this house; they were together, they were alive.

"I'm sorry," he said. "I shouldn't have lied to you."

"What did you lie about?" Belle said.

"Not knowing Oliver's name," he said. "I know it."

Belle didn't seem to care one way or another. She poured the rest of the milk in the sink, deposited the cup. "I didn't think he would hurt us. Grandma told us he was just a kid who made a stupid mistake."

"Grandma said that?"

"She said he would suffer for it the rest of his life, just as much as we would."

"Wow," Andy said. "I never knew you talked to Grandma about it."

"I used to, when I was little," Belle said. She stood in the half-darkened doorway, her lovely face invisible in a shadow. "They should probably let him out of prison by now, don't you think? He's been there a really long time. Especially if he was just a kid when the accident happened."

"I don't think so," Andy said. "I don't think they should ever let him out."

"Yeah," Belle said. "I guess." She blew him a kiss, their good-bye sign, then disappeared down the hall.

He had to remind himself that to Belle, Lou was just an idea, not a memory.

Andy reread his statement. It filled him with shame. He pressed delete, stretched his fingers, started again.

ON THE SUNNY October day Andy's mice once again refused to drink as much as he predicted they would, Lionel Shell stood outside his office for three hours with a sign around his neck that read, GENESIS 1:1. Andy was downstairs, staining slides, listening to the radio, could have stayed there for hours, but eventually Rosemary panicked and called him in his lab. "This kid's not going anywhere. He's just staring like a lunatic. What if he starts shooting the place up?"

Andy sighed, turned off the radio, *This American Life.* His thumbs were stained from methylene blue. He'd always imagined he'd have a grad student or several to help him with this kind of work. He scrubbed his fingers with Borax in his tiny industrial sink, headed upstairs slowly, thinking about the proteins in the drunk mice's brains.

When he got to the fourth-floor biology suite, he found Rosemary standing by the door, twisting her watchband. Down thirty paces stood poor Lionel, ramrod-stiff. "It doesn't look like he's packing, Rosemary."

"You never know these days."

This was true. At each new school shooting, high school or postsecondary, the entire Exton Reed faculty began assessing their classrooms for the militant or suicidal, plotting escape plans out of hard-to-open windows or heavy doors. "I'll talk to him," Andy said. It was a Friday afternoon, typically empty, and he wondered if Lionel had organized his lonely protest deliberately for a day when he wouldn't have to confront anybody.

"Hey, Lionel," he said. "Everything okay?"

Lionel blinked. He didn't turn around. Andy noticed the white earbuds.

"Hey!" he yelled. "Lionel! Turn off that iPod and talk to me."

Was it possible the kid had tears in his eyes? Lionel shrugged, turned off the music, and buckled to the floor, assuming a cross-legged slump in front of Andy's door. His sign rested against his folded legs.

"Sorry, Professor."

"It's okay." He wasn't sure if he should bend down or make Lionel stand up. "What are you doing here?"

"I'm protesting."

"Clearly," Andy said. He sighed, bent heavily to the floor himself so he could be closer to Lionel's face. "Listen, Lionel, it's fine if you want to protest, but I'm not sure what sitting outside my office on a Friday is going to do for you."

Lionel waved him away. "It's important to me that people know about what you're teaching. Or I guess it's just important to broadcast that somebody cares. It's easy to think nobody cares about anything at this place, but I do. I hate what you teach. I'm sorry," the tears filled his eyes but did not spill over, "I just hate it."

"You don't have to apologize," Andy said, although, petulantly, he did feel a little stung. Disagreement was one thing, but hate? "So why are you taking the class again if you hate it so much?"

"Because somebody has to keep tabs on what you do! Somebody has to keep an eye on you."

"Ah," Andy said, letting his butt sink down to the floor to ease the twinge in his back. Poor Lionel. The kid wore dirty sneakers, loose jeans. He probably weighed 130 pounds. Andy knew he was on a full scholarship, and there was that underfed, vulnerable look about him, that full-scholarship look. "But why don't you write letters to the editor, that sort of thing? It might get more done. I mean, I appreciate what you're trying to do here but what's the point of a protest if there's nobody here to see?"

Lionel shrugged. He fiddled with his iPod. He'd been listening to someone British read the Bible.

"My sister's an existentialist. Do you know what that is?"

"An existentialist?" Andy said. "In Delaware?"

"She's actually my twin. She goes to community college. Her name is Sara."

"That's my daughter's middle name," Andy said, to make a connection. Lionel didn't bite.

"She thinks that there's no point to anything. That we could live or die, and it doesn't really matter, and anyone who thinks it matters is a fool. She reads a lot of French writers."

"It's a pretty French idea," Andy said.

"And she's very dismissive of the way I think, that there's a God who's watching over us. And I think she's as wrong as anyone can be, but then I look around at the stuff we do to each other, the stuff we teach, and then I think maybe she's not so wrong, you know?"

"Which scares you."

Lionel shook his head no, and Andy remembered he should never accuse a young man of feeling scared. "It just makes me sad."

"I'm not an existentialist, Lionel," Andy said. "I don't know if that makes you feel better or not. I believe that life matters." As he said that, he felt it to be true, although he also knew this wasn't always what he felt.

"But how can you believe that without God?"

"Because, Lionel, I don't need the supernatural to give my life meaning."

"Then what gives you meaning?"

There was some pabulum for this, something about nature being enough of a miracle, or about how life itself contained meaning, but Andy forgot what the script was. He had been focusing on the tiniest substructures in mouse brains for hours now, and there was pain between his eyes, and in his back.

"Without God," Lionel said, "all we have is a materialistic view of the world where there's no morality, no good and bad. Everything's random, therefore nothing matters. That's where existentialism comes in."

"You know, Lionel, there's a strong argument to be made that morality evolved right alongside physical characteristics," Andy said. "You can see protomorality, or at least a sense of compassion, even in toddlers who are too young to know religion. Even in animals."

Lionel nodded. "Of course you can, because God created us all. Even the animals."

"Yes, but—"

"And I hate to point out," Lionel said, "that dictators like Hitler and Stalin used evolution to support their genocides."

"Oh, come on, Lionel," Andy said, pinching the bridge of his nose to wipe out the incipient headache. "Let's not bring those two into this."

"It's true. *Mein Kampf* is all about evolution. Hitler believed that the most evolved races, which in his mind meant Aryans, had the right to exterminate the less evolved, which in his mind meant the Jews, the gypsies, the handicapped. You know, everyone else." Lionel's owlish eyes bugged out a little when he soliloquized. "But if you're a Darwinian evolutionist, this should only seem natural, right? I mean, isn't that what evolution does? Separate the strong from the weak? The more evolved from the less evolved?"

"No, it's not."

"It totally is," Lionel said. "And Stalin thought the same thing, which is why he exterminated native peoples from Azerbaijan to Siberia. Stalin is responsible for more deaths than even Hitler is. Which is a lot of deaths we can attribute to Darwinian evolution. But, you know, whatever, Professor. Teach what you need to teach, like it doesn't matter."

Oh, God. "Lionel, you can't just slap the words *Hitler* and *Stalin* onto something you don't agree with and call it a reasoned debate."

"So let's take Hitler out of it," Lionel said. "Let's remove Stalin and Hitler and still think about a world where we've agreed in survival of the fittest. The strong vanquishing the weak. What have we got then?"

"Again, Lionel, I think you're deliberately misunderstanding the nature of Darwinian evolution."

"No more welfare, no more public health care, no more hate crime legislation, since what is a hate crime if not a crime of the strong against the less strong? You like that world, Professor? You want to live in that world?"

"Lionel, enough."

But the kid was on a roll. "Morality, human obligation toward one another, comes from the idea that life has purpose. Evolution takes away that purpose. It makes everything an accident. Everything becomes random. It takes away the necessity for humans to look out for one another."

"That's not true," Andy said, as Rosemary gave him a worried look from down the hall. "Darwinian evolution is not the same as social Darwinism. Social Darwinism is this ugly thing that people use to justify the mistreatment of others.

Darwinian evolution is the simple idea that life forms have changed in a variety of ways in response to the environment."

"And what happens to those that don't change successfully?"

"What do you mean?"

"I mean, according to Darwinian evolution, what happens to those forms of life that don't change in response to their environment? Or that don't change very well?"

"What do you mean, don't change very well?"

"They die out," said Lionel. "That's what happens. They die."

As though this meant more than it did—as though species didn't go extinct all the time, as though everything that was born didn't eventually die.

"Do you still talk to Hank Rosenblum?" Lionel asked.

"I'm sorry?" Andy said. His relationship with Rosenblum— his former relationship—was one he tried to keep to himself.

"He thanked you in one of his books," Lionel said.

"You've read Rosenblum?"

"I'm taking your class for the second time, Professor," Lionel said. "Of course I've read him."

"Right, but I mean you read *Religion's Dangerous Lie?*"

Lionel nodded. "And I have to say," and here he started to lose his Hitler-and-Stalin cool, "I have to say that when I think about that poor girl Rosenblum *murdered,* and I think about the fact that this is a man who's on our syllabus, and then I think that you just keep teaching it—that's when I start to see my sister's point a little, that really nothing matters. That I'm a fool for trying to make the world a better place. That I should just go to class and nod my head and become a *machine*—"

"Lionel—"

"That you should just go out in the world and know that when you die you're just *dead,* that's it, there's no God, there's no nothing." He wiped his eyes with the back of his wrists.

"Lionel, stop."

"That you can just *murder* someone—"

"Okay, enough. Nobody was murdered. Rosenblum didn't murder anybody."

"I read the news reports online."

"Then you should know Rosenblum was never accused of murder," Andy said, and those feelings that he had pushed away—he had a new baby, he was trying to find an academic position, and Jesus, Hank, what was wrong with you? how could you have *done* that?—came back, gurgled in him. "Nobody was murdered." And then, to calm him down, or just to change the subject, he said, "You know, I'm doing that independent study."

Lionel took a moment to collect himself. "What are you talking about?"

"With your friend . . . your friend . . ." God, how had he become so terrible with names? "With that friend you sent me."

"Oh, Melissa." Lionel sighed. "She's not really my friend—I met her at a Campus Crusade meeting. I think she's a transfer student. She wanted to do—"

"Intelligent design, I know."

"And you said yes?" Here Lionel allowed himself a small smile. His face was mottled. Andy thought that his sister should be proud of him. He also thought about the bitter way Lionel spit out that line: *when you die you're just dead.*

"I thought it might be interesting."

"You just want to change her mind."

"So?" Andy said. "You just want to change mine."

"Yeah, but you have a position of power," Lionel said. "Who am I? Who is Melissa? How are we supposed to confront people like you, like Rosenblum—"

"All right. Enough with the self-pity," Andy said. He stood, wiped his jeans, motioned for Lionel to stand up too. "You're young, you're healthy, you have a voice. I'm middle-aged and exhausted. Rosenblum is in hiding on Long Island. From an evolutionary standpoint, it's *you* who has the power, not me. So stop feeling sorry for yourself. If you've got something to say, say it. Don't cry in my hallway."

Lionel hung his head.

"And really, kid, stand up straight." Andy felt, oddly, refreshed by this interaction, a chance to buck up poor Lionel Shell, with the existentialist sister and the fear of death that crouched around all of them, even the young.

"Okay," Lionel said. "But can I ask you one question—you know that book Rosenblum thanked you in? *Religion's Dangerous Lie?*"

Andy nodded. It was an inflammatory little paperback

Rosenblum had sold for a mega-advance and dedicated to a few of his favorite people, including, for better or for worse, Andy. It had climbed to the top of the *Times* best-seller list and perched there for months, leading to appearances on *Oprah* for Rosenblum and a certain notoriety, even embarrassment, for Andy.

"So do you really believe that? That religion is a dangerous lie? My sister does."

"I don't believe that exactly."

Lionel smiled his underfed smile. "So then you believe it's a good thing?"

"I didn't say that, either," Andy said. He thought about how little he liked to talk about these things, and then he thought, without warning, about Lou. *When you die you're just dead.*

"So you're an agnostic."

"There are no agnostics in foxholes," Andy said, which he knew wasn't exactly how the saying went but at that moment he would have said anything to keep from saying Lou's name out loud. "Listen, Lionel, if you want to protest, by all means protest, but don't be so downhearted about it. Gird yourself for the fight!"

Lionel shrugged.

"And also, if you are going to protest, please don't do it on a Friday afternoon. You're freaking out the secretary."

"Okay," Lionel said, and then added, for no particular reason, "thanks," and then picked up his sign, brushed it off tenderly, and walked the opposite way down the hall, past Louisa's ghost, whom he didn't notice at all.

THAT EVENING, AS he drove down twisted Stanwick Street, Andy saw that the Halloween decorations were already up—plastic pumpkins in windows and scarecrows on lawns. Roberta Hayes, who kept chickens, had decorated their coops with paper skeletons. Halloween was still important to his girls, who relished their princess costumes and refused to put winter coats over their tulle bodices. But they hadn't mentioned anything about costumes so far this year and he wondered if they might be growing out of it, and if so, what new trick might replace princesses.

He pulled into the driveway just in time to beat them home from Janet Goldsmith's, where they spent most Friday afternoons. He put a pot of water on to boil—Friday was spaghetti night—and thought about whether it was time to turn on the heat. The house relied on oil, like so many houses in the pines, and it was expensive. A small six-room place like theirs could easily run two thousand dollars for the season. But when the girls walked in they kept their coats on, so Andy reluctantly moved toward the thermostat. "Thanks, Dad," said Rachel, who noticed these things.

They bustled while he finished dinner, mulling on the findings of the day. When would his mice act like themselves again?

How on earth was he supported to win an NSF grant with inconclusive results based on inconsiderate rodents? This chewed at him, as did the money the oil heat was costing them, and the fact that Rachel, when she took off her coat, was wearing a sparkly shirt that seemed teenagerish, and tight.

To distract himself from these worries, as they sat around the linoleum-topped table, eating spaghetti, he asked his girls what their thoughts were on Halloween. They shrugged; the radio in the background hummed the evening news.

"Maybe princesses?"

"Maybe," Rachel said, but something in her voice said she was humoring him. "We'll figure it out." Then they were quiet for a while. He thought about telling them about the problems with the alcoholic protein but doubted they would understand. He also thought about telling them about Lionel Shell, but he didn't know quite how to explain him, and worried that the story might make them feel sad.

"I think you could have done something more with this spaghetti," said Rachel, finally, after a few minutes more of listening to the radio, the inconsequential market report.

"You do, huh?"

"Definitely." Rachel had recently taken to the Food Network, and to her own little experiments in the kitchen, which was interesting to him because at the same time she'd started talking about dieting, sugar, and carbs. "I mean, what is this? Spaghetti from a box and a jar of Ragú?"

"You've never complained before."

"I like it, Dad," said Belle. "I think it's awesome."

"It's not awesome," Rachel said, "I mean, it's fine, it's certainly *edible*."

Andy smiled; he couldn't help it. Picked on all day by all these spoiled brats.

"But I mean, couldn't we make our own sauce?" Rachel jumped up to the celery-colored fridge. "Look, we've got garlic, we've got onions—why do you even buy this stuff, Dad, if you're not going to use it? We've got carrots, bacon. We could make our own sauce."

"So you should make your own sauce," he said.

"I will," Rachel said. "Although maybe not with bacon. Nitrates suck. And another thing—"

"Don't say suck," said Belle. "You're not supposed to say that."

Rachel shrugged her off. The evening was dark around them, but the house, percolating with oil heat, felt warm. There were pools of light in the kitchen, above the table, over the sink, over the range. The rest of the room receded into pleasant darkness. "Another thing I've been thinking is that I should have a key to the house. I don't need Mrs. Goldsmith to babysit me anymore."

"She's not babysitting," Andy said. "Don't you like hanging out with Tiffany?"

"Oh my God, how many times do I have to tell you Tiffany Goldsmith is like the biggest loser in school—"

"Rachel," he said, sharply.

"What I mean," she took a breath, "what I mean is that it doesn't matter how I feel about Tiffany. What I feel like is that I'm old enough to be allowed to come home after school with a key. I'm almost eleven. I'm not a baby, and I'm not—"

Her argument was interrupted by a rap on the window of the kitchen door. "Jeremy!" Belle said, jumping up, while Rachel rolled her eyes. "Hey! Look, it's Jeremy!"

Jeremy, and Sheila, whom he had barely seen in the weeks since whatever had happened between them had happened— passing her with a smile and a quick word at school drop-off, and once stopping to chat by the benches in front of Our Lady of Lourdes—they stood huddled outside his front door, filling Andy with an unpleasant anxiety. She hadn't mentioned anything about their encounter, and neither had he, and he assumed that whatever awkwardness it had engendered would soon enough evaporate in the repetition of their day-to-day routine. But she hadn't been in his house since that night, and her presence there now felt enormous. Without wanting to, he imagined her wide white body, that sturdy underwear. He opened the door. They came in, stood by the door.

"Hey, guys," he said, standing, affable. Sheila had her hands in the pocket of her sweatshirt. "Anybody want some spaghetti? Rachel here was saying that we should start making our own sauce, but I don't know—"

"Actually, what I was saying was that I should have my

own key to the house. Jeremy has his own key, right? And he's *eight*."

"Rachel—" Andy said.

Now they were all standing, and Sheila looked apologetic, as though her very presence had started a fight. "We were just taking a walk home from pizza and saw your light on. We thought we'd say hi." She paused. "It's been a while."

"Isn't that right, Mrs. Humphreys? Doesn't Jeremy have his own key?" Rachel had a hand on her hip.

"You know, Rachel," Sheila said, her expression turning from plaintive to responsible, "what your dad decides about you and your safety has nothing to do with whether Jeremy has a key—"

"Yeah, but—"

"Do you guys want to play foosball?" Belle asked. They'd found a foosball table at a rummage sale the previous weekend, set it up in the corner of the living room.

"Argh," said Rachel, who could see she was getting nowhere. Jeremy, who was short and malnourished-looking (all those chicken nuggets) followed the girls out of the room. And then Andy was alone with Sheila, in his house. Outside, the crab apple tree was just starting to shed.

He turned to the sink, began washing the pans.

"I haven't seen you much," she said, picking up a plate and ferrying it to sink.

"You don't have to do that," he said, taking the plate from

her hands. They were standing under the light by the sink, but the moody darkness was all around them, and Andy suddenly felt alarmed by how poor the lighting was in this room. Surely he could buy some lamps, some better bulbs.

"I just wanted to make sure—make sure everything was okay."

"Of course it is," Andy said. "Why wouldn't it be?"

She ferried another plate. "I don't know," she said, disingenuous. "I just wanted to check."

"Everything's great," he said. He felt all the small good parts of his day vanishing, dinner, the rousing speech to Lionel, so that when he fell asleep later that night all he would be left with would be Sheila's pinched face and the guilt blooming in his stomach. Although why be guilty? Sure, he'd never had much of a swinging bachelorhood but he was fairly sure this was how it worked, that men and women could have sex with one another casually and still be friends later. Or had he blown it? Was he supposed to have asked her out to dinner? Was he supposed to have proposed marriage? Was he supposed to be haunted?

Sheila, in the pool of light, looked resigned. She was actually prettier than he gave her credit for.

"Really," he said. "I've just been busy—I've been trying to finish this NSF grant, but I need to complete a few more studies first."

"How's it going?" she asked. The table was clear, the plates were in the dishwasher, and Sheila seemed unsure what to do next. She leaned against a counter. "Your research?"

He motioned her to sit. "Do you want decaf? If I make some? It's going—well, it's been challenging lately." He rarely made coffee after dinner but he felt a need to keep moving. "I thought I'd discovered a protein differentiation that explained why certain alcoholic mice were driven to drink past inebriation. Other studies had suggested something similar, so I thought I was on the right track, but now I'm not so sure. My experiments aren't going the way I'd hoped."

"What would that mean?" she asked. "If your experiment works?"

"Something we've long suspected but is hard to confirm," Andy said. "That there are differences—key differences—in the way alcoholic brains metabolize ethanol."

"Like mine."

"Well, I don't know about yours," he said. He scooped out the decaf, turned on the coffeemaker. "We can't necessarily correlate what happens with mouse brains and human brains. I mean, mice are a fair representation of human brains, but I wouldn't want to make any leaps about your brain from what I did in my lab today. Unless you want me to dissect you."

"What?"

He laughed a little at his own awkwardness. "Do you want anything in your coffee?"

"Black is fine." He delivered their coffees and sat down

across from her, played with a splotch of dried marinara with his thumb. "The idea of your research," Sheila said, "is that alcoholic brains function differently from nonalcoholic brains."

"Right."

"And you don't think that simply feeding them endless amounts of alcohol might change the way their brains work?"

"You mean am I turning them into alcoholics?" Andy shook his head. "I don't think so. These are mice who should drink as much as I can give them."

"But what if you never gave them any? I mean the alcoholic ones, what if you just kept them away from the sauce? Would their brains change? Would they be like normal mice?"

"I don't know," Andy said. "I haven't tried that."

"So you're just assuming they're the way they are because that's the only way you can see them?"

If she was getting at something deeper here, Andy wasn't interested. The research he was conducting was a basic study of the mechanisms of certain neuropeptides, which eventually, he hoped, might lead to a better understanding of brain chemistry under the influence of alcohol. Of course he had long stopped expecting that it would lead to a bigger or more prestigious job for himself, but he thought that maybe his own small work might help future scientists figure something out down the road. The work was important to him. He wanted to understand the mechanism of the alcoholic brain.

Sheila was fiddling with the Claddagh ring she wore in place of a wedding band. "I don't know much about the genetics here—I mean, I didn't study biology or anything—but, you know, nobody else in my family is an alcoholic."

"That doesn't necessarily—"

"And I'm not entirely sure that if certain things in my life hadn't happened—look, alcohol is a cheap and easy way of feeling better. Right? Things happened to me and I needed to feel better cheaply and easily."

"Sheila, this isn't about you."

"Let me finish," she said. "I had a small son at home. I didn't have time or inclination to go to therapy. I tried taking some Prozac but it made me nauseous and it didn't help—"

"Sheila, seriously, my research isn't about you."

"How could you say that?" She laughed, but the laugh sounded bitter, which was unlike Sheila. And he knew and hated the idea that she was bitter about him, about his behavior. "Of course your research is about me."

He sighed. "It's not. I started it before we even met."

"Not me specifically, Andy, but it's about me, or people like me. Right? You want to stick alcoholics in a box, say they are the way they are because of their genes, so that me and everyone else in AA and the guy who killed your wife, you can make some kind of simple sense of us, and I get that—"

"Don't," Andy said, surprised to feel his heart pound.

"Why not?" she said. She pushed her coffee mug on the table with one hand, then pushed it the other way with the other.

"Because my research is about more than just one person. Or even a group of people. It's about the brain." He wished he was better at explaining this. It was hard for laypeople to separate biology from sociology, he knew that, but still he wished Sheila had just a slightly more sophisticated understanding of the way animal research worked.

"I guess I'm just not comfortable with you extrapolating data from mice into a grand understanding of alcoholism."

"You might not be comfortable with it," Andy said, "but that's science. In many ways mouse genes are a decent representation of our own, and if we experiment—"

"Mice don't find pictures of their husbands on the Internet with their best friends—"

"Sheila—"

"Mice don't find out their ex-husbands gave them syphilis." He blinked.

"Don't worry, Andy. It was years ago. I took the antibiotics right away."

She stood, took her mug to the coffeemaker, even though she didn't need a refill. She put her hands on the counter. She had chipped pink polish on her fingers.

"Sheila, I'm sorry if my research makes you uncomfortable."

She was still facing the other way. "Look, you don't have to avoid me because you're afraid it will be weird. It's not going to be weird. We can still be friends."

"I'm not avoiding you," he said. "Honestly. I've just been busy."

She turned to him like she knew that he was lying. But instead of calling him on it, she said, "Fair enough."

"Really," he said. He stood too, went to where she was standing, tried patting her on the shoulder but the gesture felt forced so instead he gave her a half hug. She leaned her head against his arm for a second, but he couldn't tell if she was stiffening inside.

"You okay?" he asked.

"Sure," she said. Then she gathered her coat and called for Jeremy and said good-bye to Andy with a brief but not gingerly hug, and he felt like they'd be okay after a while, that they would still be friends. He wouldn't talk about his research with her anymore and she wouldn't talk about the guy who killed Louisa and that way they would still be friends.

But later, as he was tucking Belle into bed, she asked him if she and Jeremy were going to be brother and sister one day.

"I'm sorry? Are you what?"

"That's what he said," Belle said. "That his mother said that maybe he and I would be brother and sister one day. With Rachel."

"I don't think so," Andy said. He kissed her on the head. "He must be daydreaming."

"So you and his mom aren't getting married?"

"Belle, I promise you I would tell you if I were getting married."

"That's what I thought," she said. "Okay."

It was almost ten when he went back out to the kitchen, where Rachel was assiduously chopping garlic. Ordinarily he would have told her it was probably a little late for cooking, and ordinarily she might have either listened or ignored him, but now, humiliated, he went straight for the television, unwilling to know what his oldest daughter knew, and unable to ask her any questions.

SIX

Princeton was one of the most beautiful places Andy had ever seen — rolling lawns and dignified courtyards and cottage-like shops selling Spode china — but still he left the day after he received his PhD and never returned. In fact, he'd been in Miami four years already before the thing happened between Rosenblum and the girl. It was this thing that ended his friendship with Rosenblum, not because Andy was so ashamed of what Hank had done (although he was) but because he had been too busy with his life in Miami to reach out to him, pick up the phone. As far as he knew, Rosenblum had never forgiven him his absence. But Andy also knew he'd been replaced in the old man's heart several times in the four years between his departure from Princeton and the incident with the girl; Rosenblum was profligate with his affection, but not constant, and several graduate students had already taken Andy's place even before the girl came along. Andy heard from some of them. Others, in shock, buried their heads in their own work, too sad about the girl, whom many of them had known.

The girl. Louisa had been stunned but not surprised by the grotesque story, and Rosenblum's behavior. "I always had a feeling Hank was going to get ahead of himself one day, do something accidentally terrible."

"I still feel bad for him."

"Are you going to reach out? Here, hold her down." She was squeezing a dropperful of antibiotics into Belle's wailing maw, Belle who was plagued by ear infections until she got tubes on her second birthday.

"I will," Andy said, "I'll call him," knowing even then he wouldn't—knowing that it was possible he would never speak to Rosenblum again. After the antibiotics, they gave Belle Tylenol, then walked her in her stroller around Quail Run's pool until she fell asleep.

But although Andy never did call, he kept up, to a certain extent, with Rosenblum's whereabouts, first through the news reports and later through an informal network of postdocs who kept a lane of the Internet thrumming with news of the great man's peregrinations. It seemed Rosenblum was in Europe for a while, then South America for a valedictory tour through Darwin's Galápagos, cataloging those famous finches. Then the lawsuit went through and Rosenblum was suddenly bankrupt (Princeton refused to cover him, as he had already been dismissed when the verdict came in) and now, according to reports, Rosenblum lived near Montauk, in a small house given to him by an admirer of *Religion's Dangerous Lie.*

Andy had thought about calling him when Lou was killed, then thought again. It was selfish to look for pity where he had offered none; moreover, Rosenblum's thoughts on death were broadly admirable but, on a person-to-person level, repellant.

Regardless, Andy was haunted by his old mentor—or, if not haunted exactly (only one person was allowed to haunt Andy at a time, thank you) certainly he felt attached to his memory, and often trailed by a feeling that Rosenblum was just around the corner, smoking a pipe, pontificating. Which is why he felt both astonishment and satisfaction to find a large envelope sitting on his office desk one morning covered in Rosenblum's kindergarten penmanship. He'd been expecting this without realizing he was expecting it.

"Rosemary? Where'd this letter come from?"

"UPS just dropped it off. Why? Is it suspicious?"

"No," Andy said. "It's just . . ." He sat down on his chair to examine the envelope—it had a return address from a legal office, but the handwriting was unmistakable. Rosenblum! That old bastard. He held the letter in both hands, admiring it. A part of him wanted to kiss it. God, he'd missed him. He would not tear open the letter; he would savor it like a gift.

"Professor?" A timid knock on his open door. Lionel Shell, in a sweater-vest.

"Lionel?"

"I wanted to tell you thanks for the other day. I'm doing much better now. You really—I appreciated our talk. Thank you."

"Great," Andy said. "Glad to hear it." He gave Lionel his you're-dismissed look, turned back to the letter. He'd forgotten how even Rosenblum's toddler scrawl could inspire, in him, a sense of revelation: when he first started working with Rosenblum he wondered if he should save the memos the great man left him just in case they were worth something some day. He'd imagined himself, in his wilder flights of fancy, one day cataloging Rosenblum's papers in the scientific libraries of Princeton or Oxford or MIT, archiving both the brilliant manuscripts and the tedious minutiae, and contributing, from his own files, forgotten handwritten missives like "see notes on self-reinforcing divergence" or "I've got some pastrami in the fridge." And now, again, Rosenblum's writing in his hands.

"You got a present?"

Lionel was still in his doorway.

"I thought you left."

"You going to open it?" Lionel said, smiling. He came into the office, plopped himself on Andy's extra chair.

He was too pleased even to scowl at Lionel. "Oh, why not?" Andy enjoyed the anticipatory beat of his heart for one more second, then took a pair of scissors from his drawer and slid them along the side of the envelope, opening it to reveal a handwritten note on stationery with a legal letterhead.

"Who's it from?"

"Jesus, Lionel, could I have a little privacy?"

Lionel looked wounded. "Sure. Sorry." The boy collected himself, went away.

The letter was vintage Rosenblum:

Waite, been keeping up with yr dealings, know you filed for tenure. Assume you can't be hurt now from dealing with a semicriminal like yr old pal Hank. Proud of you for getting this far by the way, although half-ass school you gotta admit. Do you admit it? What kind of man have you become, anyway?

Wrote a book and would like your opinion if you still have time for the man who made you who you are. If not, you can fuck yrself. But if you're willing to look the thing over, send me a note care of my lawyer at Briggs Watson, New York. Thinking of you fondly. Hank Rosenblum

Stapled to the note was the manuscript's title page. The thing was called "Death and Immortality."

Death and immortality, religion's dangerous lie.

Andy turned to his laptop immediately to write to Hank via the lawyer:

Yes, I'd love the manuscript. And please, if you could send me Hank's e-mail, his phone number, anything, I'd love the chance to talk to him. It's been years and I haven't known where to find him, but if you would be so kind as to pass his information along, I'd be appreciative.

As he was pressing "print," he heard another tentative knock on his door. God, Lionel, go away.

"Professor Waite?" A female voice—not Lionel. Argh, but on the other hand, his light was on.

"Yes."

Melissa Potter, in a protective position, slightly hunched, her backpack sliding over a shoulder. "You said this was a good time to meet?"

"I did?"

She looked alarmed. "To discuss my independent study," she said. "I brought all these books," she added, letting the backpack fall to the floor. "Is it still an okay time?"

Was it an okay time? What he wanted was to spend more time with Rosenblum, reread the note once or twice (what did he mean by "keeping up with yr dealings"?) and perhaps do a little Internet stalking. See what Rosenblum had been up to. He wasn't like his students or his daughters, people who spent so much time online researching their friends and rivals they could name what everyone they knew ate for breakfast each morning. It had been a long time since Andy had poked around, looking for news on Rosenblum. But now he thought he'd spend an hour or two on the cause. And maybe that lawyer at Briggs Watson would give him something to go on.

"Professor?"

Andy looked up at the girl, sucking on her cross in his doorway. *Didn't your mother ever teach you it's rude to stand in people's doorways?*

"Can I please come in?"

She took his blank look as assent, slumped into his office and sat heavily on a chair. Then she bent down and began retrieving book after book from her backpack, piling them up on the corner of his desk. Reluctantly, Andy put Hank's letter back in its envelope, stuck it in his drawer. The books kept coming. They were all brand new and published by places he'd never heard of.

What would Rosenblum make of all this? Would Rosenblum ever have agreed to talking about intelligent design with this girl? He probably would have. Rosenblum loved a good fight, and he especially loved fighting with women. (Or maybe he wouldn't have seen it as a good fight at all—the opponent was so uninformed, and so droopy.)

"So," Andy said, "these are the texts you're going to use for research?"

Melissa nodded, stuck her gold cross into her mouth, then let it fall. "I borrowed some of them from my church," she said, bending again, fishing for more materials. "And some of them I ordered online. The bookstore didn't have them. But it's not like I was expecting them to. I mean, why would I expect diversity of opinion from a college bookstore?" She sat up with a smirk and a paperback in hand.

God Is a Rainbow. The cover, cheaply bound, showed a blurrily printed rainbow with a pot of gold at one end and a cross at the other.

"A rainbow? Is that a metaphor?"

She looked confused. "It's my favorite. It was written by my pastor."

"Ah."

Adam's Rib. The Macroevolution Myth. The Mystery of Intent, and this cover cribbed directly from the Sistine Chapel, except where God was supposed to be reaching out for Adam's finger instead he reached for a test tube.

"How many do you have here? Have you read them all?"

"Um, I think I have nineteen. These are the ones I've finished," she said, gesturing to the pile on his desk. "I thought I'd give them to you so you could get started."

"Me?" The various piles of papers on his desk looked lopsided, ready to fall, his research grant oversized and heavy—he reached out to straighten it, avoiding Melissa's narrowing gaze.

"How else are you going to understand my independent study? If you don't read these books how will you know what I'm doing? Besides, I agreed to read *your* books."

"Right," he said. "Well, you understand I'm busy. And also, as professor, it's my job to assign and yours to read." He stopped fiddling with the stack, picked up *The Macroevolution Myth.*

"So maybe you could look at just a few? Like five or six?"

Andy grunted. "How is it possible," asked the jacket copy, "for *random mutations* to turn one species into another? Is this the best Darwinians can come up with? Shouldn't there be a better explanation to this most important of human questions?"

"I think you'll like that one," Melissa said, settling herself on the chair. "It's pretty good. And here," she said, flicking through her notebook, "I've outlined the dimensions of my study, the paper I'm going to write at the end. My thesis is that intelligent design is a more realistic alternative to Darwinian evolution, if you think that sounds okay. Or something—maybe you can make it sound smarter than that for me. I'm not sure I'm in love with 'more realistic alternative.'" She pondered this for a moment. "But anyway I realized I never had you sign the paper-work, so I brought a pen, if you could just—"

"Do you even understand the basics of Darwinian evolution yet?" He channeled Rosenblum. "Have you read anything that I've asked you to read? Or are you going to start debating something you don't even really understand?"

She hunched her shoulders, a silent harrumph. "I understand Darwinian evolution," she said. "I read the books you assigned, and I took Bio 101 at County."

"So what do you think it is, exactly?"

"Evolution? Uh, you know," she said, sarcastic. "Survival of the fittest. Natural selection."

"Right," he said, "but what do those things mean?"

She sighed, heavily. She didn't like being underestimated. "Single-celled organisms evolved over countless generations, via the accumulation of small genetic mutations. The organisms that survived and passed on their genes continued to breed, and the ones that didn't went extinct. Eventually, these single-celled organisms evolved into all the different animals and plants and fungi and bacteria on the planet."

"That's right," Andy said, pleased with her succinct response, having grown accustomed, when asking questions of undergrads, to much more hemming and prevarication.

"But just because I can define it doesn't mean I believe it."

"Because?"

"Because it's patently ridiculous," she said. She stopped fiddling with her necklace. "If you're willing to accept that life came about because, I don't know, lightning struck some organic material in the primordial soup—and this, by the way, is not something I'm willing to accept—then fine, that's how life began. But to think that random mutations could be so miraculously beneficial as to create the eye, the wing, the lung—can't you see how silly that is?"

"Melissa," he said, "just because your books say it's silly doesn't mean your books are right."

"Why are you willing to ridicule books you haven't even read?"

"I'm not," he said, then started again. "It's just—books like these, with these unprovable arguments—" He stopped. He was going about this the wrong way. How would Rosenblum have done it? With more sarcasm, of course, but also he wouldn't let the undergraduate frame the argument.

"Well?"

"Look, why *couldn't* random mutations develop into an eye over eons? In fact, why wouldn't they? If you started, say, with cells that just happened to be slightly more photosensitive than others, and if organisms that were able to detect light through these photosensitive cells had that much of an advantage, in a hostile world, over organisms that couldn't detect light, why *wouldn't* successive generations of selection refine those photosensitive cells into, you know—something like an eye?"

"I think a better question is why *would* they."

"Because that's how evolution works. We have all evolved, mutation by mutation, from single-celled organisms that existed hundreds of millions of years ago. There's molecular evidence. There's proof!" And here he wished he really was Rosenblum, who always had the numbers at his disposal, the right way to recount the history of DNA.

"Your argument is so circular," Melissa said. "Evolution exists because we're the products of evolution."

"Is that what I said?" He feared it was.

Melissa sighed again, but this time she seemed almost disappointed, or, far worse, compassionate. "Sometimes I think Darwinians don't know how ridiculous they sound. Like *we're* the ridiculous ones, when all you have to go on are mutations—"

"That's not all we have to go on," said Andy.

"*Mutations!*"

Andy, who had never before found himself mocked for holding fairly conventional beliefs, was even more annoyed with himself than usual. Why did she have to keep saying "mutations" in that tone of voice?

"So that's why we're here, then," she said. "Instead of God, you choose mutants."

"All right," Andy said, "I get it. Enough."

What he knew of evolution was what he'd learned as an undergraduate and applied to the rest of his research: that genes were hereditary, that mutations in those genes expressed themselves in different behaviors or traits, and that the different behaviors or traits that led to more successful reproduction were the ones that were more likely to be passed on. This was the way of life. If it wasn't, he couldn't conduct his research. He couldn't teach biology.

"Here," Melissa said, opening *The Macroevolution Myth* to a passage she'd highlighted in pink. "Listen, Professor Waite. Just so you can see where I'm coming from. I'm quoting: in order for supposedly 'helpful' mutations to randomly arise in organisms, an organism would have to wait approximately 216 million years, according to conservative estimates, to see this mutation arise. If one accepts the secular estimation that life on this planet dates back 3.5 billion years, one only has to do simple math to realize that enough time simply hasn't occurred since life began to account for every single mutation necessary to create something as complex as the human heart, much less the brain." She closed the book triumphantly. "See?"

"You realize this language isn't particularly convincing," Andy said. "What do you mean 'conservative estimate'? What is a 'secular estimation'?"

"Do you really want all the numbers?" Melissa asked. "I mean, there are footnotes if you want them—"

"I don't need to see the footnotes," he said. "I just—listen—" and here his mind went, without bidding, to his NSF grant, his mice, the volcano he and Belle were supposed to make for her presentation on North American geology, "when I said I would oversee this independent study with you, I suppose I was hoping you'd go with a different thesis."

"Well, what thesis were you hoping for, exactly? That intelligent design is wrong? That the Great Biological Powers That Be are right because everyone says they are?" Frustration put an appealing flush in her cheeks, which Andy noted and dismissed.

"Why don't we take out the right and the wrong," he suggested, letting his voice grow more gentle, supportive. "How about we revise your thesis to be that intelligent design represents an alternative to Darwinian evolution that's, I don't know—that's worth investigating. As opposed to what you have now, which is that it's a better alternative. Because it's not, and I can't support your investigation into an untruth."

Melissa rolled her eyes. "That just sounds flaky," she said.

"And also it's not what I want to say. I want to talk about intelligent design. I want to make an argument for it. I want to prove that the world is simply too complex, too perfectly designed, to be a product of," here she wrinkled her nose again, "*mutation.*"

"But you're only saying that because the only literature you read supports your beliefs."

"I could accuse you," she said, "of the same thing."

His grant was only a quarter finished, and the first part was due in a month. He hadn't done laundry all week. Dinner, homework, the volcano.

"So are you in or are you out?"

"I don't know," he said, scratching his cheek.

Melissa's face went slack with horror. "I need these credits, Professor Waite!"

"I mean, I'm in. But only because I said I was in. Not because I think you're going to convince me that," he picked up one of her books again, Saint Jesus of the Test Tubes, "that God is a rainbow."

"Fine," she said. "As long as you sign." She bent down again to her backpack, took out a folder, removed a blue sheet of paper—the official Independent Study Faculty Agreement—and a white sheet of paper, which laid out her goals for the year: to read and analyze the following books and articles, to put together a bibliography of useful materials on intelligent design, and to write a thirty-page research paper.

"Thank you," she said.

"No problem," Andy lied.

She put her haul into her backpack and stood. Now that she was standing straight, Andy realized how tall she was. "You have young daughters, right, Professor Waite?"

How did she know? But the proof was all around him, in the photos tacked up to the bulletin board on his wall, the lunch sitting on his desk, packed in Rachel's old *Mulan* lunch box.

"If you ever need a babysitter, you know, I love kids."

Andy smiled. Once upon a time, he imagined, female students offered up their bodies. Now they offered up their Friday evenings. "That's nice of you, Melissa. I don't go out much, though."

"Well, just in case," she said. "And thanks for signing those papers."

"You bet," Andy said. As soon as she was gone, he removed Rosenblum's letter from the drawer.

What kind of man have you become, anyway?

The kind who can't slam-dunk a fight with a creationist. The kind who can't prove a simple hypothesis about drunken mice.

But, he thought to himself, reading Rosenblum's letter for the fourth, fifth, sixth time, the kind who would take on Melissa in the first place. The kind who would find the time to debate her. The kind who takes reasonable care of his girls, who's a decent enough neighbor, who tries to be cheerful most of the time. The kind who, when he becomes too resentful about the life fate has handed him, looks in at his daughters sleeping in the same bunk and feels a renewed ability to go on.

There are worse men out there, Hank.

When he was a child in Shaker Heights he would walk to Horseshoe Lake with his mother on chilly March mornings to collect paramecia. They would each have two big jelly jars, and they would crouch by the creek and dip in their jars and collect all sorts of terrific things: paramecia and amoebas and sometimes, accidentally, tiny golden fish arching like thumb-nails. They would take them back to their living room and Andy's mother would pull out the microscope, set it down on the kitchen table. She'd make pond-water slides, stick them under the scope, adjust the magnification. There the paramecia would flutter, the hydras would bulge. Andy's mother would turn up the magnification and suddenly Andy would be able to see the insides of the tiny creatures, the micronucleus and macronucleus, the vacuoles, the dozens of quivering cilia.

"Life exists on scales beyond our imagination," his mother would say, her face warm next to his by the microscope.

What kind of man have you become, Andy?

The kind who still sometimes remembered that the world is full of wonder.

He put Melissa's books in his backpack and headed home,

thinking more frequently than he wanted about the way her cheeks flushed and her fleeting smile.

THAT NIGHT, THE volcano flowed over the kitchen counter, onto stacks of dirty dishes and the remains of Rachel's chicken and broccoli casserole (low-fat sour cream, low-fat cheese). Belle squealed in delight, reminding Andy of his own reaction when his mice behaved the way they were supposed to (why wouldn't they behave the way they were supposed to?).

"This is some serious lava flow, Dad," she said, mopping up the floor with a rag. "This is like some Pompeii-level stuff."

"I was going to send Dad in with those leftovers tomorrow, FYI," Rachel said, glaring at the mess from her perch at the kitchen table. She was engaged in a back-and-forth with someone on Google Chat, which was a program Andy wasn't sure he'd permitted. House rules dictated that all computer use had to stay in the kitchen, under public eye, because Andy had read one too many articles about perverts trolling and high school bullies sexting and whatever else happened in the grubby corners of the Internet and he was not going to let any of it happen to his girls.

"He could still eat it, if he wanted," Belle said.

"Excuse me? It's been volcanoed."

"It's not real volcano, idiot," Belle snapped. "It's soda water and vinegar. Oh, and I guess a little dish soap, but not that much."

"I know you didn't just call me an idiot."

"Girls," Andy said. "Enough."

They cleaned the kitchen and bathed with a certain amount of persnicketiness and fell asleep in their respective bunks. After Rachel was out, Andy went to the laptop to see what she had been typing with such ferocity, and to whom.

Lilybeansxox. He didn't really like the sound of that at all. Rachel's handle (racherache) at least had a sort of alliteration thing happening. Who was this lilybeansxox and what did she (that was a she, right?) want with his Rachel?

Was it wrong to spy on his girls? Andy bit a nail. Perhaps it would have been if he'd had any idea what they were talking about, but the whole back-and-forth between Rachel and Lily, set up in choppy little lines, was so full of acronyms and references to things he didn't understand (what was a 303, a DGT?) that he didn't really feel like a spy as much as a visitor from another planet. What did AYTMTB mean? BBIAS?

His daughters were studying Spanish in school but they already spoke another language. This disconcerted him, as it was a language he knew he would never master, while the various languages he spoke (as parent, grown-up, biologist) would all be available to his girls should they want to know them one day. They were privileged in a way he wasn't. It didn't seem fair, that he should be raising them and yet they should be, in so many ways, profoundly unknowable.

Still they murmured in their sleep, he thought. Still he could admire them and know how lovely they were, and maybe that was his compensation. But on the other hand, what the hell was an IWIAM?

It was midnight, but the idea of getting in bed seemed depressing. He went out to the porch, fingered a cigar. He could go see if Sheila was around but—but no, he didn't feel like seeing Sheila. Four houses down, her downstairs light was still on, and he knew she'd keep him company, but the thought of her loose breasts came to mind and he inadvertently shuddered.

Back inside, he thought, well, I could work on the grant. A page at a time and by the end of the month he'd be done—but the truth was as long as his mice refused to behave the way he wanted them to, it seemed silly to ask for any more government money. Almost half a million dollars, and it would certainly come in handy, but there was no way the NSF would write him a check without first approving of his findings. And right now, for reasons that were beyond him, his findings were a mess. What would the tenure board say if they knew? Who would give him tenure on the basis of a half-dozen failures?

Still, maybe he was just looking at things the wrong way.

He opened his briefcase to take out his notebooks, but the first thing he grabbed, glossily bound, was one of Melissa's paperbacks. *God Is a Rainbow.* He opened it, took it to the bathroom, where he often got his best leisure reading done. But waiting for him in the basket next to the john was a copy of *The Onion* he'd been meaning to read, and so he sat there, chuckling to himself, until his back started to hurt, which was a sign that he was an hour closer to death and it was time to go to bed.

SEVEN

Three months after Rachel was born, Lou admitted smuggling her into church. "It wasn't my fault," she said, after she'd confessed. "I was compelled."

"What do you mean, compelled?" Andy had asked, annoyed, betrayed, but also consumed by tenderness the way he always was when he watched Louisa breast-feed.

"It was like—it was like something had taken over my body."

"Yeah, but—"

"It was almost like I was possessed."

"Give me a break, Lou."

She shrugged.

In the months and years before in the NICU, Lou witnessed the hospital chaplain perform baptisms every few months on her tiny patients, touching them gently with thumbs moistened from flasks of holy water. Once, when nobody could find the chaplain, a devout nurse performed an emergency baptism on a boy who had been born at twenty-three weeks, plum purple and monkey-faced, and who died a few minutes later. The boy's parents had asked her to do it; they watched as he was blessed and held him, together, as he died.

Throughout her pregnancy, Lou would come home and report on these baptisms, Andy listening patiently as she told him about the chaplain and the nurse and the dead babies, gauging him for his reaction. What did she want him to say? Of course he understood: if ever there was a time to be suspicious, to think toward miracles, it was when your child was struggling for life, when the distance between life and death could be measured in milligrams. And if these ritual blessings gave parents comfort . . .

"So you understand?"

"I understand," he said. "That doesn't mean I approve." For even then it was hard to discount his years with Rosenblum: fairy tales were meant for children. Adults should find their consolation in the truth.

Lou stuck her feet in his lap. "I don't know, Andy, if only you could be there—it's really beautiful to see these parents watch their children get baptized. It gives them strength to keep going, you know? And also, when you're in there for so long, and there's so little to get excited about, it's nice to have a ceremony. Something to welcome the baby into the world, not just get ready for another intervention. Worry about whether or not he's going to die."

"But isn't that what baptism is? Protection against death?"

"Andy, come on, it's more than that. It's like a declaration of love."

"Were you baptized?"

"You know I wasn't," Lou said.

"And didn't your parents love you?"

"Oh, cut it out." Lou had been raised in Arizona by parents who explored various faiths with fleeting but passionate resolve: Unitarianism and Zen Buddhism and for a brief, uncomfortable moment, Scientology. Lou and her sister had announced to their parents in early adolescence that they would no longer participate in their religious experimentation; since then they had only rarely visited a house of worship or even wished someone a happy holiday. Her father had died of cancer an evangelical Christian; her mother lived peacefully in Sedona as a yogi. Before Lou met Andy, she'd spent most Christmases by herself, handing out sandwiches to homeless people; now she and Andy did that together. But she was never as vitriolic about her faithlessness as Andy was, nor was she as smug. She had never had Hank Rosenblum as a professor.

"I wish you would just have an open mind about these things, Andrew," Lou said. She only called him Andrew when she was annoyed, so he apologized, rubbed her feet in his lap. Later on, he did the laundry.

And then the baby was born: healthy! Enormous! A full head of hair! Rachel after her father, Ray. Lou's mother came in from Arizona, Andy's mother from Ohio, and they both marveled at the baby's alertness, her solidity, her eager feeding and sound sleeping. They made soups and lasagnas and let Lou take naps and when they left Lou dissolved into tears until the baby started crying too. And then, three months after Rachel was born, Louisa confessed what she'd done. Andy had left early to go to the lab, and Louisa was panicking about the end of her maternity leave; to distract herself she took a long morning walk with the baby, in her new expensive stroller.

Unintentionally, the walk took her past Christ the King. That it was a Catholic church, that it was Tuesday morning, that the place was officially closed—Lou didn't consider any of it. She said, later, that what she did felt as instinctive as nursing her baby when she cried, as instinctive as kissing her head while she slept. "I'm telling you, Andy, I was compelled."

She parked the stroller at the base of the church's stairs and walked her up toward the double doors, cradling Rachel's solid body against her chest. Although the place was officially shut for business, one of the front doors was partway open and Louisa shimmied in. A janitor looked at her crossly, saw the baby in her arms, waved her through the vestibule into the large, chilly sanctuary with the marble basin at the rear.

Rachel, startled by the sudden cold, opened her hazel eyes wide as if she were going to yell. "Shhh," Lou said, kissing her forehead, keeping her quiet. She took the baby to the marble basin and dipped a finger in the water, then dotted the water on Rachel's forehead. The baby started to cry for real this time, and Lou rocked her and sang to her until she stopped. The janitor gave her the stink eye now but still didn't tell her to leave. And Lou couldn't leave until she said something.

But what to say?

Her early years of religious pilgrimage had not prepared her for this kind of moment. And even the things the chaplain had said—Jesus Christ, banish the devil—none of that felt right either. So, when she was sure Rachel could be quiet—for whoever else would hear this, she wanted Rachel to hear it—she made up her own small prayer: "Dear Whoever Is in Charge, if there is indeed Someone in Charge, please bless this baby. Please keep her safe from harm. Please let her live a life of joy, surrounded by people who love her. Do not let her be troubled. Protect her. Please. If You're in charge—if You're out there. Please watch over this child." She recited all this to Andy, later, during her confession.

And then, although it seemed selfish, she added, "And please watch over my husband and me so that we can always be near her, as long as she needs us to be."

It didn't seem like enough but she wasn't sure what else to say. She thought of her dead father, and Andy's dead father, whom she had never met. She thought of her grandparents, whom she had loved, and their parents, whose stories she'd heard when she was little. She imagined a great link of ancestors standing over her, watching her hold this baby in her arms. Generations of men and women who came together and created one another. And now she was here, having created this little girl. She was an ancestor too now. She remembered the way her father improvised bedtime stories, the way her mother sewed them superhero capes.

She lifted her baby toward the church ceiling, the sky. "Amen."

She said thank you to the janitor, who murmured, "God bless," and then she hurried back out of the church. "Are we gonna tell your daddy we did this, Rache? What do you think? Are we gonna get in trouble or what?" But it was too late. Someone had stolen her stroller.

WHEN MELISSA CAME back to Andy's office with a draft of her thesis statement, he found, to his relief, that she had replaced the cross around her neck with a dormitory ID on a long beaded chain. He took the paper she extended, looked at it. "Did I tell you to bring me this?"

"Why are you always asking me that?" she said, perching on the chair opposite his desk. She was wearing a black turtleneck and jeans and looked older, more serious than the last time they'd met, just a week before. "Sometimes I think you have no memory at all, Dr. Waite."

"I'm just distracted," Andy sighed. "Or it's possible you're right, I have no memory at all."

She chuckled because she thought he was kidding. Andy scanned her paragraph until he got to the meat: intelligent design is provable because studies of natural phenomena are best explained by the intervention of a Designer.

He scratched his head, wondered again why he'd said yes to this project, and how to navigate a fight he was too tired to have.

"So what do you think?"

"You've got a lot of passive voice in here." He pushed the paper back at her. "See if you can rewrite it more clearly. And be sure to be specific about 'natural phenomena.' I want to know exactly what you're referring to."

"I was going to talk about the bombardier beetle, and the explosive mix of chemicals it uses for self-defense. And also the heart of the giraffe, how it's strong enough to pump blood up its neck but doesn't get crushed by the weight of all that blood. And also I was going to talk about DNA."

"How so?"

"Well," she said, leaning forward, her breasts straining heavily against her turtleneck (why did he notice her breasts, and the way the black fabric made her skin look so white?), "DNA is a code, right? It's the code, the language, that provides instructions on how all living things develop and behave. But codes aren't random. Codes aren't created by chaos.

Codes are only the product of a design. So who could be the designer of DNA? Some kind of alien intelligence? Human beings? Or was DNA designed by mere luck? I don't think so. The only real rational explanation for the coding is an Intelligent Designer who planned it out."

Andy sighed. If he were Rosenblum, he would be able to expound briefly on the conditions of chance, on the viral proteins that almost certainly first created DNA, on energy and possibility and why God was even more unlikely than Melissa's "mere luck." If he were Rosenblum, he would say, in a voice so drippingly gentle it was cruel, "Dear girl, please don't be fooled into thinking that religion is an answer to a scientific question. We can answer the questions of why people are religious by using science, but we cannot answer basic questions of science by pointing to miracles. Don't forget, dear, that to your great-great-grandfather my crappy cell phone would have seemed like a miracle."

But Andy was not Rosenblum, so he just sighed and said, "I'd skip the giraffe and go straight to the DNA part of the thesis."

"You think?" she said. "'Cause the giraffe stuff is pretty interesting. The pressure per square inch of blood in a giraffe's vessels is so strong it should theoretically cause a stroke, but instead, the giraffe has this sponge of blood vessels under its brain that relieves the pressure. Nothing else in the animal kingdom has anything like this, so it's clearly the product of spontaneous design."

"Or else it slowly evolved along the singular branch that eventually produced the giraffe."

Melissa grinned and shook her head. "It's so crazy how Darwinists refuse the simple answer when a complicated one will do."

"It's even more crazy how intelligent designers refuse to use science when a magic wand will do."

For an instant they smiled at each other. "So if I cut the giraffe can I keep the thesis?"

What could he say? "Cut the bombardier beetle too."

She nodded, folded her paper into her backpack. "Well, thanks again, Dr. Waite. How's everything with your mice, by the way?" She'd gotten what she wanted, so now she was cordial.

"Eh," he said. "I'm supposed to finish a grant application, but it's tough going. I can't replicate my initial findings."

"So then what?"

"So then—" He flicked on his computer, a signal that he was planning on getting to work and she could leave. "So then I don't get the money." She stayed quiet. "And I suppose I start to feel even more insecure about everything my research is supposed to prove."

"Does this affect your job here?"

"Not really," he said. "But it doesn't help."

"Are you worried?"

Who would even ask that? "Sure, sometimes. I mean, it's

better to have a job than not to have one. And my girls—I need to provide for my girls."

She looked thoughtful. Her eyebrows were knitted.

"Anyway, it will all work out," he said in his class-dismissed voice. He swiveled toward his computer. The monitor was frozen on the welcome page.

"Your girls will be okay," Melissa said.

"Will they now?"

She ignored his sarcasm. "It's a cliché, but it's true—kids are so resilient. Lots of dads change jobs. I mean, I'm sure you're not in danger, but worst case—" He looked at her. She was tucking a hair behind her ear. "Worst case, I'm sure you guys will figure out another happy way to live."

"It's just that they've already been through a lot." She was still looking at him so intently. "Their mother is gone."

"My dad left when I was two. The guy I call my dad is actually my stepdad."

"Oh."

"And he's a good guy and everything but he's not so great at keeping a job. We've been foreclosed on, we had to live with my aunt for a while. Now there are five of them living in a two-bedroom apartment. They just had to move again. I'm the only one who got away."

"That sounds tough."

She shrugged. "Things aren't always easy, I guess is my point, but you know what? You ask my brothers and they'll tell you they're happy. They play football, don't really care that they get free lunch at school. And me too! I mean, I'm in college! Can you even believe it?" Had he ever met someone like her before, someone who was so literally transformed by a smile? "Anyway, your kids have a great dad. That's really what matters."

"I guess." This wasn't the sort of thing he usually discussed with students, with anybody.

"Look, I don't want to sound like a nag or anything but you really might want to take a look at some of the books I gave you. They're really good at pointing out the bigger picture."

"Melissa—"

"I'm just saying."

"Thank you," he said, curtly.

"Oh, it's no problem, really," she said, leaving him to his cluttered office and the computer that refused to turn on.

GOD IS A RAINBOW was still in his bathroom while Belle took a bath (she still preferred long, dreamy sessions in the bathtub to the brisk efficiency of the shower); he picked it up when he brought her a fresh towel, moved it to the kitchen countertop, left it there.

"Dad, what's this?" Nosy Rachel, making tomorrow's lunches. "This isn't the sort of thing you usually read. What is it, a kid's book?"

"It belongs to one of my students," he said, frowning over Rachel's shoulder as she peered at the jacket photo.

"You've got some wackadoo students," she said.

His plan that night was to go over his data, try to see any inconsistencies. In a one-man lab it was so easy to get things wrong: he could have adulterated the ethanol, mixed up the specimens, poorly recorded the levels they were drinking, fudged his brain scans. Every part of his experiment required attention to detail, which was a quality he prized in himself when he was a graduate student but now felt almost impossible to achieve. The milk in his fridge was past its expiration date; the girls had permission slips for school a week overdue. Well, at least he'd fill out the permission slips. Melissa's book glared at him from his countertop. It was that or sleep or his dysfunctional notebooks; the book disheartened him the least. He filled out the slips, then took it to the den.

The book was written and self-published by Stephen and Michelle F. Cling, the husband-and-wife pastor team who tended the flock of the Hollyville Mission Church in Hollyville, New Jersey. Melissa Potter's pastor and his wife. They were writing from the perspective of small-town theologians, not scientists, and they began by presenting a folksy summary of who they were and what their flock was like (this was a word they actually used, *flock*). But in reading their description of Hollyville and its Mission Church, Andy found himself, despite himself, charmed. This part of New Jersey, south and west of the pines, was still mostly family farms, specialty crops, tomatoes, peaches, lettuce. Not enough land for agribusiness, not enough real-estate pressure to sell out for new developments.

The Clings described their town as two stoplights and a general store, the kind of place that made Mount Deborah seem bustling by contrast. The kids drove tractors before they drove cars, and spent summer nights swimming at the quarry. And everyone went to church on Sundays: Hollyville Mission or their friendly competitors, Hollyville Baptist and Hollyville Word of God. After church, neighbors ate lunch together, and the kids and old people took naps.

It sounded like a nice enough life, or a nice enough life to keep reading about, anyway. And as he read, Andy found himself admiring the Clings for other reasons. Primarily, in their two hundred pages of Christian chitchat, they didn't pretend to know more about evolution than people who were actually trained in evolutionary biology. In fact, as the Clings moved from small-town history to introductory theology, their book spent only a few pages on evolution. It assumed that its readers believed in a God who created the earth and everything on it in seven days, so it didn't spend much time trying to argue that notion. Instead, it talked about why people were here in the first place — why God had even bothered.

And because the book wasn't trying to seem scientific, and because he found Stephen and Michelle's prose style charming, complete with anecdotes from the church and diversions into song lyrics they both liked, Andy found himself unexpectedly immersed in *God Is a Rainbow*. That first night he read until one in the morning, and the next night too, and the next, keeping it by his bed and reading from it at night when he couldn't sleep, or when an ephemerally horrifying dream woke him up at four in the morning. He found himself slowing down, in fact, so that he wouldn't finish it too fast, and underlining the passages he liked: the church luncheon menus, softball games on neighboring farms. He imagined Melissa helping her mother make fried chicken, blueberry pie with blueberries from New Jersey bogs. He was surprised by how much these images pleased him: her large forearms beating down pie dough, her cross resting above her breastbone, shining under the church's stained glass.

He read the book for two week's worth of late nights, memorizing, despite himself, the comforting words of Stephen and Michelle Cling. It wasn't all tractors and quarries and pies. There was religion here too, but under the spell of all that pie Andy couldn't help but take in the religion. "You are here because of divine will," the Clings said. "You are here because God wanted you to be here."

It was late, he was tired, he kept reading.

We are here to fulfill our divine purpose in life. To make the world a place fashioned in our image, which is, of course, to make it in the reflected image of God.

And everyone you have ever lost has fulfilled his or her divine purpose. And he or she is waiting in the presence of God until the day you will be reunited.

Andy rolled over in bed. He was becoming, now, too acquainted with four in the morning, and in the small bedroom which still felt weirdly unfurnished, papers everywhere, books everywhere, clothing in an Ikea bookshelf—what kind of grown man kept his clothing stacked in an Ikea bookshelf?—he took out his pen and underlined.

Have you ever spoken to a small, guilty child who's trying to get out of telling the truth? Ever notice how, when the child starts spinning his story, it becomes more and more complicated, more and more fanciful? He would need a mere sentence to tell the truth; to tell his elaborate tale requires paragraphs.

Life is like that. It can be read in a sentence: in the beginning, there was God. But the fabulous tales of nonbelievers require paragraphs and paragraphs, books and books, nutty theories upon nuttier theories because fiction is always more dressed up than fact. God is a fact. Atheist theory is fiction.

And even if evolution were true, how did it get started?

And even if evolution got started by some freak lightning strike, what was here on earth before that?

Nothing? What is nothing, oh atheists of the world? Oh you who think you have thought your way out of God, tell us: what was the nothing that was here before us?

By the way, haven't the scientists among you told us there is no such thing as nothing? Haven't you said there are no vacuums, no great wide emptinesses?

Thus spake Stephen and Michelle Cling, and here Andy checked out, again, their picture in the back of the book, full-color, against a Sears studio backdrop: Stephen with glasses and strawberry blond hair, Michelle, looking like any forty-ish resident of Mount Deborah, same dyed hair, same belted jeans.

There has always been something in the universe, and that something has always been God. You have never been alone in the world, reader. And those who have loved you love you still.

Andy put the book down next to his bed. He closed his eyes.

Lou's funeral had taken place in a funeral home, without preachers or guides of any sort, because nobody had any ideas about who to call. A few of her friends spoke, her uncle. Her sister sat outside with the girls for a while, then took them to McDonald's.

But during the funeral, formless, endless, Andy—desperate for anything to take him out of this place—tried to imagine Louisa in heaven. Because he had never allowed himself the lunacy of heaven (or hell, for that matter; when you were dead you were just that, dead, so relax, everybody, and be nice to one another) he had no idea exactly how to imagine it. Was

Lou dressed in a white dress? Sitting on clouds with angels? He was embarrassed at how his imagination took him to such childish places but he didn't know where else to send it. Lou sitting on a cloud, strumming a lute. Lou looking down on him, telling him it would be okay. Her figure outlined in shimmering vapor.

Stephen Cling, in his picture, wore a Hawaiian shirt printed with crocodiles. Michelle wore a bright blue polo buttoned to the top. What did these two people know that he didn't? What weren't they afraid to imagine?

Fortunately for him, his girls had never asked if their mommy was in heaven, so he had never had to lie to them. They knew where she was. They had watched him sprinkle her ashes off the dock.

So to think of that now, that Lou's body was in the Atlantic but her spirit was waiting for him, cradled by the arm of God, or cradled by clouds, or simply vaporous and translucent but watching him, knowing him—it was such a delicious idea that even to consider it felt sinful, like taking some kind of recreational drug. But *God Is a Rainbow* was so matter-of-fact about heaven and God and purpose and life. Stephen and Michelle just knew. Lou wasn't a figment of his imagination smirking in the corner.

Again, eyes closed, he gave it another shot: really, what would it look like? Lou in a white gown. Her magnificent hair. He saw the white dress she wore to Rachel's first birthday

party. That she would have worn to their fifth anniversary dinner, if they had gotten around to it. (Why hadn't they gotten
around to it? They'd just assumed they'd have more time.)

"Lou," he said. He said it out loud. "Lou, are you there?
Baby, are you there?" He closed his eyes. He tried to imagine.
He pushed out of his mind Stephen and Michelle's airbrushed
grins and instead tried to see Lou in heaven. She wasn't the
ghost who haunted him. She was an angel.

He tried to believe.

But after a while he started to feel ridiculous, so he got up,
went to the kitchen, brewed some coffee. A little after six he
completed the first part of his NSF grant. He clicked "send"
and sent it into the system. He'd figure out the rest later; he'd
make his experiments work. Then he got back in bed and reread the part of *God Is a Rainbow* about how he was here for
a reason, how everyone is on this earth for a reason, and the
reason belonged to God.

EIGHT

Because Rachel refused to spend another second in the company of Tiffany Goldsmith, and because Andy was still uncomfortable just handing her a key, he decided to hire Melissa Potter to babysit two afternoons a week. He wondered, briefly, about the ethics of this—was it okay to use undergraduates as domestic labor?—but the truth was she had offered, and he trusted her.

For her part, Melissa had decided to relax around him the moment he confessed, in office hours, to having read *God Is a Rainbow,* and to having found something worthwhile in it—which was not to say, he specified, that he thought the whole book was worthwhile, or that he accepted all its arguments, but he did appreciate Stephen and Michelle Cling's comforting tone, and he could see why they made such good pastors.

"You could meet them!" Melissa said, unable to contain

herself. "I could bring you to church! Oh, they would love to hear that you liked their book!"

"I'm not going to go to church with you, Melissa," he said. "I'm just saying I thought their book seemed, in its own way—wise."

Her smile refused to dim. "They're going to be so flattered."

"Well—"

"Really," she said. "It'll be the best news of their day."

She had become like that, more and more—unable to contain herself. And how terrific she was with Rachel and Belle! Helping Belle build a dollhouse out of shoe boxes, making endless rounds of spaghetti *pomodoro* with Rachel, and doing everything with good cheer and a willingness to listen to whatever was on the girls' minds. More than once, toward the end of the fall semester, Andy had come home from work to find Rachel and Melissa on the couch, head to head, talking about something serious—boys maybe, but could Rachel already be worrying about boys?—both of them refusing to let on to whatever it was they'd been discussing.

She wallpapered Belle's dollhouse with scraps from magazines.

She made Rachel a mix CD with—Andy checked—no Christian rock whatsoever.

"Does she ever talk to you about Jesus?" Andy asked on Friday afternoon, having given Melissa her twenty dollars and sent her back to her dorm.

"Jesus?" Belle looked confused. "Why would she do that?"

"I think she just really likes us, Dad," said Rachel. "It's not like she's trying to save our souls."

In fact, the only soul she seemed even vaguely interested in was Andy's, and this interest stemmed from her independent study as much as it did from any need to proselytize that burned in her heart. At first, she saved much of her debating for his office (where he really had no time or inclination for student visits and yet—how he brightened when he saw her!). But soon enough, she began gently teasing him at his house, his own turf, while wiping out an omelet pan or reheating macaroni and cheese for the girls—"Did I just hear you say, 'Oh my God,' Dr. Waite? Whose God are you talking to, exactly? Because I didn't know you had a particular God."

"Give me a break, Melissa. And call me Andy."

She shook her head, smiling to herself, stirring macaroni. "I can't. I was raised to respect the student-teacher relationship."

What surprised him too was how Melissa seemed to have grown into herself over these past few weeks—or how she seemed to grow more at ease in front of other people. She no longer walked into his office half hunched over, holding a notebook to herself like armor. Instead, she stood straight, looked directly into his eyes. She was prone to the occasional touch of a shoulder, which gave Andy, he couldn't help it, a tiny shiver. A young woman touching him! He was such a sucker. Invisible Lou, standing in the corner, would roll her invisible eyes.

Melissa was still awkwardly built, of course, tall, thick, and broad—had she been born a boy she might have been a linebacker—but, in the way of certain homely girls, she had a smile that lit up her entire face. She still wore her gold cross sometimes but she no longer sucked on it.

"You know you don't even have to pay me," she said, sticking his money in her back pocket one Friday afternoon. "I'd do this for free. Your girls are great."

"Don't be ridiculous," he said. "You earned it."

"But just so you know, I mean it, I'd come for free." Then she grinned at him, flounced her hips a little as she walked out the door. Or did he imagine that? When he woke up at four in the morning, why did he calm his frantic heart with the memory of her smile?

ALTHOUGH ANDY USUALLY only required Melissa's services during the afternoons or early evenings, when teaching or meetings kept him on campus late, toward the end of the semester he reserved her (insisting he would pay her, pay her overtime, even) for the second Saturday night in December. It was Marty Reuben's annual biology department holiday party, which Andy anticipated and loathed in equal measure. "I know you have finals," he said. "It's fine if you don't want—"

"No, no," she said. She was in his office, pointing out a particular passage in Dawkins which gave her offense. "I'd love to. I had nothing else Saturday night anyway."

Marty Reuben lived about an hour from Andy in Lace Point, a Philly suburb Marty despised for its muted anti-Semitism, but which he found himself unable to quit because the schools were so good and the village was so picturesque. So Marty stayed and feuded with his neighbors, stealing the signs supporting Republican candidates off their lawns. His wife, Jane, cooked beautiful dinners and shook her head at her husband's eccentricity.

"It's just inertia," Marty would say, when pressed (not that anybody pressed him, really) to defend his decade-long residence in Lace Point. "It's hard, isn't it? You got the house, you got the kid in school, you got your bank and your barber, you know. And selling a house is a pain in the ass. In this market? You gotta be crazy, really. So Lace Point it is, at least while the kid's at home." Here, the dissolute sigh. "And me, I always thought I was gonna live in Shanghai."

And oh, how Andy resented the way he enjoyed nights in Marty's fine house, eating his fine food, listening to funny tales of his fine travels (boating the canals of eastern France, climbing Guatemalan ruins). Why did Marty Reuben live in a beautiful house in a beautiful village with a gourmet wife and a lively daughter, why was his biggest problem the ongoing feud with his neighbors about Mitt Romney? Why was his life so privileged that he thought American politics were his biggest problem? And Nina Graff who brought her ridiculous vegan casserole even though the party was not a potluck, it was *never a potluck,* and Linda Schoenmeyer, the chair, who seemed to be getting fatter every year, with her doggedly devoted husband, and George Hayad with his silent wife who seemed doggedly devoted too, in her enormous bangles—why were all these people so blissful? All of them, two by two, eating hors d'oeuvres in Marty's living room, admiring Jane's kitschy antiques, sitting next to one another at the table, living their gloriously becoupled lives. Meanwhile, who did he have for a companion? Most years, nobody. This year, because he could not stand one more year of sitting solo at the end of the table, he'd asked Sheila.

"Really?" They'd stood in front of her house the previous afternoon—Andy had just dropped off the girls at their dance lessons, and Sheila had been pulling into her driveway, looking miserable, since she had just dropped Jeremy off with his dad, and would spend the weekend alone. Andy knew how lonely she was, and felt that he should do something nice for her. He hadn't been particularly nice to her, he knew that.

Still, he hedged. "I'm not promising it will be fun."

"A dinner party in Lace Point sounds like fun," Sheila said.

"But it's full of biologists."

"So? I like biology," she said. "What little I know about it." He tried not to notice how pleased she seemed, how she smiled like a prize winner. He tried to force the memory of her wide pale body from his mind. "What should I wear?" she asked.

"Nothing special," he thought, but then worried that Sheila

would take him seriously, dress in one of her pocketed sweat-shirts. "Business casual."

"So I'll wear my scrubs?"

"Right," Andy said, trying out a chuckle. "Scrubs."

"Okay," she said. "I'm looking forward to it."

Instead of wearing scrubs or a sweatshirt (or overdressing, which would have been worse) Sheila wore a navy blue dress, simple, the sort of thing you could wear comfortably to a funeral or a job interview or a faculty dinner. She had put in her contacts, let her bangs fall to the side of her face instead of straitjacketing them in that horrible barrette, and when Andy told her she looked very nice, he meant it.

"I got some wine," she said.

"You didn't have to," he said, although he was glad she did, because he'd forgotten to bring some, and it was the usual thing to bring wine to Marty's boozy dinners, but then he felt shame that the alcoholic had to remember the wine, that the alcoholic felt so obligated by this social occasion that she would walk into a liquor store to satisfy the obligations. "You really didn't have to."

"I thought it would be a good thing to do. I was actually going to bring flowers but the only thing they had at ShopRite were poinsettias, which are so Christmassy, I don't know."

"No, wine is nice. Is it hard for you to go into liquor stores?"

"Oh man, you have no idea, I just go crazy! I just rip corks out with my teeth and smash bottles in the aisles!" She laughed, she was being sarcastic. "You can say it's from you," she said, sliding into his car, giving Andy pause. Did she bring it because she knew he'd forget? Did she really know him that well?

The ride to Marty's was pleasant—they talked about their kids, Rachel's latest culinary inquisitions, Jeremy's karate. Sheila said she liked to go to the Lace Point crafts fair every November, and that she'd sometimes take a walk around the various neighborhoods, peering into the oversized Tudors and colonials. "Once I broke in."

"You what?"

"Well, it wasn't exactly criminal." She smiled, looked out the car window into the endless, impenetrable pines. "The house had a FOR SALE sign, so I thought I might just try the door. It was this mansion, Andy, the sort of thing I used to think I'd live in when I was a little girl. I couldn't help it, I just had to see—and so I did, and it was open, and the house was, I don't know. It was empty, the owners had clearly already left, but even so the place felt like Cinderella's castle or something. There was a pond in the backyard with swans."

"Did you stay?"

"All afternoon," she said. "I kept trying to leave, but I just wasn't able to."

"Why not?"

"Oh, I don't know. Real-estate dreams," she said. "The dreams of a different life. I kept decorating the rooms in my head. Picking out furniture I remembered from catalogs, a Pottery Barn sofa. All the family pictures were mine, though. The ones I imagined hanging on the walls."

"Real-estate dreams, huh?"

"Houses are symbols, aren't they?" she said, philosophizing. "You look at a house—or at least I look at a house—and if it's nice then I imagine the family who lives there is also very nice, very responsible. Earned that house somehow. Unless it's big and tacky, in which case I imagine the people who live in it are just horrible." She laughed. "I remember when we bought our house, I wondered what people would think, if they would think I was nice and responsible or just tacky. It's such a big house! But I loved it. I wanted to live in it forever. I remember driving past it when I was a kid and thinking someday I'll live there. I couldn't believe it when we moved in."

She sighed, looked at her hands. It was dark like midnight outside, only the occasional streetlight puncturing the black. "It's a good thing I didn't grow up in Lace Point, otherwise who knows what I would have dreamed of."

"So when did you finally leave?"

"I had to pick up Jeremy," she said. "And I remember thinking, I'll pick him up and I'll bring him right back here, we'll feed the swans, we'll hang up our pictures on the wall, we'll make this ours." She laughed. "Desire can make you a little crazy."

She looked at him as if she wanted to say something, but then changed her mind. "Is your colleague's house like that?"

"What, like a castle?" Andy said. "No," he said, remembering what he could of his colleague's home. "It's nice, but you'll be able to leave."

Still, Sheila seemed to grow more abashed as they traversed Marty's flagstone pathway. Marty's wife, Jane, came from wealth, and the house exuded quiet but smug good taste. Three stories, brick. A slate roof with copper gutters. Attractive outdoor landscaping, attractively lit, and a circular drive crowded with his colleagues' cars. Automatic lights beamed on them as they parked, illuminating some Japanese plantings to the side of the house, stunted trees and a miniature pagoda.

"You said this wasn't too fancy?"

"Just relax," Andy said, holding Sheila's wine.

They were welcomed in enthusiastically, the last to arrive, and the women in the department told Sheila how *happy* they were Andy had *finally* brought someone while Marty offered Andy a scotch. Andy rarely drank—it was a way to keep his discomfort with drinking at bay, simply never to do it—but he found that not drinking at Marty's made him more uncomfortable than accepting what was poured, so he took the scotch, sniffed it, made some idle chitchat from the comfort of one of Marty's leather club chairs, near the warmth of the roaring fire, while Sheila was fussed over in the kitchen.

"So, how's your semester been?" asked George Hayad, the department's polyester-clad microbiologist. "Still teaching your God class?"

"Just finished up."

"Decent students?" George asked, then coughed up something thick and wiped it into a handkerchief. "You get any loonies this time?"

"Not really," Andy said, thinking of Melissa, of Lionel Shell. "Mostly nice kids. Open-minded."

"Open-minded or just uninvested?" Marty asked. "I don't know which is worse, actually—kids who disagree with evolution or kids who just don't care."

"They care," Andy said. "But they care about a lot of other things too. They're busy kids."

"Please," Marty said, looking around his cherry-paneled living room, the oil paintings of hunting dogs on the walls. "What do they do? Listen, I worked three jobs to get my ass through Yale. I stocked groceries at night. You think any of these kids do that?"

"Some of them might."

"They drive nicer cars than I do," Marty said, which was certainly true for some of them, but Andy had always suspected that Marty drove his rusty Ford just so that he could point out that his students drove nicer cars than he did.

"We have a lot of kids on financial aid. Two thirds of them, I think."

"I don't know," Marty said, shaking his head dolefully. "I look at the student parking lot, it's full of Audis. You know how much I'd like an Audi?"

"So buy yourself an Audi," said George Hayad.

"Jane would never let me. Jane doesn't like German cars."

"Ah," George said, and the three men stared into their scotch, then at each other, trying to determine what to say next.

"So I've been trying to finish up an Advancing Theory of Biology grant for the NSF," Andy said, as the grant was his conversational Audi, impressing his colleagues into hushed submission. "I'm thinking we could really upgrade our lab equipment with the funding, maybe even hire a postdoc or two."

"Federal funding is impossible now," George said.

"You think we need a postdoc?" Marty smiled, unimpressed. Andy had overplayed his hand. "For what, may I ask?"

"Well," Andy said, "my research is complicated."

"Ah," Marty said. "You still doing whatever it is with the mice?"

"He cuts off their heads. It's like an abattoir down there." George pronounced *abattoir* with a French accent.

"That's how animal research gets done," said Marty. "Don't be a philistine." But he and George laughed together for quite some time, leaving Andy to stare into his scotch.

"Well," said Marty, after a few minutes of fraternal chuckling, "here come the ladies. Is it time to eat?"

"Mmm," said George. "Smells like roast."

Over dinner, Sheila was quiet and deferential. She mentioned twice that she was just a dental hygienist, had never even gone to college, and that she had never sat around at a table with so many doctors before. At this, Andy wanted to say that they weren't actually doctors, that none of them could cure cancer or even prescribe a Valium, but of course one was never supposed to say that to a PhD, even if you yourself had a PhD, and also Andy had somehow forgotten how much people drank at these parties. (Had he forgotten? Or had he just not felt like remembering?) He himself was drinking more than usual, had already put down a glass and a half of red by the time the soup was cleared, plus the scotch.

"So Sheila, tell us, do you ever see any really gory teeth?" asked Nina Graff, whose own teeth were stained wine red. "Like just disgusting mouthfuls you *cannot believe?*"

"Oh man, I could tell you stories."

Please, thought Andy, don't.

But Sheila was suddenly in her element; she launched into detailed accounts of the various malocclusions and enamel rot she encountered day to day, unaware she was being humored (was she being humored?) while the biology department sliced and swallowed their tenderloin. And then, soon enough, it was time for cake—"puds," said George, who had studied eight million years ago at Cambridge—and then it would be over, and Andy could go home to his girls, his little house.

"And toddlers are the worst. Parents putting juice in their kids' bottles."

"Really?" Nina said, putting down her glass. "I don't believe you. Who would do such a thing? Who would do that?"

"It's true. And not just poor kids, either. Educated parents give their kids milk all day, not knowing milk has sugars that rot kids' teeth. I've seen two-year-olds who need their entire mouths replaced."

"But that's *horrible*!" Nina said. "Oh, don't go on. I can't bear it. Two-year-olds? I just can't bear it."

"Nina gets very exercised," said Nina's husband, the orthopedist, and then he kissed his drunk vegan wife on the head, and this was the moment that Andy realized it was late, his head was pounding, he really had to go.

"So many parents have no idea how to handle their kids' oral health." Sheila put down her ice water, made a large gesture with her hands. "You ask them if they brush their kids' teeth, they say no, they let their kids do it themselves. I'm like, great, I'm all for self-directed kids, but you're talking toddlers! Twenty months old, they know how to brush their own teeth?"

"Can you see it?" asked Nina. "When you look in their mouths?"

"Of course!" Sheila laughed. "Brown teeth, soft spots. You want to shake these parents, you really do. And then the best one, one time we find a two-year-old with eleven cavities. So clearly, the kid's going to need anesthesia, which is a major thing on a small child, and probably at least one root canal—and then he comes back for a follow up visit and he's drinking a bottle of *Coca-Cola*!"

"No!" said Nina and Linda as one.

"I swear. Our receptionist wanted to call the authorities."

"I can't say I blame her!" Nina said. "I would have called them myself!"

"Except it's not a crime to give a kid a bottle of Coke."

"Under some circumstances," Nina said. "Under some circumstances it certainly is a crime."

"Nina believes in the nanny state," said her husband.

"I'm just reasonable," Nina said. "I'm sorry, but I think I'm just a reasonable person." She flushed. Sheila was nodding her head in agreement, pouring herself more ice water.

"Well, it's probably time to get going."

Nina looked alarmed. "Andy, Andy, you can't leave! We haven't even talked about *you* yet."

"What is there to say?" He pushed back his chair but did not stand.

"Did you know," Linda asked, addressing the table, picking up her glass as though she were about to give a toast, "did you know that Andy here is sponsoring an independent study with some student on—get this—*intelligent design*? I couldn't believe it. The paperwork came by my desk just the other week."

"You're kidding," said Nina. "An independent study in ID? But is that even science?"

"That's what I thought. I thought, Andy, is this even science?"

"It's a route to science," Andy said. "It's a . . .," and this was where he relented, poured himself a final half glass, "it's a pathway to talk about real issues in evolution," he said. "So that she'll have to confront the full scope of the science."

"Who's the student?"

"Melissa Potter. She's a community college transfer."

"What would your old friend Rosenblum say to that?" Nina asked, chuckling. "To you taking on a community college student's work on intelligent design? I bet Rosenblum would be very annoyed." Nina had met Rosenblum once twenty years ago at a book signing and still liked to talk about the meeting, her momentary encounter with infamy.

"Actually, he'd love it," Andy said. "And she's not in community college anymore. She's one of ours."

"Oh, but *Andy*, honestly," Nina said. "I mean, *honestly*."

"Melissa Potter?" George wondered, aloud. "Do I know her?"

"Big girl," Marty said. "I've seen her."

"Well, don't you think she'll come around?" Linda said. She reached, with her fingers, for a scrap of Jane Reuben's sugar-glazed orange cake.

Andy knew he should bid his leave, but didn't. "What do you mean?"

"She'll separate truth from fiction," Linda said. She leaned back in her brocade chair, expansive, chewing on cake. Her husband gazed at her adoringly. "Don't you think you'll be able to open her eyes to see the world as it is? Not the world she wants it to be? I mean, I think that's your responsibility as her teacher, Andy. She's old enough to stop believing in fairy tales. And you're such a good teacher. You can get her to stop believing in that garbage."

His head pounded. The buried sizzle of heartburn. "But it's not garbage—it's not a fairy tale to her."

"Garbage, bullshit, pick your terms," said Linda. "I prefer fairy tale. That the world was created in seven days, etcetera, etcetera."

Though Sheila kept a pleasant smile plastered on her face, he could tell she was lost. Weren't they just talking about dentition? She took frequent, anxious sips of her ice water.

"It just—I don't think it helps to call it a fairy tale," Andy said. "She has done a lot of research into irreducible complexity, Behe's work in the theory."

Sheila fiddled with her bracelet. "Sheila, that's the idea," Linda said, kindly, "that certain organisms are so complex that they couldn't have developed generation after generation, via selective pressure. According to this guy Behe, a scientist out of—where is he, Nina?"

"Lehigh."

"Lehigh!" Linda snorted. "A legit school! Anyway, this guy proposes that a particular part of a kind of bacteria contains parts that would be useless on their own, and therefore would never have arisen independently. The flagellum had to be designed, he said, because it's too complex to have come about via evolution."

"Oh," Sheila said.

"It's nonsense, of course. Total crapola, as they say. But reassuring to the Jesus crowd, I suppose. Lehigh! Amazing."

"You're really supporting this student's research?" asked Marty, pouring himself another. He was growing out his beard, gray-striped, like a skunk. "Do you think that's morally sound?"

"Of course I do," Andy said, trying to keep the peevishness from his voice. "Why wouldn't I? How could it be unsound to support a student's inquiry into—anything? Isn't the point that she's inquiring? Isn't that a good thing?"

"Yes, but for her to inquire into a belief system rather than a scientifically provable theory—at the very least, it seems a waste of time," Marty said. He stroked his fledgling beard.

"Look, the fact that she wants to research an avenue of science seems laudable to me. Besides, she believes what she believes, and if we demean it—"

"Of course she believes it," Linda said, "but that doesn't mean we can't lead her to the truth. You're such a sweet guy, Andy. You respect your students, which is great. But you're a biology professor, first and foremost. It is your job to inform the students about the realities of biology."

"Your realities," Andy said.

"What? No," Linda said. "The realities. This isn't subjective, Andy. You know that, right? Science is objective? As is the truth?"

"I—sure," he said. He knew science was objective, and that

truth was objective, but what every person needed to get through their lives—that was not quite as black-and-white. "Listen, I better get going," he said. "Sheila needs to get back."

"I don't—"

"Oh, but Andy—you didn't finish your cake! Let me wrap up some for you, for the girls. Sheila, could I get you some to take home?" and before he could stop her Jane Reuben was up and bustling, the conversation was once again bustling, Linda was pontificating about something new but still she stopped for a second to give Andy what seemed to be a distinctly wary eye.

"Before you go, just tell me—you aren't going to validate Melissa Potter's intelligent design crap, are you, Andy? Irreducible complexity?" Linda said. "You're not going to stamp that crap with department approval, are you?"

"I don't have a stamp, Linda."

"Just tell me you're not. This is a serious biology department. Nina? Wouldn't you say we're a serious biology department?"

Nina was half-slumped. "It is so serious, Linda. We are so very serious."

Andy drained his glass, stood to go. Sheila stood too, smoothed her dress.

"The thing is, Andy, it has to start with us. We have to be the bulwark," Linda opined, from her comfortable seat in the beautiful house. "And I get it, Andy, you're such a sweet guy, you want to be nice to your students, but remember you're doing them no favors if you let them believe in lies."

"Gotcha," Andy said.

"You can't validate the lies."

"Jane, where's the bathroom?" Andy asked, even though he knew. Under an oil painting of a sunrise, Andy took a long, dribbly piss. Then he rifled through a basket under the sink for an aspirin but he found only tampons and condoms. For whom? What kind of guest bathroom stored condoms? Tantalized, rebellious, he pocketed a handful.

"Sheila, it was so nice to meet you," Linda said, as Andy took his Tupperwared wedge of cake, his pocketed condoms, Sheila to the door.

"Thank you," Sheila said. "Thank you. I had the loveliest time."

The condoms felt heavy in his pocket. Sheila offered to drive, but he said no, he was fine, he would do it.

"Who is this Melissa character?" she asked him as they departed Lace Point, got back on Church Road toward their own forsaken strip of New Jersey. "They certainly seemed up in arms about her work."

"Oh, just a student," Andy said. "She's nobody."

"Then why were they so freaked out?"

"You ever hear of the Scopes monkey trial?"

"Tennessee, right? William Jennings Bryan?"

Andy was surprised; he hadn't expected her to know it. "Well, Melissa might have come out on the other side."

The lights which led them out of town abruptly turned dark as they crossed an invisible border. They were in the country.

"So she's a religious fanatic," Sheila said.

"If you believe in God are you automatically a fanatic?"

"Hey, whoa," Sheila said, pressing an imaginary brake with her palm. "That's not what I said. I'm just trying to figure out why you seem defensive when you talk about her."

Andy didn't say anything. The road twisted into the pines.

"At dinner, I mean."

"I wasn't trying to be defensive."

"Well nobody ever does—"

"She's my babysitter."

"Ah," Sheila said. She smiled like she understood. "And you like her."

"I trust her with my girls," Andy said. When he pulled in front of her house, she did not immediately open the door to get out. He wondered if he was supposed to open the door for her. Well, he wouldn't. He was tired and his head still pounded.

"So," she said, "you have a babysitter?" She turned to him with a heavy-lidded smile.

"Yes," he said. "And I better get back to her. It's late."

"Oh," Sheila said. "Okay." She paused another second before opening her car door. "Well, thanks again. I really had a lovely time."

"Me too," Andy said, and because he was a gentleman, he waited to make sure she was safely in the house before backing out of her driveway to his own darkened home.

• • •

BUT WALKING TO his own front door, he felt lighter. Melissa had heard him jam his key into the lock and opened the door for him, smiling, leaning against the jamb. "Hey, Doctor." She was so young, so untainted by that preposterous dinner party. And now that they hung out more often she called him Doctor, or sometimes Doc, although not Andy, never Andy.

"The girls were good?"

"They were great," she said. "Noncombative."

He followed her into the kitchen. It was starting to get icy out, and the windows were steaming; water was boiling in the kettle. She had put out a mug with a tea bag in it. Two mugs, in fact; two tea bags. She planned on staying, and she knew where he kept the tea bags.

"So did you like hanging out with the other biology teachers?" she asked. "What did you guys talk about? Did you talk about your students?" Here she turned and made a kissy face, the first adorable gesture he'd ever seen her make.

"Eh, nothing important," he said, ignoring Melissa's adorability, watching her pour water into the mugs.

"What's nothing important?"

"Politics," he said. "Family. I don't know, what people talk about. Not students," he lied. "There was too much booze, but otherwise it was fine."

"You didn't drink, though, did you?" Melissa asked, as she sat down with the tea, pushed a mug toward him across the table.

"I'm sorry?"

"You didn't drink, right?" And here Andy wondered if he'd committed some foul, because when he counted up everything and included the scotch, he drank four alcoholic beverages over four hours, which wasn't enough to become impaired but which was certainly more than he ever drank in ordinary circumstances. In ordinary circumstances, in fact, he didn't drink at all! Should he tell her that? He couldn't remember whether alcohol was specifically against whatever religious rules Melissa subscribed to but he didn't feel like apologizing for it. She had never been subjected to one of Marty Reuben's dinner parties and never would be.

She blew on her tea, casual. "Just because, you know, you had to drive. So you wouldn't want to be drinking."

"I know," he said.

She sipped her tea. She probably wasn't aware that she was needling him. She was twenty-one, with a twenty-one-year-old's idea of right and wrong, a twenty-one-year-old's unmalleable morality. And she had no real idea of his biography.

"Well, anyway, the girls really were great tonight," she said. "I helped Rachel with her science homework. She's doing a project on rock porosity? So we've been soaking those rocks. You'll see, we left a bunch of buckets in their bedroom."

"Melissa, I don't drink and drive," Andy said, although he knew he must be drunk, at least a little, to even begin this conversation. Why was he defending himself? Why were they drinking tea together? The clock above the sink said it was

162 I LAUREN GRODSTEIN

almost midnight and there was no reason for her to still be in his house. She had a Honda Civic parked in his driveway. He could give her money and she could leave.

"No, of course," she said, quickly. She held her mug with both hands. "I didn't mean to sound like I was—"

"My wife was killed by a drunk driver," he said. And again, why say this? Except the look on Melissa's face, of fresh horror and shame, made him feel stronger. Powerful. What had happened to him could still horrify people. And he was drunk, he'd admit it, four glasses in four hours, but he was drunk with something else too, loneliness, he supposed, and it felt an awful lot like being drunk on alcohol, the same resentment, the same headache. He thought about how he'd treated Sheila, like he didn't know better, except he did, and he felt guilty about that, and resentful that Sheila made him feel guilty, and all that plus having to live every day with Louisa's ghost.

"I knew your wife was gone," Melissa said. Her eyes looked damp. "I didn't know why."

"Forget it," he said. "It's nothing we have to talk about."

"I didn't know what I was saying. I'm sorry."

Andy was quiet. Melissa looked down at her tea bag, plopped it up and down a few times in the hot water to leech out the tea.

"She's in heaven, you know."

"Melissa," he said. His head was pounding. Tomorrow, Sunday, a long Sunday with the girls at home, and if he remembered right the weathermen were calling for snow. What would they do with themselves all day? Homework? Would he have to supervise homework? Would the girls feel trapped, start picking on each other, bickering, would he have to send them to Jeremy's house? Would he have to sit there and make chitchat with Sheila while the kids shot at each other on Jeremy's PlayStation? Would he have to change Sheila's lightbulbs? Fix her faucet? Stay for dinner?

He wanted Melissa to leave right away but also he wanted her to never leave.

"I know you don't necessarily believe what I believe," Melissa said. "I tease you and everything but I know you don't really believe in a loving God the way I do, and I'm really not trying to change your mind."

Let an undergraduate into your house and she'll think you've let her into your heart.

"And I would never say this to the girls, don't worry—we never talk about their mother and I never would bring that up—but I just want you to know . . ." She trailed off.

He could have stopped her there, but, again, he didn't. All his life he'd been like that, forgoing the small good decision in favor of entropy, letting the chips fall where they may. "I want you to know that her spirit lives on, Professor Waite," Melissa said.

Above her the clock read 12:03.

"She watches over all three of you, all the time."

She kept her voice low. She was looking down at the table, cheeks red. She knew she was taking liberties, but still she took them. It was perplexing to Andy that he'd never been better at stopping other people or himself from doing the wrong thing. If he'd been as powerful as he believed he might not even be at this kitchen table right now. And yet he wanted her to keep saying what she was saying, because she believed it, and it felt wonderful to hear her proclaim this particular belief.

"She's always there."

In that moment, he saw that everything Melissa had introduced him to—the books, the beliefs, the way she interacted with his daughters—it had all brought him more comfort than anything else he had found since Lou's accident. Posttraumatic grief counseling and the awkward words of the therapist, the hugs of friends and family, the good, quiet time alone, the self-help books—none of it felt as good as Melissa's quiet affirmation, the Clings' affirmation. Lou was with God, watching over them. It was so simple. What would be the point of resistance?

He put his fingers on his temples and rubbed. "You know, this is nothing I've ever really talked about before."

"I'm sorry."

"Don't apologize," he said, but could think of nothing else to reassure her. Really she shouldn't be talking about his dead wife at all. Really he should have stopped her. And yet the comfort of thinking his wife was alive, watching them, the comfort of this large awkward girl in his house . . .

She took their mugs to the sink, rinsed them. She was hunched again. She picked up a dish towel to dry the mugs.

"Melissa, it's late. I can do that."

"Okay," she said, but she finished wiping the mugs clean anyway, and that simple domestic gesture—he was exhausted, half-drunk, dreading tomorrow, full of entropy, unable to use force—and something in that simple domestic gesture made him fall in love just like that with this girl. Melissa believed in something. Melissa believed his wife was looking down at him. He wanted to borrow her belief. He loved her in that moment for having belief he wanted to borrow.

"Melissa," he said. "Can I ask you something? Is God merciful? Or is he just? And don't say both—"

"He is just," Melissa said, definitively. She didn't ask him why he wanted to know. And before he could stop himself—he was terrible at stopping himself—he was behind her with his hands on her shoulders and she had turned around and turned her face up at him, her broad face, damp eyes, but somehow pretty when she was happy, and he pressed his lips against hers. Why? Why? He tilted her chin with his finger.

Maybe he was just hoping to be slapped awake.

But she did not slap him; instead she pressed herself more firmly against him, opened her mouth a bit so that their tongues pressed against one another's—and how odd, this feeling, another woman's tongue, but how pleasurable too. Had he been celibate for seven years? Almost entirely he had. A quickie at the Academic Biology conference in Fresno four years ago, and then another at the same conference, a year later, in Atlanta. That second one he stuck around for breakfast, where he got his first good look at the woman, a grad student, at least fifteen years younger than he was. She was impoverished-looking, scooped up her hotel coffee shop eggs like a starving person. She didn't say much but kept smirking up at him from behind droopy lids. "You going to eat that?" she asked, pointing to his bacon.

And then, a few months ago, Sheila.

And that was it. In seven years.

He put his arms, gingerly, around Melissa's wide, firm waist. She pulled him closer. They could have moved to a couch or a chair or even the bedroom, but instead they stayed where they were, leaning against the kitchen sink. He put his hands in her soft hair. She ran a tentative hand against his waistband. God, he had those condoms in his pocket. Had he known in his subconscious, when he stole them from Marty's marble powder room? Had some part of him known or planned this?

"Melissa," he breathed into her hot puffy hair.

She moved her head back and he looked at her face, pink-cheeked, pink-lipped. She wore a smile, half-apologetic, as though she had been the one who instigated this.

"I've never done this before," he said. "I mean, since my wife died—I've rarely—and especially not a student."

"I know," she said. "You're not the type."

The type? He took a step back. "I don't—I can't take advantage of you. You should go home."

"I don't want to."

"I know, but—"

"I won't tell anyone."

He sighed, heavily, as his heart ticktocked. "Melissa," he said again; her name was wonderful to say. Together they had done something they would have to keep secret. It had been a long time since he'd kept a secret, and the idea of it thrilled him. He kept his hands on her firm sides. He still felt that grace, that comfort, from just having her around. He leaned forward again. His mouth was on hers again. She pulled back, smiled, kissed him once more, and they stayed that way for many long minutes, Andy's head swimming, her mouth soft and pliant, and above him—could he hear it?—watching over him, forgiving, understanding, Lou among the chorus of angels.

Eventually he walked her to her car. He felt pleased and horny like a teenager. "Will I see you again?" he asked.

"Of course," she said.

He didn't touch himself after he got into bed; instead, he assessed his bedroom, his shelves, clothes spilling out of them, coffee cups leaving rings on the nightstand, the journals. He wondered if he was losing his mind. Perhaps he was—but didn't he deserve to, for just a little while? He'd held out for so long. Beside him, one of Melissa's books. It made him happy just to hold something that was hers: *The Mystery of Intent*. He opened it up to the first page. "What believers understand," said the author, but in his head he heard Melissa's husky voice, "is that there is no peace like the peace that comes from trusting God. If you don't believe, ask yourself, what do you have to lose by turning to belief? And what might you gain?"

Heart singing, angels singing, Andy thought to himself that really he had nothing to lose, and already, just from considering the possibility of belief, he had already gained so much. God is just. God wanted Oliver McGee in jail. He'd had a feeling this was how it was supposed to be.

Too thrilled to sleep, head still half-pounding, Andy got out of bed and stood by the window, leaned his forehead against the window. He stayed that way, head soothed by the cold, until the first fat snowflakes started to fall.

NINE

The girl's name had been Anita Lim. She was the daughter of Korean immigrants who had established a small grocery store in Brooklyn during the first year of the Reagan administration, and who had hung by their shop's front door a large framed photograph of that president, along with a reasonable facsimile of a handwritten note from him, thanking them for their good wishes in the wake of his shooting. It spoke to how well the Lims were liked in their part of Brooklyn that none of their friendly and pushy customers ever gave them shit about that photograph, even as the old conservative Italians died out and were replaced by tattooed mothers pushing fancy strollers and novelists buying cigarettes at two in the morning.

As the years went on, the Lims sold fewer cans of tomatoes, more boxes of organic soy milk, and continued to do a brisk trade in cat food, toilet paper, and soap. They remembered their customers' names and preferences, never ran out of Progresso chicken noodle for Chris and Julie Butler's boys, never ran out of energy bars for Catherine Marcello, the marathoner. They had fresh flowers out front, seasonal and expensive, and a wide variety of craft and regional beers in the coolers in the back.

The Lims lived in an apartment above the store, which they had secured, rent-controlled, for three hundred dollars a month when they moved to Brooklyn from Pusan, and which they eventually bought when their landlord, a cranky old Italian, announced a sudden and hasty move to North Carolina in 1982. What was he going to North Carolina for? The Lims never found out, but they rallied their family in Korea, took out some loans, bought the building, watched its value rise precipitously during the first years of the century, and paid back their family with interest.

In 1979 and '80 they had their children, who, because the Lims themselves were always working, seemed to grow up in the store, between the shelves of soup and the shelves of macaroni. Eddie and Anita attended the public school down the block from the store when the school wasn't considered particularly good, and attended the Bethany Presbyterian Church in Sunset Park even though there was a bigger, fancier Korean church in Manhattan. But the Lims liked Bethany, its homey feel, its pastor practically an old neighbor from Pusan. Eddie, their elder child, did them proud by believing the Word of God. Anita, on the other hand, did not believe, and in fact often refused to go to church at all, but although this rejection made her parents sad they agreed with each other, at night, when Anita's light still burned from behind her bedroom door—my goodness, how many hours could that girl study without wearing out her eyes?—that she was such a marvelous daughter, such a credit to them in so many ways, that truly they could not be too saddened by her. Besides, were they really going to force her to go to church when all she wanted was to play the cello, play tennis, study biology, study chemistry, write short stories, and win so many high school prizes and medals that her father actually built her a trophy case for her room? Were they really going to complain about a daughter whose teachers called home not just occasionally but on a regular basis to exclaim that they'd never met a kid quite like her, so articulate, so self-possessed, so conscientious, so very, very brilliant?

Some Sundays other churchgoers wondered out loud, "So where is your Anita this morning?" Well, usually she was traveling to Washington DC for her model UN or perfecting her experiment for the Intel Science Talent Search or playing cello in France with the International Youth Symphony. Eventually the other churchgoers grew sick of hearing about Anita and left the Lims in peace.

Had Mrs. Lim felt truly connected to any of the ladies at church, the ones who masked their jealousy with probing questions, she might have said: "I do not wish that Anita were here at church by my side so she could walk with God. I wish she were here so that I could spend some time with my daughter." It was her fondest secret that she wanted the kind of relationship she suspected American women had with their daughters, the kind where they shopped together for shoes or went out for lunch at restaurants in Manhattan. This was foolish, she knew, but it was still what she longed for, and if she couldn't have that (there were a million reasons why she would never have that) she would settle for church, for Anita sitting at her side the way that Jackie Park sat next to Mun-hee Park and Casey Rho sat next to Soo Rho.

Nevertheless, despite these quiet disappointments, the Lim family prospered in a general American way. They bought a car. They perfected their English, although they still preferred reading newspapers and watching movies in Korean. They replaced their car with a nicer car, installed air-conditioning and a high-tech security system in their store. They lamented that Eddie was not quite the student his sister was, but still he graduated from high school and gained admission to Hunter College and the Lims were delighted to send him there and hang a Hunter bumper sticker on the wall of pride next to their shop's front door, where it joined the photo of Reagan and also Bushes I and II, a signed portrait of Billy Graham, and postcards from customers' travels around the world.

A year later, when Anita graduated as Stuyvesant's valedictorian and headed off to Harvard, Mrs. Lim worried about whether or not she should place a Harvard bumper sticker near the Hunter one on their wall. She didn't want to embarrass Eddie; moreover, she didn't want their customers to think she was a braggart. She had already received innumerable e-mails of congratulations from distant cousins in Korea, and her sister back in Pusan told her that their mother, practically deaf, practically bald, subsiding on nothing but tea and gruel, had smiled her first smile of the month upon hearing the news. Harvard!

In typical Anita style, the girl herself was sanguine about the whole thing; she liked Harvard but she'd also liked Stanford and MIT and Yale, and only chose the former because their financial aid package was comprised mostly of grants instead of loans.

So Anita went to Harvard, and Eddie went to Hunter, and the Lims stocked Seventh Generation diapers and coconut water and baked seitan in their store, and found themselves, against all expectations, having detailed conversations about Korean food with almost obnoxiously knowledgeable white kids from the neighborhood who wanted Mrs. Lim's take on their home-brewed kimchi or crispy handmade squid pancake. Mrs. Lim asked Anita, on the phone, what it was with these white kids.

"They're called foodies, Mom," said Anita, far away in Cambridge, sounding as distracted as ever. "They're looking for authentic food experiences."

"Why don't they make their own authentic food?" Mrs. Lim wondered.

"They don't have any," Anita said. But Mrs. Lim knew this wasn't true, because her own children had raised themselves on white food whenever she turned her back; until they left the house, she hadn't realized how much pizza they used to eat, how much spaghetti, how many (grimace) turkey sandwiches. Now that they were gone, Eddie in an apartment with some roommates on the Upper East Side, Anita in Cambridge, she and her husband ate omelets or English muffins or nothing at all. They drank endless cups of coffee, like real Americans.

"Anita? Will you be coming home for Thanksgiving?"

"I don't know, Mom. I have so much work to do."

"Maybe we'll come up there? We could bring Eddie?"

"I guess," Anita said. "But don't you have to work?"

Another fond secret—Thanksgiving was Mrs. Lim's favorite holiday. More than Christmas, more even, God forgive her, than Easter. Her old Italian landlord had taught her to make pumpkin pie with ricotta in it and the kids ate it up every year, even her husband asked for seconds, and then they would watch football together on the television, the one game of the year they watched, Eddie explaining everything, play by play.

"So we'll come up to Cambridge then," Mrs. Lim said.

"God, Mom, I don't know, let me check my schedule, okay?"

Mrs. Lim imagined, across the country, American daughters helping their mothers bake pies.

"What are you so busy with, anyway?"

"Um, I don't know, only everything?"

"Come on, Hae Sun. Tell me."

"Graduate school applications, midterms, GREs, everything."

"GRE?"

"You know—that test. For graduate school. Forget it, you wouldn't understand."

Mrs. Lim sighed. She would understand, of course, but it helped Anita to shut her out and concentrate if she thought her mother was just a storekeeper, nobody she had to pay too much attention to. Then she thought, don't be silly, don't be sorry for yourself. Think here of everything you have. A sweet son, a brilliant daughter, even though it might have been nicer to have it the other way around.

Of course Anita could have majored in anything—English or anthropology, French or chemistry—but after a class with Stephen Pinker of linguistics fame, she chose to study linguistics, specifically the way that the evolution and dispersal of various language patterns mimicked biological evolutionary trends. Pinker had suggested to her that she continue her studies at Princeton, which had an excellent evolutionary biology program, helmed by the brilliant Henry Rosenblum, the author of *The Homo Sapiens' Backbone* and *Religion's Dangerous Lie*. This sounded like a good plan to Anita, who was beginning to formulate a plan for her life: school, more school, a PhD, and a tenured job at a school. In her spare time she would continue to play the cello and tennis.

She met Rosenblum for the first time at a conference at

MIT's Whitehead Institute, where she was presenting a paper she'd coauthored with one of her lesser professors. He introduced himself after her presentation, told her he'd heard a lot about her, looked forward to working with her in the fall. She should look for an official acceptance letter in the mail in the next few weeks. "That's it?" Anita asked him. She was startled by Rosenblum's enthusiasm; she had taken him for a cheerfully drunk old man when he'd first approached her. He was tall, with a large belly and ears full of protruding white hairs; the pictures she'd seen of him had clearly been taken twenty years earlier.

"That's it," Rosenblum said. "You'll be working closely with me. I look forward to it."

"So do I," Anita said, startled and a bit underwhelmed.

"Princeton!" Mrs. Lim's mother was dead in Pusan at this point but she could feel her spirit smiling down at her, whispering praise.

"I barely even had to apply," Anita said. Even she sounded impressed with herself.

"And you'll be close again! New Jersey!"

"Yes," Anita said, and suddenly that distracted sound was back in her voice. "I guess I will."

Eddie, at this point, was at seminary in upstate New York, studying to be a pastor, and was dating a nice girl and collecting some nice friends, including a roommate, Charles, whom he spoke of fondly and frequently. Charles was from

Los Angeles, his family originally from Seoul, and everything he did seemed to be haloed with luck and success. Charles was the smartest in the class, Charles spoke three languages fluently, Charles delivered sermons with such grace that he could make their weathered old teachers weep with newfound devotion. The Lims met Charles on their trips to visit Eddie upstate and were impressed by him, if a little put off by his fierce-eyed determined belief in not just the Lord, but himself. He offered to pay for dinner for everyone when they went out, as though the Lims wouldn't be happy to pay, or as if they couldn't.

As for Anita, she lived in a tiny apartment in Princeton, across from a record store, one room with a hot plate and a bathroom that even a tiny girl like her could barely squeeze into. No closet. One window. The Lims offered to help her with something better but Anita declined, said she was happy there, and anyway she spent so much time in Rosenblum's lab she was rarely home anyway. Her research was incomprehensible to her parents, although this new, satisfied Anita—as satisfied as they'd ever seen her, although still distracted, and more focused than ever on academic success—this new PhD-candidate daughter did try to explain to them what she was doing. Her research worried them because it seemed to be less about language at this point and more about evolution, strict Darwinian evolution, which contradicted everything they knew from church and everything they believed in their hearts. But they knew that they had let Anita go her own way all those years ago when they allowed her to play cello instead of go to church, study chemistry instead of read the Bible, so whose fault was it, really, that she was now studying Darwinian evolution? Could they blame anyone but themselves?

And surely devout Eddie was making up for whatever lapses they'd allowed in Anita.

They met this Rosenblum several times in Princeton, and he seemed to be a nice enough man ("But so foul-mouthed!") who praised Anita constantly and without moderation. "She's doing brilliant work, Mrs. Lim. I've honestly never met a student like her in my life. Her theory on the viral origins of life—has she explained it to you? In our field this is groundbreaking stuff. And for someone like her, doesn't even have her PhD yet—for someone like her to be publishing these kinds of papers, it's really unbelievable. You must be very proud."

On their drive back to Brooklyn, Mrs. Lim noticed how worried her husband looked. "That professor," he said, "what do you think he wants with her?"

"No, no," Mrs. Lim said, glad that her husband had articulated what they were both worried about so that she could reassure him, and thus herself. "He really just thinks she's very smart, that's all. He doesn't want anything else."

"But why is he always around? Every time we visit, there he is."

"She works in his lab," Mrs. Lim said. "They have a very close professional relationship."

"What if he takes advantage of her?" he said. "She's still so innocent."

This was something Mrs. Lim wondered about too, although she knew better than to bring it up with her daughter (and here too she imagined those American mothers and their daughters, eating their lunches, talking about boyfriends)—why exactly was this Rosenblum so high on their Anita? Why that possessed look in his eye when he told them how brilliant she was?

"No, Mom, you don't understand. We're doing research together. If anything it's an intellectual affair, not a sexual one. I mean, if it helps you to think of it like that."

This didn't help Mrs. Lim at all, not that it mattered much. Anita was a grown woman now, and her life was her own. She could study Darwinian evolution, have an intellectual affair with her professor, live in a room like the room she herself had once shared with three friends in Pusan, before she met her husband, before she followed him to America, before she worked calluses on her fingers to give her children something more.

In April Anita won another award, something big and important with money attached. Evidently this was the first time a person without a PhD had won this particular award, and she and Rosenblum traveled together to London to receive it. Mrs. Lim wanted to meet them at the airport on their return— ever since she had moved to this country, bewildered, exhausted, and was met by representatives of the Bethany church,

Mrs. Lim had been a firm believer in meeting people at airports. But Anita, of course, said no. A car service would be provided for them. They would be ferried right back to Princeton. Why would she even want to go to the airport on the middle of a Tuesday? Didn't she have to work? And there it was, the sneer in Anita's voice, and Mrs. Lim, when she hung up the phone, didn't wish for another daughter this time nor lament the daughter she had. Instead, she took down the Harvard bumper sticker, and then she went back to work.

In May Anita passed her orals.

In June Eddie was married.

The wedding was held at the home of the bride, who was not, of course, planning to be a pastor herself (in the Korean Presbyterian church, women were not ordained), but who wanted to teach youth Bible, perhaps in New York, perhaps back home in Dallas. She was a second-generation American, and when Mrs. Lim met her parents, she was surprised at their heavy Texas accents—she had never met Koreans with Texas accents before—and from the way that they regarded her son, she knew he was not exactly what they had imagined for their daughter.

Still, a wedding was a joyful thing, a hot Texas wedding in June, and Anita agreed to take a break from Princeton and her work with Hank Rosenblum (Eddie had wanted to bet someone she'd just bring him along to the wedding so as not to interrupt her studies) and put on a peach-colored organza dress and be one of Diana's eleven bridesmaids. At the rehearsal dinner, a big Texas barbecue, Korean food on the side, Anita was seated next to Eddie's seminary friend Charles.

That night, in the corridor of the Holiday Inn, outside their adjoining rooms: had anyone seen Anita?

The next morning Anita was neither sleepy nor hungover but instead was as happy as Mrs. Lim had ever seen her. Gushing. Glowing! She didn't need any makeup whatsoever but still she happily submitted to the makeup artist, who drew long lines around her eyes, lines around her lips, filled in the lines with sparkly colors. She floated into her peach dress. She walked down that aisle carrying her flowers like one of the heroines in the British novels she and Mrs. Lim both used to read. From the front pew where Mrs. Lim sat, regarding the processional, she thought: Oh, for heaven's sake. Anita's in love.

How she changed! Immediately she changed. She was happy. She was polite! She allowed them to tease her, kindly, about the size and squalor of her Princeton living conditions. She allowed them to bring her another glass of champagne. When it was time for her to say something to the bride and her brother, she raised her glass and spoke with more loving kindness toward Eddie than Mrs. Lim had ever heard her express. And she danced with all of them, with her brother, with her father, but especially with Charles, who escorted her onto the dance floor with a gentlemanly hand on her back and whom she gazed up at with eyes wide and joyful, never mind the sparkly makeup sliding off them in a welter of Texas heat.

She didn't go directly back to Princeton but instead came to her parents' house in Brooklyn, borrowed their car, and drove up to Rochester, where Charles was now an apprentice pastor. "Don't worry, Mom, I'll stay with one of the ladies from his church, Charles is old-fashioned about these things," and Mrs. Lim thought that she had just been in London with Rosenblum and hadn't even told her the name of their hotel.

Suddenly she was in Brooklyn all the time. Suddenly Charles was their guest for dinner, along with Eddie and Diana, and nobody could quite believe the girl Anita was or had become: demure, friendly, and most of all, smiling. Finally, finally, she helped Mrs. Lim prepare food in the kitchen. They ate together, like a family, in the dining room, the television turned off, the conversation friendly and engaged. Diana talked about her wish to start a big family, soon, and instead of rolling her eyes (Anita had always had strange ideas about children, thought the best thing to do was not have any in the first place) Anita just smiled.

All she asked of them throughout these performances—and Mrs. Lim couldn't help but think of them as performances, because how else to understand these radical changes? How else to understand the daughter who now asked her how her day was, who asked if she could help out any, who wanted—and here Mrs. Lim almost dropped the phone—who wanted to meet them at church on Sunday before taking the train back to Princeton? All Anita asked of them in return was that they not discuss in any particular detail her work at Princeton, in part because she wanted to explain it all to Charles herself, and in part because she was kind of rethinking, she said, the whole thing. She was rethinking everything she'd ever believed.

On a busy Friday morning at the store, October, Halloween season, Mrs. Lim received a strange phone call. The man on the other end was frantic, speaking so quickly that at first Mrs. Lim didn't understand.

"Anita!" he finally said. "Where is she?"

Anita, at that moment, had just stepped out of the store to go for a jog in Prospect Park with Charles.

"I'm sorry?"

"Mrs. Lim, she hasn't returned my calls. She hasn't come to the lab. I've seen her on campus and she's told me to leave her alone. Is she sick? Is she depressed? What's happened to her?"

"How did you get this number?" Mrs. Lim said. That miserable unwashed professor at Princeton chasing her down like this—it was unprofessional. Maybe it was even criminal? Mrs. Lim thought briefly about calling the police.

"Can you tell me where she is?"

"I'm sorry," Mrs. Lim said. "I don't think I should."

"Mrs. Lim, no disrespect here, but do you know anything about the award Anita won this spring?"

"Yes," she said, and even here was she saying too much? "She went to London."

"Right, but do you understand what a big huge deal this award is? Her viral theory—Mrs. Lim, this is one of the biggest deals in evolutionary biology in a generation. Did she tell you, Mrs. Lim? Have you seen the newspaper articles? Do you understand? I need to find her, Mrs. Lim. I need to talk to her."

If there was anything she was sick of, it was people assuming she didn't understand. "I'd like to end this conversation now, Mister."

"Did she tell you about the money, Mrs. Lim?"

The money? "I must hang up the phone."

"Two hundred thousand dollars, more or less, depending on the exchange rate. That's the money that comes with the Kent-Hughes. She didn't tell you?"

"Anita doesn't talk about these kinds of things," said Mrs. Lim, even though she felt her insides growing cold. What kind of daughter wouldn't tell her about two hundred thousand dollars?

"Mrs. Lim—I—" the voice on the other end sounded less frantic now, now just broken. "She didn't tell you?"

What was she supposed to say to this stranger? What she and her daughter talked about, didn't talk about—the kind of daughter Anita was, or had been, was no business of his.

"Mrs. Lim, your daughter is the sort of genius I've been waiting to meet all my life. In all my pursuits, in everything—I think, if she continues the track she's on—Mrs. Lim, I think

Anita might explain some of the very fundamentals of life itself. How it started. Where it comes from. The very origins, the lightning in a bottle. Do you understand, Mrs. Lim? We need to continue working together because—because if we don't, Mrs. Lim, I just worry—I worry about all the people who will suffer. That's what I think about. That's what a big deal she is."

Oh, the grandiosity of these people. Mrs. Lim was glad she'd taken the Harvard sticker off the wall.

"Do you understand, Mrs. Lim?"

"I have to go now."

"Do you understand what's at stake?"

"Good day."

She did, of course, have every intention of asking Anita about the phone call and the money and the prize—two hundred thousand dollars never even mentioned—and maybe she would even ask about all the people who would suffer, but instead, an hour later, when Anita jogged into the store, sweaty and trailed by a beaming Charles, she ran straight behind the counter and into her mother's arms. "Anita!" This hadn't happened since she was a toddler. "What's happening?" Between this and the phone call—Mrs. Lim wondered about her own nervous heart.

Instead of answering, Anita stuck out her left hand, where a modest but not insignificant diamond was perched on the ring finger. And now Mrs. Lim couldn't help it—she brought a hand to her chest to make sure what she was feeling was just a nervous flutter, not an attack.

"I asked your husband for permission last night," Charles said. "I hope this is okay with you as well, *Uhmuhni.*"

The Korean word for mother. "Of course," Mrs. Lim said. "Oh, I am so happy."

Forget the two hundred thousand dollars. It didn't matter. Because now she really was so happy, planning the second family wedding of the year, and this time she had so much more to do with it, and this time—for the first time—she was included in the major affairs of Anita's life. Although Anita still lived in Princeton, and Charles still lived in Rochester, the wedding was going to be held in Brooklyn, at the Bethany Presbyterian Church, and officiated by Eddie.

Pregnant Diana told them to hurry up and get it done so she could still fit into her bridesmaid's dress when she walked down the aisle. A January wedding, then. Followed by a Hawaiian honeymoon, and then the couple would move to Rochester, where Charles would finish his term as an assistant pastor before moving on to a church of his own, or perhaps even doing missionary work. Charles had long felt a desire to spread the Word of God in Africa.

"And what about Princeton?" Mrs. Lim asked, cautiously, as she and Anita sat in the kitchen, addressing wedding invitations. "When will you finish your studies?"

"I'm not sure," Anita said. She put down her pen, rested her cheek on her hand. Everything about Anita looked different than it had a year ago. Her hair was longer, falling in shiny sheets down her back. She'd started wearing contacts, so her eyes seemed more expressive, less obscured by the heavy black frames she'd favored since her freshman year at Stuyvesant. Her clothing too—where once she wore only the kind of clothing that made a girl disappear (dark turtlenecks, dark cords), now she wore knee-length skirts and open-collared shirts with patterns on them. She wore lipstick and high-heeled shoes and earrings and her diamond engagement ring. She looked, more and more, not at all like a scientist and a lot like a pastor's wife.

Mrs. Lim neatly stacked her invitations back into the cardboard box they'd arrived in and reached out her hands for her daughter's. This was a gesture she wasn't used to making but it felt natural. Her daughter's hands were so small and soft. Mrs. Lim didn't say anything, but enjoyed the feeling of her daughter's hands in her own.

"It's, like, my entire life I was searching for something, you know? I kept searching and searching, thought I'd find it in school—thought I'd find out the reason that we were here, the reason that I'd been born in the first place. Because I wasn't very happy, I don't think. I couldn't figure out the reason for my own life. But I thought if I could—maybe I wouldn't be happy, but at least the world might make a little more sense."

Mrs. Lim remembered Anita as a baby. So watchful. Never cried. Slept still as a stone.

"But no matter how much I studied, no matter how much I understood—no matter how many awards I won, even—I was never very happy. And it was only after I met Charles, after he opened up the way I saw the world—only then did everything start to make true sense to me. Only then did life fundamentally start to mean something to me."

Mrs. Lim held tight to her daughter's hands. "I understand," she said.

"I know."

They were quiet for a while. The kitchen in which Mrs. Lim had done so much raising of her family hadn't changed much in the thirty years she'd been using it—same linoleum tile, same gray chipped counters, same view, out the back window, of the small, fenced-in yards of her Brooklyn neighbors, and the tall poles in each yard, with clotheslines controlled by pulleys—but Mrs. Lim noticed that the kitchen seemed new to her in some small way. She wanted to stand to make tea but she didn't want to risk this sense of newness.

"I have to tell Hank, but he's not going to understand."

"He's called me," Mrs. Lim said.

"You?" Without their glasses to guard them Mrs. Lim could see worry in her daughter's eyes. "He got your number?"

"He told me that you won two hundred thousand dollars."

Anita took her hands back, shaded her brow for a second. "That's a lot of money."

"I'm going to give it to Charles's mission in Africa," she said. "I mean, I know I'm supposed to use it for research, but

I can get around that, I think. I'll use a little for the wedding, and the rest of it will go to Charles."

"You don't have to use it for the wedding," Mrs. Lim said. "We're your parents. We'll pay for that. Give it to the mission." She said this even though she knew it meant that, with the money, the mission would take Anita to Africa, and she would lose her daughter just months after she had finally found her. But that was fine, that would be fine. She'd be closer in Africa in some ways than she'd ever been in Princeton. And hadn't Mrs. Lim herself spent her adult life thousands of miles from her own mother? And though they'd missed one another, assuredly—hadn't they both survived?

THREE WEEKS LATER, just before Thanksgiving, another phone call in the middle of the night. "Can you stop her, Mrs. Lim? She is destroying her life. She is destroying everything! You can't let her go to Africa with that charlatan."

"Do not call this number again," Mrs. Lim whispered, her husband slumbering, snoring beside her. "Do not ever call this number."

"I'm begging you," said the voice. Was he drunk? He sounded drunk to her, or on drugs, some kind of drugs that made his voice waver and slur and go very quiet, and then start again. "You have to stop her, please. It's your duty! I mean—your duty, Mrs. Lim, to free thought. To the world."

"Do not call here," she said.

"Mrs. Lim, I'm begging you."

She hung up the phone.

WHAT HAPPENED IN the next few days was never entirely clear to Mrs. Lim, not in the years when she thought about it, nor in the years she spent trying to forget. Evidently Anita had returned to her hovel in Princeton and sat down with a Bible, a new shiny Bible that had been a gift from her brother. She stayed up all night—it must have taken her all night—going through it with scissors, cutting out every paragraph that contradicted what she had learned in her Ivy League schools about the history of the universe and the origin of man. When she was done with this exercise, the Bible almost came apart in her hands. Hundreds of paragraphs and even pages had been excised.

She brought this remnant of the Bible to Rosenblum. She said, "This is what your studies have done to the Word of God. I will not be part of this anymore."

Rosenblum evidently picked up the Bible and threw it in the toilet. Although eviscerated, the book was still too big to flush down.

That afternoon, an e-mail was sent to Charles's personal account, detailing Anita's research into the viral origins of life, hundreds of millions of years ago. "You see?" said the e-mail.

"This is the woman you will marry. This is what she truly believes."

That evening, Rosenblum placed phone calls to Charles's cell phone and his office in Rochester, but nobody picked up, and he left no voice mails.

The following day, quarter-page ads appeared in the *Princeton Packet,* the *Trentonian,* and the Rochester *Democrat and Chronicle,* accusing Charles Park, assistant pastor of the Bethel Mission Church, of brainwashing a certain Anita Lim, one of the most promising scientists of her generation. The ads also accused Pastor Park of stealing Ms. Lim's two hundred thousand dollars of Kent-Hughes prize money and funneling it to his own mission in Africa. Photos of Charles, looking surly in his pastoral garb, were placed centrally in the ads.

That evening, Charles drove to Ms. Lim's apartment in Princeton. He admitted to the police that he and Anita fought. He admitted to the police that he had broken off their engagement. But he left the apartment around 9:20, and several witnesses at the record store reported seeing him storm out of the building, angrily, slamming doors.

They saw Anita leave the apartment a few minutes after, sit on the stoop, and sob.

The following afternoon, upon the report of a flood in a downstairs apartment, Anita's landlord discovered her body, in a sodden ochre heap, on the floor of her one-room apartment.

She had hanged herself to a pipe, which had broken after she'd died, dropping her on the floor and leaking water all over her corpse. She'd left her note on the table, however, so it had stayed dry.

AT THE FUNERAL at Bethany, Mrs. Lim told well-wishers—and there were hundreds of well-wishers, customers, friends—that these past few months had been the happiest of her daughter's life, and therefore the happiest of her own.

TEN

Andy's mother's flight left Ohio just ahead of a storm that would have kept her Akron-bound for days. It was always tricky to fly in and out of that airport, little planes and shortened runways, and Andy wondered what he would have done if she hadn't made it. He could have cancelled his own ticket, let this one pass. He looked at himself in the mirror, the receding hairline, jackrabbit eyelids, brownish purple bags under the eyes.

There was no way he would have let this one pass.

They picked his mother up at the Atlantic City airport, took her to the White House Sub Shop where the four of them shared a White House special—no word from Rachel about the nitrates—and got back to Mount Deborah around ten at night, Belle asleep in the backseat and Rachel halfway there.

"You sure you want to do this?" his mother asked the next morning. She'd gotten up at five a.m. to see him off, made her specialty, blueberry pancakes. "You could just go to Florida and relax," she said. "Go the beach for a couple of days."

"I don't want to go to the beach."

She nodded, sat down across from him at the table. "You didn't have maple syrup," she said. "I used powdered sugar instead."

"I'm on the docket, Mom." His mother had just turned seventy, and he noticed for what felt like the first time that she'd started to look old, chin drawn. Her eyebrows were growing sparse. She had always seemed comfortably Midwestern to him: cardigans, pastel turtlenecks, a no-nonsense haircut like the kind you'd give a boy in kindergarten. Her hair had started going gray years ago but only now did he realize there was no more brown in it.

"How long has it been since you've gone on vacation?" she asked.

"We were in Ohio in August."

"I don't mean to visit me. I mean on vacation. A break. Andy," she said, and touched his hand briefly, "you need a break, I think. You need to—"

"Please don't tell me to let this go."

She put down her fork. She looked into her coffee. "I wouldn't."

The flight to West Palm Beach was a seamless two hours, retirees going home, exhausted, after visits with their Northeastern grandchildren. Andy rented his car at the Budget counter, smiled grimly at the kind rental agent when she told him he was being upgraded to a PT Cruiser. He stopped for an early lunch at a Chili's off 708, even though he wasn't hungry, even though he couldn't imagine ever being hungry again, the White House sub, the blueberry pancakes, the impotent anger percolating through him, but still, he needed to stay fueled. He ordered a hamburger from a waitress whom he thought, for a moment, was the same woman he'd rented his car from, and wondered how she could handle two such different jobs at once. The waitress did not ask him why he was ordering a hamburger at 10:50 in the morning, nor did she seem to judge him when he left most of it uneaten. He got back in his car with grease on his tie. About thirty miles northwest of West Palm, he peed on the side of the highway.

The first time he'd presented a victim impact statement, four years ago, he'd felt almost thrilled with anxiety and rage, almost hysterical at the opportunity to look at Oliver McGee and tell him exactly what he had done to their family, sentence by beautifully articulated sentence. He had culled the letters he'd written all those five-thirty mornings for the language that most inspired him—"a hell of missing moments," "and one day these girls will have families of their own"—but he spoke them in a voice so emotion-choked that he barely pronounced the words at all; his hands were shaking so that he could barely read. Years of teaching, years of presenting research, burying his father and giving his eulogy, never once had he been unable to give a talk. Yet this time, it was him and his paper and his shaking hands and his blurry eyes and he only managed to get out half of it. Was Oliver McGee even in the room? He heard weeping, furtively, a seat a few yards from where he stood. Oliver's mother. The grandmother. He sat down without finishing what he'd wanted to say.

The next time, eighteen months later, Andy refused to indulge in grief-stricken theatrics; this time he would just lay it bare. This was what his daughters were doing; this was what he was doing; this was what it was like to do all of it without Lou. He was escorted by the corrections officer from the waiting room into the windowless hearing room. He'd been there just a year and a half before, same room, same panel, but the room felt like nowhere he'd ever been before. Even Oliver seemed like nobody he'd ever seen before; the image that haunted his imagination was of a soft-faced, soft-bellied teenager, but this Oliver was not that person. He was skinny, chiseled. Andy imagined he'd joined some kind of gang. Probably a white-power gang. The mother and grandmother cried through this hearing too but Andy paid them no attention and read his statement clearly. Barely trembled. Sat down at the end and almost expected applause; drove back to PBI airport with the windows down and Led Zeppelin on the radio, blasting. When he found out three weeks later that Oliver had again been denied parole he did not indulge himself in tears or any kind of whispered words to Lou but kept it curt on the phone. "Thank you, Officer. That's good to hear."

And now this time. This time, he knew, the kid's chances were better; he'd served six years of an eight to twelve, and Florida prisons, like prisons everywhere, were overcrowded. He must have been behaving himself if he kept coming up for parole. Working overtime at the license-plate shop? Tutoring at the prison library? Andy had been to the Okeechobee Correctional Institution twice but still all his imaginings of prison life came from the movies.

Tomorrow's hearing was at eight thirty; he had a room waiting at the Okeechobee Travelodge. He thought he'd spend the afternoon working out—maybe he'd lift weights in the Travelodge's tiny fitness area, maybe swim in the bathtub-warm pool. But the skies were overcast—January in Florida wasn't necessarily the paradise Northerners imagined—and the idea of spending an afternoon in a tiny chain-hotel fitness room, prisoner to the television's Fox News rotation—it was impossible. Thirty miles from Okeechobee, he turned around. Flew south down the highway, past the exits that were as familiar to him as nursery rhymes: Woolbright, Jog Road, Glades Road, Ives Dairy. Two and a half hours later, he was in Kendall. He didn't stop to think about what he was doing or why he was doing it. What was to be gained by doing it? But when he got off the highway he was so far south that 95—the great eastern highway which connected Florida to Maine—no longer existed. Down here it was called Highway 1. He took the Manor exit. He circled to Eighty-seventh. He pulled into the Blockbuster parking lot but it was no longer a Blockbuster, just an empty storefront, the outlines of where the letters used to be leaving dark marks on the store's façade, a ghost. He got out of the car.

"Mister! Hey, Mister!" Was someone calling him? He paid no mind. "Mister! Hey you!" He stopped, he looked. Nobody was there. He kept walking.

What was he expecting from this visit except gravity? That's all he wanted: to have the gravity he needed to walk into that small, windowless hearing room tomorrow, face the three members of the parole board, refreshed and reanimated by the sight of the very location where Oliver McGee had killed his wife. He would have gravity. He would be grave. He would read the statement he'd prepared with a serious face and steady hands. Here it was, the intersection he hadn't visited in the seven years since she'd been killed. The rain started falling in that ominous Florida way as Andy walked along the side of the road, the only pedestrian in a square mile, toward McDonald's.

"Mister! Hey!" A woman's voice.

Cars flew back and forth across the intersection. More cars lined up outside the drive-thru. Here, under that streetlight. Oliver had slammed into her at fifty miles an hour and forced her car through the intersection, where it spun and ricocheted into the side of the Steak 'n Shake and then back out into the street. Like in an action movie. Like in a horror movie. Parts of Lou's skull forced through the windshield. What was left of her forced back into her seat. She didn't have an air bag. It had been an ancient car.

There was no plaque to mark what had happened, no memorial like those tattered teddy bears you sometimes saw along highways. People lined up in their cars to buy their Big Macs and chicken nuggets. The Steak 'n Shake was open too. Rachel had loved their milkshakes, he'd forgotten that. She used to pronounce *strawberry* "staw-verry."

And if he was going to continue to tour this haunted museum then why not get back in the car and drive two miles west and two south until he arrived at Quail Run? Now the rain was clearing, because that's what rain did in Florida, come fast and hard and retreat like a coward; now the skies were opening gentle and blue. Quail Run had gotten a face-lift, a new sign with navy lettering and gold trim. The parking lot too had been newly paved, and Andy tried not to feel his heart's lunatic pounding as he pulled into a spot, his old spot, right next to Lou's, and got out of the car. The balcony of 13C that looked out over the parking lot: there was a small grill, a Weber, nicer than the one he and Lou used to have. A kid's tricycle. She was there. Was she still there? Was she watching him?

This thought surprised him.

"Mister!"

That voice again, only now there was a body to match it: a woman in her sixties in a blue flowered dress, getting out of her car. He knew her. "That's a reserved spot," she said.

She saw his face and her own went pale. "Oh Jesus. Andy."

"Joyce," he said, wondering how he had heard her voice all day—for now that he heard it, he was sure.

"What are you doing here?" she asked.

"Nothing," Andy said. "Visiting."

Like his own mother, she had grown old in a short span of time. He remembered her as a lean tan woman with a shaggy haircut, cold blue eyes, smoker's lines around her mouth. Now she wore this dress that an old woman would wear, and her hair was tied up behind her head. Orthopedic shoes. "You came down for the hearing?"

Andy nodded. He knew very little about Joyce McGee; when they were neighbors, they were barely even neighborly. There was a Christmas party in the complex's garden every year, but the McGees never went, nor did they open their door to trick-or-treaters. She was never by the pool, like Oliver often was. The television in that end-unit town house was always blasting.

He knew that she managed a salon near the Miami campus. He knew she worked late hours, and that she kept trying to get Oliver a job there, sweeping up, washing hair.

Oliver. When he was sentenced she kept crying his name, softly, behind an oversized wad of Kleenex. Oliver: maybe her dreams for him were in that very name, three syllables, a good man's name. She had wanted her son to be an artist or some kind of thinker, with a name like that—an intellectual-property lawyer, a translator at the UN. Andy wondered if he'd been teased growing up, a fancy-pants name in a classroom full of Johnnys and Lupes and Juans. Oliver McGee. Joyce was still standing there, her keys dumbly in her hand.

"How's your mother?" he asked.

"She died last year," Joyce McGee said. She closed the door to her car. "Pancreatic cancer."

"I'm sorry," Andy said.

Joyce nodded. She didn't seem to be able to leave—was she afraid he'd smash her car or scream at her across the lot?—but she didn't have anything to say. She'd come to Lou's funeral, sat in the back of the funeral home, by herself. She'd had the courtesy not to cry, as far as Andy could see, or to say anything to anyone after. She did, however, sign the guest book: *Joyce Marie McGee* in a schoolteacher hand.

"How's Oliver doing?"

"He got his college degree," Joyce said, then looked abashed, like she shouldn't be bragging. "Do you want to see your old apartment? I know who lives there. I'm sure they'd let you in."

"I don't want to see it," Andy said.

"Why are you here, then? Are you here to see me?"

"I'm just here," Andy said.

Joyce nodded. Had there ever been a Mr. McGee? What had happened to him? Andy had no idea.

"And your girls?" she asked. "How are they?"

"They're fine," he said. "They're doing very well," he added, then wished he hadn't, because he didn't want her to know they were doing well. As far as he was concerned, he wanted her to think, forever, that his girls were the stricken babies in their matching yellow dresses at their mother's funeral. He wanted to think that they were motherless and suffering.

"I'm glad," she said. "Andy—" she started. She loosened her grip on her keys, closed the car door, walked around to where he was standing next to his rental car. His old parking space.

"Andy," she said again, a few feet from him now, so that he could smell her smell of cigarettes and hair spray. She wasn't wearing a blue flowered dress, just a blue flowered smock over a T-shirt and a skirt. This made him feel better; she wasn't elderly, she just worked in a hair salon. Fine. He didn't need to pity her. "Andy, look—"

"Yes?"

She bit the corner of a nail.

"What is it?"

"Look, I have no right to ask you this, I know, and I—I really don't know how even to begin—"

He remembered himself four years ago, the first parole hearing, his own trembling.

"Andy, I know you're here for the hearing tomorrow and I know I have no right but if you would just consider—if you would just consider—"

She bit a corner of a different nail while he stared.

"He was just a boy, Andy, when it happened. When he was sentenced." She realized she was chewing on her nails and stopped. "If he gets out now he could still have some kind of life."

"What do you want me to consider?"

"What happened to your wife will never be undone, Andy. No matter how long my son is in jail, no matter how guilty he feels, everybody feels, no matter how much we hurt for the rest of our lives we cannot bring back your wife, and my son sitting in jail will not bring back your wife."

He didn't say anything, but he could feel the anger coming on.

"He got his degree in industrial drawing, Andy. He's a real good—he's always been a talented artist and he wants to work at a factory somewhere, designing, I don't know. He's the first member of our family to get a college degree, you know that? You're a college professor, right? It's an accomplishment."

"He got his degree in jail," Andy said, thinking of Exton Reed, its shabby quad, its lumbering architecture. He found that he was chewing the inside of his cheek. "What kind of accomplishment is it to get a degree in jail?"

"Well, you could argue—maybe you could argue it's an even bigger accomplishment, because there are all sorts of obstacles. Things happen—things happen there you don't even want to know about, and there are fights, and people fight him all the time. He's had to get really hard in jail, he was never such a hard kid, but he's had to get very hard and learn to protect himself and at the same time he got an arts degree from the University of Florida, there was even a graduation ceremony at the jail." She fumbled through her purse for a cigarette.

"Could you not?" Andy asked, as she lit it. "Could you not smoke?"

She inhaled, then stubbed the thing out with her orthopedic shoe. Andy thought he had never had a more pathetic conversation in his life.

"I guess what I'm asking is—"

"I know what you're asking, Joyce—"

"Is for a little mercy."

He felt the parking lot start to spin, held onto the car roof to steady himself. A little mercy. Sure, there were probably evolved people out in the world who were more than capable of being merciful, those nuns who campaigned for killers on death row, the 9/11 families who opposed the war in Afghanistan, the mothers of murdered sons who paid for their killers' defense. He had read these stories, he knew they happened—and one time, in the office, Linda Schoenmeyer said to him, casually, "So do you have a correspondence with the person who did it?" meaning did he and Oliver McGee correspond, and although Andy was not a particularly icy person he heard the ice in his voice: "What kind of correspondence do you mean, Linda?"

"I just wondered—you know, if he's written to you. Apologized, that sort of thing."

"Why would he do that?"

Fat-faced Linda blanched by the coffeemaker.

"My life isn't a movie," he'd said to her, and left her there in the faculty lounge, and she'd avoided him for weeks after that rather than apologize.

But maybe, maybe if a drunken Oliver McGee had mowed down Linda's lumpy husband in front of a Steak 'n Shake, maybe if she'd had to raise her children alone, maybe evolved Linda would have struck up a correspondence with the killer in his cell, maybe they would have exchanged Christmas cards, maybe she would have visited him in prison and advocated for his rehabilitation and testified on his behalf the first time he was up for parole. Maybe Linda Schoenmeyer was that kind of excellent person. Maybe that's what divided the good people of the earth from the bad, their capacity for mercy.

You are here for a reason.

His reason, at this moment, was to keep Oliver McGee in jail for as long as he possibly could. He had no capacity for mercy nor did he want any.

"I cannot be merciful about this, Joyce."

She lit another cigarette because, fuck him. "I'm sorry to hear that," she said. "But he's paid for this crime, you know that, Andy? He's paid and paid and paid."

"He hasn't even served his full term."

"The things that have happened to him in there," and now,

yes, she was shaking, "the things that happen to a nineteen-year-old boy, and he wasn't hard when he went in there. And I thought *you,* a college professor—you might understand—"

"My children don't have a mother, Joyce."

"*I'm losing my son!*" She brought the cigarette to her mouth and inhaled on it like it was saving her life.

Andy opened the car door, got in the car. There was nothing to be gained by this conversation because the next thing he wanted to say to her was fuck you, Joyce, you lost your son when you didn't get him into fucking treatment seven years ago. That would have been a fucking accomplishment, Joyce.

He peeled out of the parking lot without looking where he was going and drove blindly until he found 95, took it to 708, got to his room at the Travelodge, took a Valium, fell asleep. He was up at 6:00 before the alarm and was waiting at the prison gates by 7:15. The corrections officer who accompanied him to the waiting room asked him how he was doing. "Just fine," Andy said, and meant it.

The same windowless room. A three-member panel, but different members this time. Joyce McGee in her orthopedic shoes. Oliver McGee in his orange jumpsuit. Andy read his statement clearly: "Members of the parole board, it is with great sadness that I discuss with you the myriad reasons that Oliver McGee, prisoner N24633, should probably never be released from prison, and certainly not released before his time is served. Let me begin with my scientific research into alcoholism and behavior—"

He finished his statement. He signaled to the corrections officer that he wanted to leave before any statements were made in support of Oliver McGee's quest for parole.

He was back home in Mount Deborah by seven o'clock that night. As he walked up the path to his house, his mother opened the front door. "Oh, honey," she said. "Oh, honey, I'm so glad you're home."

ELEVEN

The parole board would take several weeks to make its decision, and Andy knew better than to wait by the phone. He busied himself preparing elaborate tests, attending to his daughters' homework, and seeing Melissa Potter. He was, in fact, seeing too much of Melissa. She babysat for him all the time, occasionally just showing up at his house to see if he needed a hand. When she arrived, she urged him to get research done, to go to campus, even. "Don't you want me to stay?" he'd ask her, when his daughters were in another room.

"Go on," she'd say. "Do what you need to do. I'm here to help."

"But you don't have to," and then he stopped protesting. Why should he protest? She cleaned the house while he was gone, she ferried his girls to dance, she helped Rachel bake fat-free angel food cakes with strawberry sauce. She knitted Belle a blue and white striped scarf. She admired the trophy Rachel brought home at the end of soccer season, and polished it for her with Sparkle Wax.

"Did you hire, like, a nanny?" Sheila asked him, Sheila who noticed Melissa's dented Civic parked in his driveway at all hours.

"I guess I did," Andy said, embarrassed to be caught out. "She's a student. She needs a job."

"Ah," Sheila said. "I was starting to think you were dating her." She let the silence fester for a minute, then broke it with uproarious laughter.

Andy felt his jaw tighten, but forced himself to laugh along. "Like I would ever date a student. C'mon."

Yet how his heart flooded when he heard her pull into the drive.

"You know, I mean it, you don't have to pay me, Doc," she said. "I like doing this. I like being here."

"Take the money, Melissa."

"What are you even paying me for? Playing with your daughters?"

"I'm paying you for your time," he said, thinking, please don't ask me why I'm paying you. Thinking, I need to keep up this pretense.

In truth he and Melissa were rarely alone. When they were, they usually coexisted in a froth of stanched erotic feeling. (Didn't they? Didn't she tingle the way he did when he accidentally-on-purpose brushed her arm?) "I just like being near you," she said, "and your family." The girls were in their bedroom, he was looking for his wallet, and he couldn't help it, he kissed her on the mouth and neck, the girls only a door and a hallway away. Then he gave her a twenty and practically pushed her out the door. She honked her horn twice on the way out.

"When is Melissa coming over?" Rachel asked one icy Saturday morning in February as she laid out clothing on her bedroom floor. The fifth-grade father-daughter dance was at the end of March and evidently this required wardrobing. She stretched out a pair of jeans with rhinestones on them he couldn't remember buying her, black T-shirts. A pink miniskirt with zebra-print trim.

"Where'd you get all that stuff?"

"Borrowed," she said. Belle was sitting on the top bunk, surveying the landscape. "A lot of it came from Lily Dreisinger."

"Who's Lily Dreisinger?"

Rachel shrugged, as if it would be too difficult to explain. "I hate all this stuff anyway. When is Melissa coming over? She said she'd take me to the Cherry Hill Mall."

"I'll take you to the Cherry Hill Mall," Andy said, sitting down on the floor to riffle through his daughter's clothing. Some of it was in women's sizes now, 2 or 4. He had thought she was a kid's size 14; in fact, was proud of himself for knowing not only who his kids' teachers were and the names of their dentists and dance teachers but also their sizes in both shirt and shoe. "Is this a training bra?"

"God, Dad, no! Ew! It's a tank top!"

"Yeah, but it has—"

"Give it to me!" Rachel said, snatching it away, her cheeks red, her arms folded around the top as though it were a victim.

"It's like a tank top with a bra inside," Belle explained from the top bunk. "It was Lily Dreisinger's sister's."

"Oh my God, Belle, shut up," Rachel said.

"Don't say shut up," Andy said, absently, wondering what to make of Lily Dreisinger and her sister. Were these enemies or friends of his cause? Did Rachel need a bra? Was he supposed to notice? *How* was he supposed to notice? He was unable and unwilling to inspect his daughter's chest, and, unlike his plan to handle menstruation (on her twelfth birthday, he would put a box of maxi pads in her T-shirt drawer) he couldn't just buy her some training bras (did they still call them training bras?) and stick them in her T-shirt drawer. Unless he could. Maybe that's what he would do.

He'd ask Melissa.

"What about this?" Andy said, picking up a flowered skirt his mother had bought Rachel when they were in Ohio over the summer. It was from the Gap, a store he thought she liked.

"Too small."

"It's mine now," Belle said.

"But we just got it," Andy protested, feebly. "Shouldn't it still fit you?" What did he know about skirts, or girl's sizes, or his daughters at all? What did he know about girls? Wasn't it unfair that he had to know it at all? He knew about his mice and his students, he knew their teacher's names and their dentist's name, he knew—

His phone buzzed. Thank God it was her. "Did you say you were going to take the girls to the mall?"

"I did," Melissa said. "Is that okay? Rachel wanted to find an outfit for the father-daughter dance."

"Sure," he said, wondering if he could ask her about bras, not her bras, which he hadn't seen enough of—and here, he remembered, in a flash, Sheila's beige no-nonsense bra, and his dead wife's, who had small breasts and wore lacy things without wires, who should be here now, who should be here, who wasn't here.

Melissa appeared in his driveway half an hour later and returned with the girls at the end of the afternoon; both flounced into the house with more clothing than he had given them money for, and he knew Melissa had bought them things with her earnings, and he also knew he wasn't going to ask her about it. They displayed their wares fashion-show style: cut-off shorts, a tight-ish plaid shirt for Rachel, purple with lace for Belle. "What do you think?"

He had no idea how to judge a fashion show; the whole thing made him irritable. But he thanked Melissa chastely, waved to her from the door, and she waved and disappeared, and Sheila Humphreys waved too, from her front yard, bundled into her winter coat, because she mistook the direction of his good-bye.

THOSE EARLY WEEKS of the semester, Melissa still came into his office to talk about intelligent design, and about God generally, only now she was starting to talk about God in a more relaxed manner, as though he were a friend she thought Andy should meet. In the office, they would tangle with each other's feet, or he would brush the back of her hand as it riffled through the pages of one of her books, but they didn't touch each other more than that, and he didn't argue with her when she talked about her beliefs. He was glad he was not teaching There Is No God this new spring semester. He didn't know how he would be able to argue with Lionel Shell with the necessary vigor.

"Tell me more about this God of yours, anyway."

"What else do you want to know?"

Really, he just liked hearing her talk, and he liked letting her talk him into things. "I mean, how do you imagine him? Does he have a white beard? Sit on a throne?"

"What does God look like? I have no idea," Melissa said. "We're supposed to be created in his reflection but I really don't know—I don't think that means we look just like him. I think it means that we're supposed to operate the way he would, do our best to be godly." She paused, absently scratched her knee like a child might. She was wearing a short blue skirt which showed off blocky knees. Andy wanted to lick them.

"I've been trying to picture him," he said.

"Have you?"

"Just to have—just to have some idea of what you're talking about when you talk about God. You act like you have a personal relationship with him, but the only God I ever thought about was distant, not really involved in, you know," he felt silly, "in our day-to-day lives."

"When did you think about God?"

"As a kid—I don't know. It's been a long time. Until I met you."

"A little kid or older?"

"I can't really remember," he said, although he knew that even as a small child, he didn't take the God idea seriously. He came from a proud line of teachers, Midwesterners, nonbelievers. "I guess the last time I really considered the subject was in high school history class. Learning about pilgrims, Cotton Mather, Jonathan Edwards. Sinners in the hands of an angry God. I still remember that one—being dangled over the fires of hell."

"You didn't go to church as a kid?"

Andy shook his head. "My mother taught high school biology," he said. "She didn't have the time or patience for church. I remember I asked her where people came from—I was talking about babies, seeing if I could goad her into telling me about sex—but instead she started talking about Darwin. I guess I was eight."

"Where was your dad?"

"He worked all the time. He ran a handyman business," Andy said. "He died when I was twenty."

"Oh." She looked saddened; he loved her expression when she was sad. Her eyes grew crinkled at the corners, mouth fell open. "You've lost a lot of people in your life."

"It's really Lou," he said. "Nobody else matters as much to me. She's the loss that stings."

Melissa wasn't going to try to analyze this, which was good—she only touched his wrist for a minute.

"Did Lou believe in God?"

"No," Andy said. "We were compatible that way," although of course it was more complicated than that: Lou believed in more than she admitted—she'd baptized Rachel—and Andy believed in ghosts.

And now it was time to change the subject. Although they were in his office, he leaned toward her, kissed her neck, the softest part.

"No, not here," she said. "We're talking."

"Are we?" But she had pulled away, adjusted her collar primly. He found this girlishness so attractive; Louisa had been sexy, but not particularly girlish, and he had never before reveled in the softness of the skin on the inside of a twenty-one-year-old's wrist. The softness of the skin under her neck. He touched her neck where he had just kissed it.

"What about art?" Melissa said.

"What do you mean?"

"You know, music, art. Classical music is often religious—Bach's works, Handel's *Messiah*. And if you look at old paintings they're all like Jesus and the Madonna over and over again. I took art history at Salem County," she said. "It was impossible to tell all those old paintings apart. But you can't look at them and not think about, you know, the spirit."

His honeymoon had been to Paris, a whole day at the Louvre. The Renaissance galleries: Botticelli, Raphael, Caravaggio. An entire afternoon, hand in hand with Lou, admiring the slope of the pregnant Madonna's belly, or the baby Jesus with the receding hairline. And the rolling Tuscan hillsides standing in for ancient Bethlehem, and the sheep, and John the Baptist, and the thin halos painted on in real gold. The altarpieces and the triptychs and the miniatures. An afternoon in Lou's hand.

They were not going to talk about this. His hand in Lou's. He leaned forward to kiss Melissa, and this time he did not let her pull away.

THE FOLLOWING MONDAY, UPS delivered Rosenblum's manuscript in an envelope labeled Briggs Watson, Attorneys-at-Law. The note attached: "As per your request." Andy snickered out loud with joy. Rosenblum!

The manuscript itself was surprisingly thin, fifty-odd pages, and he wondered if this was just an excerpt, or if Rosenblum was planning to reemerge on the world stage with a brief manifesto, the kind of thing that could be sold cheaply and attractively packaged at the check-out counter at Barnes & Noble. Not a bad idea, Andy thought. Take back the world a little at a time.

Andy shook out the envelope to see if the lawyer had included any contact information for Rosenblum, an e-mail address, but there was nothing. He went online, looked up Briggs Watson, Attorneys-at-Law, found a simple website, the kind of thing he could put up in fifteen minutes. No phone number. There was an address, though—the same address as the one on Rosenblum's envelope, a PO box in Manhattan. Jesus, Rosenblum. This was the best he could do for a lawyer?

Well, surely there was an office somewhere. Maybe after the semester was over, Andy would take the Greyhound to Manhattan, do a little investigating. He suddenly wanted very much to talk to Rosenblum, to tell him all he was doing with his research, to tell him about his failures to get the mice to behave the way he wanted. To tell him that, despite the recalcitrant mice, he was finally doing well again, after all these years.

He would not, of course, mention Melissa, or God.

The manuscript, "Death and Immortality," was typed out hastily and covered in cross-outs and handwritten interjections as per Rosenblum's fiendish style—the old man thought much faster than he could type, and although he occasionally dictated to typists, he was paranoid that one of them would steal his ideas, hand them to a competing biologist, a graduate student. And he couldn't write longhand, since he was unable to read his own handwriting. So he worked like this on one of the new Apple computers he bought every other year, a mishmash of type and script, marginalia, scratch marks, coffee rings, very occasional drops of what looked to be blood. Andy wanted to breathe in the paper, to smell it—and then he realized he was alone in his office, so what the hell. He picked up the manuscript and held it to his nose, but it only smelled like paper, and a little dust.

He started on the first page.

Death and Immortality
Henry Rosenblum
Professor Emeritus of Evolutionary Biology,
Princeton University

When I was sixty-one years old, a time in a man's life when certain things become apparent (and to deny these apparent things is to make yourself a fool), I met a young girl who was unlike anyone I had met before. She was capable, calm, and without the desperate need for affirmation that I find so irritating in young people (in most people). She was able to see what was true.

Her name was Anita Lim, and her parents were immigrants from Korea. Most of what I know about her family I learned after her death, although she did tell me some things about them. Her father's family had been separated during the Korean War, and she had several uncles and cousins starving somewhere north of Pyongyang. She did not dwell on this, as she resented how lucky these accidental circumstances made her feel. But she mentioned it. She also had a brother whom she did not like to talk about, and parents whom she respected and avoided because she felt, by simply being who she was, she disappointed them. I was certain this couldn't be true, although I met her parents both before and after her death, and it's true they seemed ignorant and hostile. But what I know of Korean parents is informed entirely too much by stereotype; I will admit this now. Anita's parents fit that bill.

Upon arriving as a graduate student at Princeton University in 2001, the girl attached herself to a project of uncovering the origins of DNA. Specifically, this meant she worked on sequencing the genomes of the viruses that might have participated in the building of the first DNA molecules on the earth over a billion years ago. Although she worked, nominally, with a team of viral geneticists, she spent most of her time in the laboratory by herself. Solitary and ceaseless, she made more progress into the origins of life than any scientist I had previously met. It wasn't just me who thought so. Any scientist capable of understanding what she was up to found himself almost unnerved at her youth and her brilliance. She won the Kent-Hughes prize, a prize usually given to scientists at the peak of their careers, when she was twenty-three years old.

I firmly believed that Anita would have solved one of the quandaries I've been waiting for someone else to solve my entire life. I believed, given enough time, that Anita would have exposed the foundation of life on earth.

Now, it is clear to me that very soon somebody will tell us how, and under what conditions, this once-sterile earth became fertile. We already know that carbon molecules began to join with oxygen molecules to create the first organic compounds over a billionfold years ago. The question is how this led to DNA, the building block of human life. But some scientist, somewhere, will figure this out soon. He will tell us where DNA came from. For we already know that once DNA existed, it began evolving, according to the processes that Darwin made clear, and once it began evolving, we became inevitable. We are both lucky and inevitable, was how Anita would put it, if you pressed her, which I did.

I spent most of my working hours with Anita, in those brief years we had together, and occasionally my colleagues would tease me about being in love with her in a romantic way. This is, I think, because in my younger days I was rather roguish. (I was married four times for a cumulative six years.) I'd slowed down by the time I was in my sixties, finding that a good night's sleep more than replaced whatever pleasure sex used to provide, but I think my colleagues still liked to imagine that I was capable or even interested in seducing a young girl. It is hard for us to see that others are aging and changing around us, because it reminds us that we too are aging and changing. I am not the first to notice this, of course. If I am still roguish then you are still youthful, etcetera.

Anyway, I was not in love with Anita. I think, in fact, she frightened me. I think I was frightened of her capacity to find the truth. Regardless, I liked her, if one can like such a quiet and solitary person, and as I said I worked closely with her. She was interested in Darwinian evolution, and we talked about the subject often, as Darwinian evolution has been the subject I have studied most of my life, and in so doing have developed whatever expertise I have developed.

And then, in a case that has been well-documented (a case that led to my being placed on academic leave from Princeton, where I had been a fixture of the biology department for more than thirty years), Anita was killed by a madman.

Who that madman was is a question I still believe is up for debate.

This book is my own short discussion of death. It is about the death of a young girl, and the death of an idea, and, I suppose, my own death, and yours.

I have spent my entire career thinking about the scale of time. I told myself I could appreciate it, what a billion years might mean, but I think I was lying to myself. I don't think a human being has the capacity to understand a billion years, and I don't think human beings ever come to terms with the fact that yes, they too will die. Even suicides don't really believe it. They know they don't want to live anymore, but that's not quite the same thing.

Before Anita died, she found herself a convert to Christianity, and decided that she would no longer pursue her research into the viral origins of DNA. People often speak of deathbed conversions, and there are few of us, I imagine, who, in our darkest times, don't want to reach for supernatural comfort. What is about to happen to us is so beyond our understanding that we need to be comforted by something else that is beyond our understanding. Death—our own, or others'—is the only thing powerful enough to allow adults to believe in what is otherwise impossible to believe. All religion is a response to the undeniable: that there is death, and that we will cease to be. That the people we love will also cease to be here anymore. This is the story of Jesus, is it not? He died, but didn't really die? And isn't this what people say when they talk about giving "meaning" to life? Not, *why was I here at all* but *why can't I be here forever?*

Anita's narrative is that she died after she turned to God, but I wonder if she turned to God because she knew that soon she would die?

Andy closed the manuscript. He still missed Rosenblum dreadfully but this all felt like nonsense to him, self-indulgent nonsense. (*Who was this madman who killed Anita?* Come on, Rosenblum, cut the shit.) He put the manuscript on top of a pile of papers on a chair, turned to the NSF grant it seemed more and more likely he would never finish writing. He added some language, deleted some language. Changed around a few numbers. His computer froze, shut down without allowing him to save his files. He would have been angry about the work he lost except he hadn't been doing any real work. Rosenblum's manuscript on the chair was like having Rosenblum himself on the chair. He didn't want to fight with Rosenblum right now. His excitement over having Rosenblum back in his life made him feel oddly vulnerable to whatever Rosenblum might say. He would wrestle with that later.

For the moment he would visit his befuddling mice.

The forty-two C56BL/6s were climbing along the bars of their cages, scratching madly; he checked the log, and the tech hadn't come around since yesterday morning. Well, Andy knew how to clean out some mouse cages. It wasn't so long ago he'd been in charge of this kind of messy work. He put on some gloves, put his small slippery mice in a plastic box, cage by cage, emptied out their shavings, refreshed their food. Eight cages of six mice each, stacked on top of each other in the vivarium. The six DBA/2s in cage 4 were scheduled to be bred soon; he had to make a note to the tech. On the margin of the note, he scribbled, then crossed out, "goddammit Rosenblum!!!"

Cautiously, Andy checked the levels of ethanol to see if his C56BL/6s were drinking as much as they were supposed to. Please, he thought, bending down to look at the measures; come on, you little alkies, drink yourselves blind. But no: once again, his little black mice had drunk only in moderation, as though they were at a cocktail mixer, not a frat party. What was wrong with these rodents? Didn't they want him to get his grant? Why were they conspiring against him?

"Professor?"

Lionel Shell, whom he hadn't seen in months. He was grim-looking, unshaven, circles under the eyes. Much like Andy felt. He was wearing a sweater-vest with a T-shirt under it and a small rip near the hem.

Andy put down his notebook on top of one of the little mouse cages. One of the rodents gave him what seemed to be a dirty look.

"Can I help you, Lionel?"

"What are you doing down here?" Lionel asked. "Am I interrupting?"

"Just checking some numbers," Andy said. "Maybe cleaning out a cage or two."

Lionel stuck his hands deep in his pockets. The laboratory space was dingy, pale green, windowless. The walls were lined with plastic equipment, some of which hadn't been used in generations; there were computers, microscopes, and boxes of slides along each wall. In the corner of the room stood the small wood and metal guillotine where a few times a month Andy would behead his mice, and next to it was the machine that let him make prosciutto-thin slices of their brains. Lionel went over to the guillotine. It had brown splotches on it, even though Andy did his best to keep it clean.

"Lionel? You here for a reason?" Andy felt itchy, wanted a fight.

The boy fingered the edge of the guillotine for a moment. "Can I help you clean the cages?"

"You want to?" Andy said, hoping Lionel hadn't come here to finally lose his mind. "Why?"

"I just feel like being useful," Lionel said. He met Andy's quizzical gaze. "It's the least I can do."

So they went from cage to cage, refreshing the pellets and the water, taking their time. He wanted to concentrate on something useful; he also wanted to get Rosenblum out of his head. He hated the blanket way that Rosenblum equated religion with fear of death—it was just like him to be so reductive. Surely the world's great religious traditions were about more than staving off the fear of death. They were about teaching morality, they were about separating right from wrong, they were about providing signposts on how to live in a complicated world.

Oh, but he could hear Rosenblum in his ear: *The only thing that motivates us is the preservation of our genes. Religion it-self is a response to that need to preserve. And there are clearly no lengths to which our DNA will not go to preserve itself— building a cathedral is nothing compared to outwitting several ice ages.*

Come on, Andy, didn't I teach you anything?

"Lionel, I've been thinking a lot about God lately," he said. He felt a need to confess this, or to change the subject from the fight he was having with Rosenblum in his head.

"Have you?" Lionel didn't seem as interested as Andy would have liked.

"Well, I've been working with Melissa Potter on that project, and she's given me some books which are quite eye-opening."

Lionel looked confused.

"Remember? Melissa Potter? You met her at the Campus Crusade, sent her my way—"

"I remember," Lionel said. "I just don't go to the Crusade much anymore."

"Why not?"

"I just—I'm not sure they matter to me anymore, or some-thing. It's hard to say." The boy was quiet. He was looking with spooky intensity toward the guillotine.

"Lionel?"

"I've been rereading some of the books you assigned. *The Blind Watchmaker.*"

"That's a good one."

"He's very convincing, that Dawkins. I also read Rosenblum's book *Religion's Dangerous Lie*."

"Lionel, come on, you don't have to read that stuff anymore." In their cages, the mice were happily burrowing into their fresh shavings.

"It's really depressing."

"It's not supposed to be," Andy said. "It's just supposed to be provocative. Eye-opening."

"But what are you supposed to open your eyes to? That's what I don't understand. You're supposed to open your eyes and instead of God find . . . nothing?"

"You're supposed to find evolution, Lionel."

Lionel sighed. "It doesn't quite fill the void."

"You don't have to read that stuff if you don't want to. Just because it's out there doesn't mean you have to read it."

"But you assigned it."

"Class is over, Lionel," Andy said. "You did well, didn't you?"

"I got an A for the second time in a row."

Andy smiled. "I can't believe you let the registrar give you credit for taking the same class twice."

Lionel snickered, but it was a pale imitation of his old, dismissive snort.

"What I want to tell you is that I've been thinking about believing in God, Lionel," Andy said. It was true. He had been thinking about believing in God, and in that consideration

228 | LAUREN GRODSTEIN

came the very seeds of belief. He had opened himself to the possibility, and now that he had, there was no turning back. God was a legitimate possibility, a possibility that answered questions of the heart the way that Darwin answered the questions of the mind, and accepting the possibility of God made Andy newly aware of his heart, and its capacity to heal. He felt his body unwind. "Belief has started to make more sense to me," Andy said. "I think I can get where you've been coming from all these years."

The admission made him feel pure and clean. He felt that if he could admit this to Lionel, he could admit it to Rosenblum, and to himself.

But Lionel did not look victorious. He just looked sad. "Congratulations," he said to Andy. "You're a lucky man."

"Aren't you surprised? You won this fight!"

"This wasn't a fight, Professor."

"Of course it was a fight! Why did you take my class if not to fight me, or fight Darwin? Didn't you say that yourself?"

But Lionel just shook his head. Then he hitched his backpack over his shoulder and walked, shoulders hunched, out the door.

What would Rosenblum say to all this? To Lionel, he would say: Buck up, kid. The world is more magical than even Santa Claus, and you should be glad you figured it out. Then he'd turn to Andy and say: so I leave you alone and you turn into a schmuck.

And he'd tell him to get back to work.

The work. The mice. The misbehaving mice. The drunks who didn't feel like drinking anymore. Andy looked through his notebooks.

If he had made some mistakes breeding his specimens, if he had adulterated the ethanol, if he had mismeasured their brain chemistries, if he had taken the wrong notes, if he had a research assistant to blame (could he blame the tech?) then his results would be easier to swallow. But he had never made these kinds of basic mistakes in the past, so why would he have started now?

Had he ordered the wrong kind of mice? Had the facility sent out a mislabeled supply?

Andy bent down to one of the cages, where his alcoholic mice slumbered. These tiny beasts were patented; according to the government, they were not animals but inventions. Which was the trouble: Andy could accept that animals might not be-have the way they were supposed to (as a child, he was master of a series of mischievous dogs) but an invention, a laboratory-designed product—wasn't that supposed to be foolproof?

Andy watched his small black mouse breathe in and out in its sleep. Its sleek tiny body took in air and expelled it, its whis-kers fluttered, its soft ears quivered faintly in the still air. This animal had been designed in a laboratory, yes, but designed with DNA, the building block of life, the thing this mouse had in common with a whale and a tree and with Rachel and Belle.

DNA, God's tool kit, which man had tried to take charge of to design this small sleeping mouse.

Yet the mouse refused to behave the way the person who designed it expected it to behave.

Well, mistakes get made, said Rosenblum. Don't get all mystical on me.

Andy watched the mouse breathe in and out. Sure, fine, mistakes get made—but what was the nature of the mistake? Did something go wrong in the design of this (twitching, breathing, marvelous) mouse, or was the problem the idea that we were the ones to design this animal in the first place?

TWELVE

November 30, 2003

Dear Appa, Umma, and Oppa,

And my dearest Charles, if you should read this some day, and forgive me,

I want you to know that first of all I am sorry for whatever sadness this note brings you, or discovering my mortal body. I hope you find some comfort knowing we will see each other soon in Heaven, in the Lord's embrace. Until that time, please remember me as kindly as you can. By the time you find this I will be with God, and I will be happy. As I write this note, now, it seems to me that my work on this Earth has been completed and there is nothing left for my journey here. It is time for me to meet my Lord. I want to meet the Lord. I have so little to do on this Earth now and I can hear the Lord calling me home.

Before I knew the Lord, I thought that this Earth was all there was, and that we were supposed to "make the most of it." So that's what I did, I tried to make the most of it but all the things that should have brought me joy (a successful recital, a history prize, acceptance to Harvard) brought, instead, only brief flares of pride. Was the point of life really to bounce from one moment of vanity to the next? To try as hard as possible to succeed at trivialities? To be rewarded with money or the admiration of less successful people? Was that happiness? Even helping other people seemed mostly to point out how destitute and miserable other people's lives were, and how limited anyone's own capacity to really help. Like when my mother's church group made its monthly visit to some Bed-Stuy food pantry, let's not pretend they ever made any difference in the world, at least not in the big picture of it.

So then I thought: Okay, I know the problem. The problem is I don't know the reason *why*. The scientific reason. I decided I would do my best to uncover the origins of life, so that maybe this stupid life of ours would make sense.

So ah, how horrible when my research into the origins of life brought me nothing but more frustration and sadness! How miserable when it seemed to me the point of it all was only more pointlessness! The more I pushed my research, the more it became clear that human beings were nothing but the improbable evolution of a misfiring virus. Our ancestors were bits of DNA electrified and sent out into the world. Our bodies, our very souls, were nothing but mechanisms to keep this pointless DNA alive! Henry Rosenblum, the only person in the world I ever trusted, before Charles, said to me that my research was magnificent. He said that uncovering the origins of human life was the equivalent of finding the God particle. In fact, it *was* the God particle! GOD WAS A VIRUS!

Only once, on our way to the Kent-Hughes ceremony in London, I tried to discuss my worries with Henry. I had never been to London before, and had packed the new raincoat my mother gave me for my birthday, and was wearing an old pearl ring she'd given me that had been my grandmother's. I kept twisting the ring, since I was nervous; I'd never really liked to fly. I remember looking out at the clouds and thinking about all those kids I went to Sunday school with when my mother would force me to go, and how all those kids would look up at the clouds and believe that's where God lived. And here I was, going to London to win money for erasing that belief.

I said, "Henry, do you think my work is destroying the meaning of life? Like when other people learn that all life started out as a virus, they'll think life doesn't have any purpose anymore?"

He said, "Don't be ridiculous." He said, "Only children need something besides life itself to give life meaning. Children, or depressives."

I asked him if he thought I was depressive.

"Well," he said, "well, Anita, sometimes I do worry."

They gave me my check. I wore my new raincoat. I went back to school and to Henry's lab but the more I learned, the more I despaired.

Henry noticed I was sad and tried to cheer me up the best way he knew how. He took me to fancy restaurants even though I don't really like restaurants and prodded me to spend more time in the lab even when I didn't feel like it. Because I didn't have anything else to do, I'd go back to the lab. Sometimes I'd spend late nights engaged in the riddles of my research, and I'd almost feel enthusiasm, before I remembered what it was I was proving, and then, again, I'd despair.

And then I met Charles, who said to me, "If you need joy in your life, why don't you come to the one place you'll find it?" He said, "Just listen to me preach, and if you don't feel true joy I'll keep bringing you back until you do." I had nothing to lose. I listened to him preach that very first night. We walked into the sweaty humid Dallas night on the river near the Holiday Inn, and I sat down on a bench, and I listened to Charles preach just to me. He told me: "God loves you." He told me: "God is waiting to see you at home again, when our work on this Earth is done." He told me that the noble life is more than winning awards. He told me that the true good life is something a person knows only when she lets Jesus into her heart.

I felt hopeful for the first time in my memory. I spent that night with Charles, reading the Bible, and praying. And in the morning I felt happy.

I knew I was hurting Henry—I knew I was driving him crazy, even—but I couldn't help the fact that Jesus had found a home in my heart. My world had purpose now, and that purpose was not in a lab, and it was not in a virus. In fact, now my purpose was to stop my viral research from ever happening. I was the only one who could perform the research, so I was the one who could end it. Right then, I ended it.

I wanted to explain all this to Charles, but I never got the chance. He accused me of faking it, of faking who I really was, of setting him up to look like a thief and a fool. He told me he never wanted to see me again. Charles is a man of his word, so I believed him when he told me this. And although he is the best man I have ever known, he is still only a man, and therefore capable only of man's flawed mercy—if he were ever to show me any mercy at all. But God's mercy is perfect and perpetual. When my life is over (I guess now my life is over) I look forward to spending eternity in his shining light, under the cloak of his forgiveness.

I hope you can forgive me too.

I loved you all as best I could.

Sincerely,

Anita

THIRTEEN

Now that Andy had admitted it to Lionel, he could admit it to anyone who asked. He would no longer teach There Is No God. He would teach evolution, but he would teach it with the essential truth in mind: God got this whole ball rolling.

It wasn't that he found faith, necessarily, as much as he seemed to have rediscovered something he lost a long time ago, before he'd begun to form memories. How else to explain the comfort it gave him, and the feeling of retrieval? Lionel was right—he was a lucky man. Every small moment in his day started to make sense again, in the same way these moments had made sense to him when he was a child. A neon sunset, a perfect tonal chord at the end of a piece of music, the way his daughters' careless gestures reminded him of his own and their mother's. There was meaning in these things now, or there was again.

"Does this mean we have to start going to church?" Belle

asked before dinner one night, when Andy suggested they bow their heads for a moment in gratitude for the meal they were about to eat. Rachel had cooked spaghetti with turkey meatballs and Belle had made a salad and Andy was so grateful for all of it, so filled with appreciation for the blessings in his life. Before God, he would have felt gratitude, perhaps, but mostly absence. He'd thought it had been Lou's absence. Maybe it had been something more.

"I don't know," Andy said. "I was thinking maybe we could try it out."

"I don't want to," Rachel said.

"I do," Belle said. "Everybody goes to church."

"Church is boring."

"How do you know?" Belle asked. "You've never been."

"I just do."

"Actually you don't know everything," Belle said. "Not to, like, shock you or anything."

Andy sprinkled parmesan cheese on his spaghetti. Rachel really was turning into an excellent cook—she'd used garlic in the sauce, and two kinds of olives. "I haven't decided on anything in particular," he said. "Except that there should be a little room for God in our lives."

"Yeah, but why?" Rachel asked. "CCD is supposed to be the most boring thing in the world, by the way. I always felt really lucky that I didn't have to go to CCD."

"We're not Catholic," Andy said.

"Fine," said Rachel. "Then what are we?"

"Do we have to be something?" Andy asked. "Can't we just be generic believers?"

"I don't even know what that means," said Belle. She picked up a forkful of spaghetti.

"Is this because of Melissa?" Rachel asked. "Since she believes in Jesus now we do too?"

"Is Melissa your girlfriend?" Belle asked.

"No!" Andy said, reflexively. His relationship with Melissa was so amorphous. How could his daughters have picked up on it? But of course his daughters, maybe all daughters, were perceptive. Maybe they'd sensed her in the house the few times she'd come over late at night. Maybe they'd sensed how eagerly he wanted to talk about her.

"But Melissa believes in God," Rachel said. "She told me all about her church in Hollyville."

"That's true," Andy said. "And certainly some of the books Melissa gave me have opened my eyes a little, and certainly talking to her has—but no, I don't believe because Melissa believes. And you guys don't have to believe just because I do. I just know that ever since I've accepted the possibility of God I've felt happier. More secure. And I want the same for you."

The girls were quiet. Belle slurped her spaghetti, and drops of tomato sauce splashed on her shirt.

"Were you not happy before?" she asked, through a mouthful of food.

"I was," Andy said. "But I missed your mom so much that sometimes it was hard to think about anything else."

"Don't you still miss her though?"

"Of course, honey. I'll always miss her."

The girls went quiet. The quiet lasted eerily throughout dinner, throughout dishes, and toward bedtime. He tucked them both in and kissed them each on their forehead, and later, when he went to check on them, just to make sure they were warm and their covers hadn't slipped off, he found Belle in Rachel's bed, and Rachel on the floor. Belle's arm hung off the side, and her hand dangled toward her sister. He adjusted her arm; she murmured, annoyed, and rolled over. Andy placed a pillow under Rachel's head, tucked a blanket under her shoulders. Rachel mumbled something in her sleep that sounded like "thank you."

The nights were starting to grow perceptibly shorter; it was the second week in March already. Andy settled himself in front of his computer to poke aimlessly around the Internet, see if Melissa had written. She hadn't, and Andy felt a momentary loss, but he quickly recovered himself. He turned on NPR, sat in the den with a book he'd taken out from the library, essays about the afterlife by C. S. Lewis. It still bothered him that he couldn't get in touch with Rosenblum. The Internet told him nothing.

On NPR, someone nattered about climate change, but outside, the lion of mid-March, it was still freezing.

Next week it would be spring break. On spring breaks past he'd visited his mother in Ohio, and once, with the girls, he took an all-inclusive junket to Puerto Rico. The girls had angled for Disney World but for years Andy didn't think he could face taking them there. Now he thought, sure, he could take them to Florida. Orlando was nowhere near Miami or Okeechobee but even if it was, even if they wanted to see Miami, visit the shores where Lou's ashes had been sprinkled, wouldn't that be fine? Wasn't Lou all around them, no matter where they went?

He had barely started reading the Lewis but already he'd found something he liked: "No one ever told me that grief felt so like fear."

He turned down the radio. If the house had a fireplace, he would have lit a fire. For so long he had only been aware of his grief and fear.

But now that he remembered his body, and his body's soulless needs, they were becoming harder to put away. Oh, Melissa, with the soft skin and the wheat-colored hair—he couldn't get enough of her. What would Lou think of that? He could imagine her shaking her head, her expression indulgent, saying, really, Andrew? A student?

Andy put down the Lewis, closed his eyes. Lou in the chair opposite him. After all these years, Andrew, this was the best you could do? A chubby mousy student? Even now, chastising him in his imagination, she felt closer than she had in a long time. Andy smiled. "I like her, baby, because she brought me back to you."

Don't be ridiculous, Lou said in his imagination. You like her because she felt you up.

The other night—two in the morning, only the second time Melissa had come over that late (she couldn't sleep, she said, and neither could he)—he and Melissa sat out on the porch. In the darkness, across the street, a family of deer wandered by. Melissa was wearing a big fuzzy sweater, pumpkin-colored (she grinned when he complimented it), and in the darkness she seemed to him to be a series of textures rather than colors, soft skin, puffy hair, fuzzy sweater. It was cold out but she was warm, and his leg was warm where it pressed against hers.

They had not slept together yet. Andy wasn't sure they would. It seemed wrong, not only morally wrong, but also temperamentally wrong, like it would ruin the fragile equilibrium of desire and trust and hope that lived between them. Or maybe Andy was just scared of the consequences. He reached for her hand.

There, in the cold, on his back steps, they talked for an hour, until they realized how cold they were, and that they should either go inside and risk whatever they might do inside, or else Melissa should go home. She decided to go home. But first she asked him what he was doing over spring break because she was trying to decide whether or not to go home to Hollyville. Usually she went to her parents' house, but this year she wasn't sure.

"Will your parents miss you?"

"I doubt it," she said. "They're awfully busy." From what he could gather about Melissa's parents, they each worked several part-time jobs in convenience stores, fast-food outlets, the mall. They only saw each other for any quality time on Sundays, at church.

"Well, I think we're staying here," Andy said. "We don't have any big plans but we'd be happy to spend time with you."

"I was hoping," she said, shy.

"I think I might take the girls to the beach one day if you want to come."

"In March?"

"It's sort of fun to see the ocean in the winter," Andy said. "You feel like outlaws, since you're the only people there. We stay for a little while and then we go eat fried fish or something at a seafood shack in Absecon. It's like a vacation."

"That sounds like fun," Melissa said. "I'd love to come."

They grew colder. She went home. But first they kissed in the shy darkness, on his back step, decorously, like teenagers from a long-ago era, an era that maybe even then was make-believe—was anyone ever really so decorous?—or maybe they kissed like visitors from Melissa's world, where people behaved righteously and according to some plan of God's; they behaved like good citizens, like just, modest citizens, except that when she reached her hand inside his jeans he shuddered and let her keep doing exactly what she seemed to know how to do surprisingly well.

THE PHONE CALL came just before he headed off to his final class before spring break. The woman on the other end had a thick North Florida accent, the kind that pronounced *alligator* "ally-gay-tor." Not that she was calling to discuss alligators.

"On behalf of the Florida Parole Commission I wanted to inform you that Oliver McGee, prisoner N24633, has been denied parole, and will not be eligible again for another two years, at which point he will have served his term's limit."

Andy leaned back against his desk. "Thank you," he said. "Thank you for calling."

"Have a nice day," said the woman, and clicked off. Three times, then. Three times he had managed to keep McGee behind bars, and wasn't that a wonderful thing? Wasn't that the best thing? Because no matter his current ambiguities, if his research had proven anything it was that alcoholics were always alcoholics. (And just ask one, right? Go to an AA meeting and what do you learn? Ask Sheila and what will she tell you? They can never drink again! They can never handle it again!) Moreover, McGee had proven, not just in the murder of his wife but in the two DUIs that preceded it, that he himself was irredeemable. He would never be cured, he would never not be a drunk. The only safe place for someone like him was in prison.

So why was Joyce McGee's voice everywhere?

Mister! Hey, Mister!

The first time Oliver had been denied, Andy was ecstatic, and the second time he was pleased; but now—now he wished Joyce McGee would stop talking. He wanted Lou to talk to him instead, but he couldn't hear her. All these other voices in his head: Rosenblum, McGee, Melissa, God. Lou? Lou—say something.

Oliver McGee had gotten his BA in prison. *I thought you, a college professor, would understand.*

A knock on the door, the soft familiar knock. He threw open the door like he'd been waiting for her his whole life.

"I thought I'd find you here," she said. He shut the door behind Melissa, put his arms around her wide, warm body, pulled her face toward his. He hadn't seen her all day and hadn't realized that he'd missed her. "What happened?"

"I just got some news," he whispered into her cheek. She reared back to look at him, alarmed.

"I mean, I'm fine—I just, the man who killed my wife. He was denied parole again."

"That's good news, right?" she said, and bless her for not acting like an undergraduate, bouncing up and down and saying "awesome!" She understood the gravity of it (that's what he needed, he needed gravity) and took a step back from him and leaned against his desk, a precarious pile of midterms. "That's what you wanted, right? When you went to Florida?"

"I feel strange about it, though."

"Guilty?"

He looked at her, the broad planes of her open face. Her soft, youthful skin. "I guess I do."

"That's crazy. I mean, no offense, but that's crazy. This is the man who killed your wife. Who deprived your daughters of their mother. He should stay in jail forever—"

"Yes, but—"

"Remember when I told you God was just? Is this why you asked me?"

He nodded. He loved her.

"Listen, not only is God just, but this is what is just. This is the punishment that is just, right? Parole—what is parole? It's a way of getting out early. A way of not serving out your punishment. That's all it is. A way of dodging the bullet. Why should this man get parole? He's a murderer! Why should he dodge the bullet? He should probably rot in there, shouldn't he? I mean, if that's what the state sentenced him to? To rot in there?"

He loved her, so he tried not to notice that he disagreed with her. Especially because he wanted so much to agree.

"I don't know," Andy said, miserable.

"Well I do," she said. "I know. You asked me if God is just. The answer is yes, and the proof is that this man was denied parole. See?"

Andy tried to see, but he couldn't. He wanted Lou back. That's all he could see. He had loved Melissa Potter five seconds ago but now he wasn't so sure. Still, when she came to him and hugged him, he let her, and when she kissed him—how rarely she initiated any sort of contact!—she kissed him, and he let himself be kissed.

"See?" she whispered again, his overweight seductress.

And suddenly she was kissing him hard, in the mess that was his office. They were pressed against the wall as though by centrifugal force. He put his hands inside her shirt, felt the warm firm folds of her back. Papers everywhere, books strewn around them, he moved his hands to her cheeks, held her head against the wall, next to the Exton Reed calendar that was stuck there with a thumbtack. "Andy!" she gasped. Here, it would happen here. She put her hands in his pants—he hadn't fucked her yet, why hadn't he fucked her yet?—and yanked at his waistband.

Another knock, twice, firm, the twist of the doorknob. He jumped away, almost tripped over the carpet of books. From tragedy to comedy. The door opened. Melissa Potter still stood against the wall, her face red, her hair messy. Her shirt untucked.

"Everything okay in here?" asked Rosemary. "I got a call from your 202 class. They're waiting for their midterms."

"Right," Andy said. "We were just finishing up a discussion."

Rosemary looked at Melissa, then back at him. "Okay," she said. Her tone was so flat it was impossible to know if he should read suspicion there or just boredom. "It's a quarter after eleven," she said then. "In case your clock doesn't work." And then she closed the door.

Melissa blinked at him.

"I better get to class."

"Right," she said. "I'll see you soon."

"Melissa," he said. He put his arms around her one more time and kissed her more gently, because the door was closed, because he didn't know what had come over him, because McGee was in jail. "Are you okay?"

"I'm great," she said. "I'm just worried about *you.*"

FROM THIS MOMENT on, perhaps a wiser man might have cooled it with Melissa. How close had they come to being caught? And what if they'd been caught? How humiliating for everyone, for him, for Rosemary, but especially poor Melissa, getting manhandled in the office of a biology professor.

"Cool it, Andy," he told himself, driving home along Deborah Boulevard. "Cool it now." Or, if not, just tell her look, let's put this thing on hold, whatever it is—we can wait a year and then whatever it is between us will be scandalous, but not actionable. Or maybe just say thanks for the memories, sweetheart. It's been grand.

But how could he say that to her? How could he look at her open, honest face, and not want to cradle it between his hands?

"You look great," Melissa said. She'd come that night to watch Belle while he and Rachel went to the fifth-grade father-daughter dance. Andy was wearing a new tie. He'd bought Rachel a corsage, an orchid, which was staying fresh in the refrigerator, wrapped in green paper. She was in her bedroom, getting ready, while Belle watched television in the den. "This is a new tie, right?" Melissa said.

"It is," he said, and again that urge to take her face in his hands, but he didn't—he just let her adjust his tie.

"I don't understand why Rachel always gets to do these special things and I don't ever get to do anything special," Belle said, plopping onto a kitchen chair. "It's always like Rachel's soccer game or Rachel's dance show or whatever and my question to you is, how is that fair?"

"How is what fair?"

"I want to do something special too," she said. She stood, draped herself against the kitchen counter in the melodramatic pose she'd learned from her older sister. "Like, it's always Rachel's special day and Rachel gets a new outfit and Rachel gets to stay out late and I'm stuck with a babysitter and my question to you is, how is that fair?"

"Since when do you care about new outfits?" First Rachel, now Belle. Who was about to turn nine.

"Wow!" said Melissa, as Rachel made her entrance. "Look at you!" She had pulled her hair off her face with a sparkling white band, and she was wearing a white skirt and a white shirt with rhinestones around the collar. She looked a bit like a fairy princess and a bit like a teenager and entirely like her mother. And she was growing up. And one day, only a few years away now, she would leave. All of them—they all would leave.

"You look terrific, Rache," Andy said. Gutted, he was gutted. He removed the corsage from the refrigerator and strapped it to her wrist. "There you go."

Rachel twirled excitedly across the kitchen, stopping only when she hit the counter. "What's *your* problem?"

"I am so, so sick of you!" Belle sputtered. "It's always special Rachel day and I am so sick of it!"

"Oh my God, would you relax?"

"I will not relax!" And Belle sat down again on a kitchen chair and started to sob. Melissa sat next to her, rubbed her back. Whispered something in her ear.

"C'mon, Dad, we've got to go."

"Rachel, we can't leave her like that," Andy said, marveling at the compact way Melissa was able to soothe Belle, whose back stopped heaving after a few minutes, who stopped making panting sounds.

Melissa whispered something else, and Belle, head still hidden behind her arms, nodded.

"Should I ask your dad?" Melissa said, and Belle nodded again. "Belle would like to be baptized."

"I'm sorry?"

"In a white dress."

"You're kidding," Rachel said. "Why?"

Again, from behind her arms, Belle started to sob. "Because Rachel was baptized when she was a baby and I want to be too! Because it's not fair that Rachel gets everything and I get nothing!"

"Baptized, Belle?"

"Rachel's going to heaven and I want to go too!"

"Heaven?" Gutted, and now he had been steamrolled too.

"I told her we could do it at my church, if you guys wouldn't mind the drive. Of course, we could do it anywhere, the beach if you wanted—"

"No," Belle said. "I want to do it in a church, like Rachel had it. With our mom. I want to do it in Melissa's church."

He was going to Melissa's church. A wiser man would have cooled it.

"Please, Dad?"

"We'll see."

"Why we'll see?"

"Because I—"

"You were the one who said we should try going to a church," Belle said.

"Did you say that, Andy?" Melissa asked. "Oh, I'm so glad. I think it would be so good for you too."

"Dad, can we go already?" said Rachel.

"You really want to do this?" Andy asked Belle. She looked

up at him with reddened eyes. She looked half-hopeful, half-scared. She reminded him as she so often did of himself, the deepest part of him. She nodded. "So then we'll do it."

"Fine, good, let's go," Rachel said, grabbing him by the hand, dragging him to the door.

"Really? And it'll be my day, not Rachel's?"

"Oh my God, what's your problem?"

"It'll be your day, Belle," Andy said, as Rachel pushed him out of the house and out toward the car.

THE DANCE WAS all streamers and Kool-Aid and music Andy couldn't abide and girls dancing in circles with each other while their tubby, embarrassed fathers stood in corners of the room and watched them and talked about the Phillies' spring training. Every so often Rachel would find him, make sure he was okay—what a thoughtful girl!—and then return to her friends in the center of the room. Rachel did seem to have lots of friends. They spent a lot of time giggling. Andy didn't know how to talk to the other dads.

In all, a junior high dance, which meant that nobody was spiking the punch. Did kids still spike punch? He remembered, during Oliver McGee's trial, someone talked about a particular high school dance, and Oliver showing up wasted, throwing up all over a popular girl's new shoes. The popular girl's boyfriend beat the shit out of him in the parking lot.

Was that justice?

Mister. Hey, Mister. The lyrics of a song he could not get out of his head.

At five thirty the next morning, he woke up to the cloudless sparkle of a March day.

Dear Mr. McGee:

It's been a while since I've written, but I don't want you to think I've forgotten you. Just the other day I received a phone call telling me that your application for parole has once again been denied, and I'd be lying if I said that I didn't feel some sort of relief, some sort of vindication — okay, some sort of joy — at knowing that you'll be in that shithole for another two years, playing dodgeball with your white-power friends or cowering in the shower or whatever it is you do in there. I know that I can't keep you in jail for the rest of your life, no matter how much I'd like to, but it seems a fair thing to keep you there for at least these next two years, minimum.

But at the same time — and this is what's been bothering me lately, McGee, as much as I wish it weren't — at the same time I've been trying to forge some kind of relationship with God, which is difficult, as God is a concept I've never had much patience for, and even now find a little peculiar. I have it on good authority that God is a figure of justice, and I have no doubt that the God of justice would smile upon someone like you being locked away for two more years. But at the same time I can't help but feel—it's hard for me not to feel—I worry for you, McGee. I worry for you there, and I worry for your mother, and I worry most of all for myself, and what this glee means, this glee that you have been punished and will continue to be punished, and what it means that I cannot forgive you, or that I'm so unwilling to try.

It took him forever to write these letters. It was seven, and the girls wouldn't be up for another two hours. Head throbbing, heart sagging, Andy could think of nothing good to add and so he went back to bed.

FOURTEEN

The baptism would be on the Wednesday of spring break—this was the only free time the pastor could spare. "You're going to come with us, right?" Belle asked.

"Should I?" asked Melissa, so willing to be part of their family yet so hesitant to intrude. She looked at Andy, a bit tremulously, and as much as he sometimes thought he loved her there were other times when he still wanted her to just stand up straight.

"Of course you should," said Andy, who did not want to sound impatient. "We're going up there because of you."

So the Wednesday of spring break, just after breakfast, she met them at their house for the drive down to Hollyville. She brought coffee for him, hot chocolates for the sleepy girls. They spent what felt like an eternity on country roads toward nowhere but they lightened the mood with showtunes, *Guys and Dolls* and *Fiddler on the Roof*. Finally they pulled into the

Hollyville Mission Church, the parking lot empty at ten a.m. on a Wednesday.

From the outside the church looked, as Melissa had warned, like the shell of the supermarket the place used to be, one whose reach had extended to all its neighbors in the mini-mall. To its left, the Hollyville Mission Senior Center; to its right, the Hollyville Mission Community Bookstore. And everywhere, signs of construction, Dumpsters in the parking lot, pallets of building materials left out in the damp March sun.

Andy, strangely nervous, feeling as though he were on some covert operation, and yet glad too, to do this thing for Belle—he parked in a spot near the church's double doors and let the girls out of the car. Rachel was wearing her white outfit from the father-daughter dance; Belle, not to be outdone, was wearing the princess costume that she'd worn, after a certain amount of debate, for Halloween, a shimmering ball skirt, a cheap satin bodice. Melissa wore her fuzzy sweater. Andy wore his new tie.

"Shall we?" he asked his girls.

"We shall," Belle said, and Rachel agreed.

The chapel they entered was enormous, flooded with multi-colored light—the old Acme windows had been replaced by stained glass—with endless pews on either side of them and a navy blue runner connecting the front door to the vast altar. For a strong minute Andy wanted to hustle his daughters out of there and run, but then he remembered that he was trying to bring God into his heart and that he wanted Belle and Rachel to do so as well, and, moreover, they had schlepped all the way here. And Melissa, at his side—she seemed right at home here. If he concentrated on her, maybe she could make him feel almost at home?

They moved up the carpet toward the altar, Melissa in the lead, and a jovial man bounced through the pews toward them. Andy recognized the comb-over, the Hawaiian shirt. "Pastor Cling," he said.

"Professor Waite, what an honor," he said. "Melissa has told me so much about you."

"Only good things," Melissa said, as the pastor pulled her to his side for a half hug.

"I've read your book," Andy said. "It was inspiring."

"Ah," said the man, bigger than Andy would have expected, almost bearlike. He waved his hand in front of his face in a modest gesture, then ruffled Melissa's hair with one of his paws. "You're the academic, sir. I'm just a humble servant of God. And Melissa has told me you're quite a big deal, isn't that right? You're a biology professor?"

"Well," Andy said, thinking of Rosenblum: *a half-ass school you gotta admit.* Belle took a step backward into his legs. Rachel lifted a book from one of the pews and wrinkled her nose at it. For a moment, there was nothing to say, and again, the instinct to run. But no. "So how does this work?"

"It's a simple enough process," Pastor Cling said. "Happens

all around the world, thousands of times a day. That's one of the beauties of baptism, that it's a universal blessing. Some cultures, as you probably know, immerse the baptismal candidate, while others, like we do, just use a symbolic sprinkle of water. Point's the same — the baptism washes away sin, allows you to become clean in front of God. Usually we have baptisms in front of a big group — you want your community to witness you — but in this case, I think we have a good group of witnesses right here. Your family, your friends, and God. We'll all watch you become born again clean."

"Okay," said Andy, although Belle — hadn't she been born clean? When had his little girl ever sinned?

"But first I want to ask a few questions of your daughter, here, if that's okay with everyone."

"Belle," Andy asked, "is that okay?" She nodded that it was.

Pastor Cling bent down with his hands on his knees so that he could look Belle straight on. He was probably fifty, with a shiny reddish complexion and kind brown eyes. The accent was hard to place — not Southern, exactly, but drawling, or folksy; he sounded to Andy like a Republican candidate. Which maybe he was, or one day could be. He put his hands on Belle's round shoulders. He said a few things to her that were hard to hear, then he spoke again more loudly.

"Belle, let me ask you — do you promise, here, in front of your friends and family, in front of God, to try to do what's right and try not to do what's wrong?"

Belle nodded somberly. "I do."

"And do you promise to try to understand God's path for you and follow that path?"

Oh Lord, what had he done? Forcing God on these girls—it seemed so absurd, so self-indulgent, except that Belle was smiling broadly. "Yes," she said. She made eye contact with Andy. She wanted him to be proud. "Very much."

"And not follow the devil?"

"No, never," said Belle. And Rachel was shaking her head in agreement. "Never."

"Then we're all set," Pastor Cling said. "You're ready to be baptized." Belle turned and smiled at them, then followed Pastor Cling up to the altar. The rest of them followed two steps behind.

Behind the blond-wood pulpit, in a pool of stained-glass light, a table was set with a silver bowl. "Now, in some denominations, the baptism can be a fancy thing, with lots of Latin and fooling around," said Pastor Cling, "but that's not how we do things here. Instead, I'm going to say a few words and sprinkle water on your head three times, once for the Father, once for the Son, and once for the Holy Ghost. Just a sprinkle. That okay with you?"

Belle nodded. "I thought I was going to have to dive into a swimming pool. That's what someone at school had to do."

"Nah," Pastor Cling said. "Like I said, we don't go in for that kind of stuff here at Hollyville."

He ushered Belle into the pool of light, and gently turned her chin up so that her forehead tilted back. The silver net of her princess gown caught the light and shimmered. The pastor dipped his fingers into the bowl. "You ready, Belle?"

"I'm ready," she said, and despite his reservations, Andy felt chills.

"I hereby baptize you, Belle Louisa Waite, in the name of the Father, the Son, and the Holy Ghost." He sprinkled the water on Belle's small smooth forehead three times. Her eyes were closed. The water beaded and fell down her face, but she kept her neck tilted, as though looking at the sky.

"And I would like to add, if I may," Pastor Cling said, his hands now on Belle's shoulders, "I would like to add that Belle, you are a truly lucky young girl, for you were born to a family that loves you, and you are now part of God's family too. When you need protection, when you need reassurance, you will always be able to turn to your family, and turn to God. You will never be alone."

Melissa, beside him, squeezed a tissue into Andy's hand.

"I know that life has dealt you some unfair blows, and that you must miss your mother something awful. I can only imagine what it is for a young girl to grow up without her mom."

Andy put his arm around Rachel. Was the water dripping on his daughter's face baptismal? Tears? He wrapped Melissa's tissue in his fist. He wanted to dry Belle's face.

"But if I know anything in the world, I know this. Your

mother is with God right now, and she is watching you. She knows that you have been baptized in his name, and she knows that when your long and wonderful life is over, she will take you in her arms again, and that you and she will live together, in eternity, in God's house."

Pastor Cling bent down again, so that he could look at Belle squarely. He tipped her face down toward him, and Andy thought he had never seen Belle look so understanding, so wise—so old. "And listen, Belle, there's something else you should know. This God who loves you is a God of love and kindness and mercy. If you make a mistake in your life—and of course you will, for you're a human being, a little girl—if and when you make mistakes, know that God loves you anyway. God knows your good heart, Belle. His love is merciful and unconditional."

Merciful and unconditional.

Andy felt snapped like a rubber band.

Who was this God? Hadn't Melissa said that God was foremost a God of justice? Isn't that what he'd asked her, and that's what she said? Hadn't she repeated it in his office, God is just? And there she stood in that chapel, beaming at him and his daughter.

Which one was it, Melissa? Justice or mercy?

Pastor Cling touched Belle's forehead again, and the spot where he touched her glistened. He had anointed her with oil.

Justice or mercy? Justice or mercy? No, no, he told himself— it could not be both.

Belle wasn't crying, but Andy could feel his own eyes start to prickle, and this worried him. He did not cry in front of his daughters. He hid his eyes behind a tissue.

And who was he crying for, anyway? His daughter? His dead wife? Oliver McGee? Oliver's mother? Rosenblum? Himself?

"Okay, Belle. Congratulations." The pastor picked a small square of paper off the table next to the bowl of water, and handed it to Andy. "This is Belle's baptismal certificate. Keep it in a special place."

Andy blotted his eyes. "I will," he said. He shook Pastor Cling's hand. This God was a merciful God. He wanted to live in God's image. He wanted God to stay near him, to keep Lou near him. He didn't want to lose what he had worked so hard to gain. This God understood him. This God took pity on him, on his poor wretched soul.

"And if you ever want to come back—"

"Thank you, Pastor—"

"Please do come back." The pastor walked them out into the sunshine. "Melissa will tell you, our doors are always open."

And so, with a hug for Melissa, and a hug for Rachel and Belle, and another handshake for Andy, the pastor retreated back into the church, leaving the four of them on the sidewalk in front of the church where shopping carts used to idle.

"What should we do now?" Rachel asked. "Philadelphia, maybe?"

"Absecon!" Belle said. "I want lobster!"

"You do?" Andy said. The sunlight felt too bright. "Since when do you like lobster?" He shielded his eyes from the sun.

"Ever since we had it at Jeremy's house," Belle said.

"You liked that?"

"I loved it! They were so good!"

Rachel let out an annoyed sigh, but Belle was unstoppable. "Please, Dad? You said it was my special day."

The voices wouldn't stop. Once upon a time it had only been Lou, but now it was a whole chorus. He had invited God in but instead of hearing God all he heard was this chorus.

Melissa, sitting next to Andy in the front seat, wore the look of disquiet that he imagined was on his own face.

"Are you okay?"

She had said God was just. Rosenblum had said God was to protect us from the dead. From our fear of the dead. Oliver was going to rot in jail. Joyce McGee was losing her only son.

"Come on, Dad, start the car. I want lobster."

"Dad, what's wrong with you?"

"But you *said.* "

Mechanically, silently, he found his way to the Garden State Parkway, to the exit for Absecon, just across the bay from Atlantic City. He had done nothing wrong. He had done nothing wrong. And yet the guilt was heavy like a stone.

"Keep going," Melissa murmured, as they passed signs on

Route 9 for the beach. He realized that he hadn't heard her voice the entire drive.

"Where are we going, Dad?"

"To the ocean," Melissa said, turning around to answer. "After that we can go get lunch."

Mechanically, silently, he followed the signs. He parked in the empty parking lot by the beach. "What now?" he asked Melissa.

"Get out of the car."

The sky was brilliant and the air less chilly than it had been in Hollyville, but the breeze brought in a frosty kick of salt. He followed Melissa out of the car, and the girls followed him. When Melissa took off her shoes by the plywood staircase to the beach, the girls and then Andy did too.

"What are we doing, exactly?"

"We're washing it off," Melissa said. "We wash it off, we come out clean. We come out new."

Belle, in her princess dress, surveyed the landscape. Sandpipers hopped back and forth across the shoreline, crossing over and back again the long skatelike track of a horseshoe crab.

"So are we going in?" she asked.

"Don't be ridiculous," Andy said. "The water's freezing."

"I'm not scared of a little cold water," Rachel said. "Are you?"

"Guys, don't even joke," Andy said. "You're not going in. It's probably fifty degrees."

But Melissa was holding each of their hands.

"You coming, Andy?" she asked.

"You'll get pneumonia," he said. "You are not going in."

The three of them looked at each other and shrugged. "Wash it off," Melissa said. "Wash it clean."

And then, with a whoop, the three girls raced across the empty beach and into the frothy surf, Belle's dress sparkling in the froth, up to their knees in the frigid water. From where he stood, he could hear their giddy screams.

"Dad! Dad, you've got to come!"

"Absolutely not!" he yelled, but he knew they couldn't hear him. He thought, again, of Joyce McGee, and her son, Oliver. Another two years at least. Oliver, who had earned his bachelor's. Oliver, who was suffering. He had prolonged the boy's suffering. That was not merciful, nor was it just.

"Dad!" Was that Rachel? Was that Belle? "Dad!"

He walked down to the edge of the water. The touch of surf on his toes felt like ice. How could his daughters jump around in the frosty ocean? But he remembered, they were like seals. They were born in pools of water. They jumped in, they splashed, they washed it off.

He bent his face toward the Atlantic but he did not come out clean.

FIFTEEN

Reading Rosenblum felt like spending time in the company of a friend, and it felt good to spend the night with a friend's troubles, distant as they were, instead of his own. As he read, the style of the manuscript emerged as confessional, discursive, not at all like the direct and impatient *Religion's Dangerous Lie* or the more scientifically reasoned earlier works. The only thing it read like was a meditation, thoughts circling around other thoughts.

Reading, Andy thought to himself: why didn't I know Hank was such a religious man?

After my exile from Princeton, I spent a few years traveling the world, knowing but trying not to care that if the Lims won their civil suit, whatever I had in the bank would be theirs. What did I have in the bank, you're asking? Unfortunately, a tidy bundle. A healthy nest egg. Oh,

why be coy? I had just under six million dollars, plus my
dusty little house in Princeton, plus the dustier place in
Vermont where I liked to retreat, ski in my younger days,
write as I got older. These properties were liquidated
and the proceeds handed to the Lims in 2007, when the
court's verdict rendered me guilty of criminal harrass-
ment. The Lims got my nice Lexus with the heated seats
and my retirement fund and every asset I had ever relied
on, celebrated, jetted off to Paris with. However, because
I'd had the foresight to spend a lot of what I had when I
had it, the Lims weren't able to touch the trips I'd taken
(the Himalayas, Cartagena, Cape Verde, Siem Reap) nor
the cigars I'd smoked (Cohiba, Arturo Fuente) nor the
ex-wives, whose favors I'd once won with diamond jewelry
and fancy dinners. The Lims would never get their greedy
hands on my fancy dinners. But they had everything else
that had once been mine; I was bankrupt; I was old; I was
supposed to be penitent.

I remember that day in 2007 looking in the mirror, and
seeing, reflected back, a man much older than the one I
had remembered. I had gone fat and bald, my beard had
turned mostly white, and when my lawyer said, "Well,
listen, Hank, we'll appeal," I told him there was no way in
hell. I was done, you see. Very much done. I looked like the
prophet my former admirers had once thought me and
I decided it was time to live like a prophet, like a mystic,

like a crazy old hermit in the woods. A man I knew who
appreciated my books offered me his cabin on Long Island,
on the outskirts of Montauk, a place I had never been.
"You'll like it," he said. "You'll learn to fish." I had fantasies
of growing my beard down to my belly and writing my
great manifesto. I had fantasies of coming back to Princeton infirm but triumphant. Instead, I moved to this cot-
tage on Montauk, which had not been renovated since the
1950s, and wasn't really winterized, and didn't have the
right wiring to support a space heater, and I put my books
on the bookshelves and decided I would love it. I would
learn to love living there in the salty air and the freezing
cold. It felt right to be cold.

But what was I affirming? Why did I need to live in this
place, broke and alone? Had I done something wrong? Did
I feel that I had? The Old Testament (I went to yeshiva as
a boy, and it has become impossible lately to rid myself of
that decrepit testament) tells the story of Moses dying
within sight of Israel, but before he is allowed to finally put
his tired feet down on that blessed land. Moses, who has
freed the Jewish people from the Pharoah's shackles, who
has led them across the desert, who has engaged in a half-
dozen mano-a-mano's with the Lord our God himself, is
not allowed into the Holy Land. He is not allowed to fulfill
his life's dream. This is his punishment, God says, for the
sins of vanity and faithlessness. God tells Moses this just

before he dies, the crabby bastard. "You are being punished." So Moses dies in exile, as he lived.

I risk sounding grandiose here, but it seems that I will die like Moses, having seen the promised land of life's beginnings but never having stepped foot in its truth. Anita offered the promised land of truth, of knowledge, but now she is gone. And I was never the scientist to find this truth for myself. My gift was always to make the most of what other people uncovered. Anita died and took with her the promise of knowledge, and I was left with my vanity and my faithlessness, or my faith in her, unanswered.

(When people ask me what religion offers I tell them a host of lovely parables.)

A few people demanded, after Anita's death, that I expound about how terrible I felt. Stupidly, I railed against them. I told them to go to hell, to join Anita there. People gasped. But what did they want me to say? Apology has never been my form, even though the truth is that I have never recovered from her death. I am here, in this freezing cold cabin, because she died. And I do not grieve for what her loss cost me materially, truly; I grieve only for her.

Still I do not think her death was my fault—and this is something I've interrogated myself upon for many, many days now. For days and months and years. I do not think I did anything wrong, and I can't imagine having done anything differently.

Of course, Andy thought. Hank Rosenblum never thought of doing anything differently. The first time he saw him in the classroom, smelling like pipe smoke, expounding for hours about the stupidity of those Americans who taught their children to love Jesus, about the idiocy of grammar school teachers in the Bible Belt, about the losers in Kentucky and Texas who wanted to make sure their biology teachers taught that evolution was an unproven idea—that first day he excoriated more than he taught, even as grad student after grad student slipped out of the classroom. Hank lived up to his reputation as a man whose brilliance was outweighed by his crankiness. At the end of the screed, Hank wiped his mouth with both his hands and smiled at the few who were left. "So I have eight of you, huh? Eight true believers."

Andy looked around. Actually there were only six, including him. It had never occurred to Andy to leave; he'd loved the heat of Hank Rosenblum's lecturing and hectoring, the way he confirmed everything his mother had ever told him about meddling school boards and idiot parents who threatened to fire her for teaching Darwin. Rosenblum was standing up for reason and what his mother had taught him—standing up tall, with spittle in the corner of his mouth.

Andy himself had always been mild and agreeable—or at least that's how he considered himself—and his professors had always been mild and incomprehensible. But here, his first day of graduate school (Princeton, fully funded!) was the man who would teach him to be smart and furious, a fully formed adult.

Andy thought back to his twenty-one-year-old self. How long human beings take to grow up. At twenty-one, he was still young enough to mistake Hank Rosenblum for a fully formed adult.

It is night in my cabin in Montauk as I write this, and night as I imagine you reading this, my good reader. I am typing by the light of a 60-watt desk lamp. But when the pain becomes too much, I stop for a few minutes and let my mind wander (the privilege of this life is that my mind can wander far and wide and nobody asks it to come home). I have been thinking tonight of my four ex-wives, three of whom are still alive, each of whom enjoyed a happy and profitable marriage after their brief dalliance with yours truly. They have eleven children between them and two of them still count me as a friend. Those two still look out for me, and think it very sad that I will die alone. I imagine they will sit together at my funeral, shaking their heads at the waste. If I am to have a funeral at all. I still haven't decided. Who would pay for it? Who, besides these ex-wives, might come?

I would come, Andy thought.

But enough about death! Now onward, friends, to immortality.

The immortality I believe in is the immortality of DNA. Our bodies have been designed and refined over generations, innumerable generations, for one purpose: to protect the dogged DNA inside each one of our cells. That is it.

But if another kind of immortality pleases you, the kind where people live forever, and not just the DNA inside them — well, I have thought about it, and I believe in this type of immortality too. And if you are the sort to take heart from what a deranged old scientist with a long white beard thinks —

Here, again, Andy put down the page. He was just the sort to take heart from what a deranged old scientist might think. He had taken heart twenty years ago and would take heart now. He needed to take heart from someone, and right now Melissa, Pastor Cling, C. S. Lewis — they weren't working for him. It was too late at night, too close to dawn.

Was Rosenblum going to tell him that life was eternal? Had Rosenblum decided to believe? Give him permission to believe too?

Lou's ghost, in the corner, smirking. He hated how angry he'd been with her and for how long. A fight came back to him, one of the worst they'd had after the girls were born. She told him that life would be easier if they had more money. Louisa made a crack about leaving him for the rich old grandfather visiting some baby in the NICU. Andy was just then combing through grant applications, and the joke was unkind, and he yelled at her and went out and slammed the door on his way. A week later, she died going out for McDonald's.

"Louisa?" he said, the first time he'd spoken out loud to her in many months. Could he have her back even if he didn't take God too? Or was this the only way: to believe in Louisa's immortality was to unwrap the entire package, the heavens above, the long white dresses, the angels strumming lutes, the Lord our Father, the crabby old bastard who denied Moses a foot in the promised land for reasons mostly of touchiness.

"Lou, I miss you so much."

In the days after she died, he found himself believing she was everywhere: she was the seagull watching him in the parking lot, the blinking light on the tip of an airplane's wing. And then her ghost started showing up in the kitchen, the bedroom, while he was alone. She never talked to him, but she had such an expressive face that he could tell what she was thinking: Cool it, Andy. Calm down. The girls will be fine. I'm here. I love you too.

"I miss you so much," he said again. The ghost was wearing what she always wore, a white T-shirt, a bloody bandage around her wrist. She had a different look on her face now, frank, apologetic. She was sorry she had died. She had wanted to live a long life with him and his girls. She should have buckled her seat belt. She should have been paying more attention to the road. Oliver McGee had been swerving, driving erratically. She had been taking a French fry from the bag. She had been dipping it in ketchup. She had never seen what was coming because she wasn't paying attention.

The whistle outside of a bird swooping down for her prey. Andy turned back to the manuscript.

My grandfather died when I was a small boy. He died the way that people used to die, at home, in bed, surrounded by family. (Far preferable, by the way, than our current system of hospitals and machines and expensive and useless procedures, and even if we lived a few years less back then, oh the majesty of that old-fashioned deathbed!) I remember a little about my grandfather: his heavy Yiddish accent, the way he sucked on an eternal supply of butterscotch candies, the nickels he slipped me when my mother wasn't looking. And I remember too, he had these startling blue eyes, like the Swedish flag. My father's eyes were the same exact color (it was these eyes, my mother said, that drew her to him at that 1929 meeting of the City College Communists, those eyes that got my own ball rolling) and so were my younger brother Teddy's. A startling blue, a bottomless blue. (My own eyes are the muddy coffee of my mother's, for which she apologized.)

Anyway, I remember sitting in that clammy bedroom on the ground floor of my grandparents' little house in the Bronx, some kids playing stickball outside, my grandmother crying, my littlest sister playing with toys on the floor. My baby cousin wailing in the hallway. The endless wait for what we all knew was coming, and the boredom and excitement of waiting for it. My grandfather's labored breath. A nurse stationed outside in the living room, and a doctor who came, then left and said he'd come back in a little while. Nobody knew exactly what my grandfather was dying of, some kind of heart condition, I suppose — but he was seventy years old and it had been a good life, and now it was time to say good-bye. That was the way of things back then. I don't think I'm romanticizing this. My father held the old man's cramped hand. I had loved my grandfather and felt sad that he was dying but also understood that it wouldn't do to cry. Only my grandmother could cry, and the baby in the hallway.

Still, it felt sad and unfair that he wouldn't be with us forever. I would miss his nickels, his butterscotch candies, the gentle way he spoke to me, the way he folded newspapers into caps.

And then, a few seconds before he finally died, my grandfather opened his eyes — he hadn't opened them for many hours — and although he didn't say anything, I can remember that moment like it was seared into me. Those Swedish flag eyes. Bottomless blue. My father's eyes, the very same color. And my brother's. And because those three were all crammed next to each other in that crowded room, I saw the three of them in the same screen, as it were — the blue of my grandfather's and father's and brother's eyes, the blue that transcends generations. And in that searing moment I understood that my grandfather would die today, yes, but also he would live for as long as my brother did, because my brother carried a part of my grandfather. The color of his eyes. And it seemed to me a fair enough bargain. We cannot live forever ourselves, but a small piece of us can, and will, as long as we keep having children.

It was during that moment I became a Darwinian.

I know that this is not enough for some people, and I am sorry about that. Some people need to believe that it is not just the color of our eyes, not just the texture of our skin, not just the predilection for foreign languages or the long piano fingers that will survive, but that they themselves will somehow live into eternity. Perhaps with their loved ones, and a few favored mementos and pets.

This feeling is especially strong, I believe, among those who have lost their children. As it should be, I suppose. This is why I do not begrudge the Lims their thirteen-million-dollar settlement. They do not want my money. They want their daughter back. The money is a poor sub-stitute, but it is all I can give them.

So now what?

I'm on eighteen pills a day and I take some in the morn-ing and some at night, except for those mornings when I just can't face it or those nights when I'm too damn tired. The pills are keeping me alive unless they're not—unless what's keeping me alive is just me being feisty, which I've been told I am. *Feisty.* This is a word people use for pets and old people, and that's fine. Although I've never been anybody's pet.

Listen, Anita. I was so panicky at the thought of losing you that I never told you the things I should have. What should I have said? That love is important, of course. That if you have found this man who you think is a good guy, and who makes you happy, and will love you and take care of you and father your children, yadda yadda (and even now, here I am making fun, yadda yadda, I can't help myself). No, really, Anita—if this man loves you, and you love him, then you are a lucky woman, and congratulations to you both.

You should have children. Many children.

And also! Listen, Anita—listen to me. Right now you may think that you have discovered the truth, and that the truth isn't in a laboratory like you always thought, but the truth is in a chapel somewhere, or a holy book. Okay, fine. You're wrong, but fine. Believe in that chapel or that holy book or the words of your husband but just keep a little part of your brain (your heart, your intestines, take your metaphor) and leave it open to doubt. Or to wonder. To curiosity. Ask yourself, one day (the kids are grown, the husband is in his study, those awful parents of yours are memories in a photo album), how *did* this God of mine put life on earth? Through what mechanism? Was it really as simple as his Word, or was perhaps the Word a more complicated story?

I am sorry for what I did to you. I am sorry for the world, of course, and sorry for myself, but mostly I am sorry that I caused you such despair. That was never, ever my intention.

I know there is no heaven but now that I am older I have become able to conjure one up. This, they say, is one of the hazards of growing older, but I don't care. I don't care that my mind is failing, and there are long periods these days that I spend quite happily back in my childhood, eating my mother's cooking, going to yeshiva, playing stickball with my friends. I liked yeshiva. People say I didn't, that my life's work was in the main a rejection of a religious childhood, but this is quite untrue. I liked my schooling, I liked the rabbis, I liked some of the fairy tales they told us. I didn't like our angry God very much but Adam and Eve, them I found appealing. Abraham and Isaac. Poor old Moses. Those stories were good stories.

And I loved my mother and father, my brother and sisters, my grandparents, our apartment in the Bronx, the foyer I slept in, the elevator with the gate and the porthole window, the cousins in every neighboring building, the pretty girls, the overactive radiator in the winter and the nonexistent air-conditioning in the summer. I loved them all; I miss them all.

Ah—I'll stop! Although I was just there this morning.

So yes, time travel is one of the small graces of growing older, and within that time travel is, perhaps, a little bit of clairvoyance, the ability to see what's on the other side, or to imagine it with a certain amount of anticipation. I imagine you on the other side, Anita. You look exactly as you did when I knew you. You are small and serious. You are always at a computer. When you realize something enormously important, when you make a crucial connection, when you win two hundred thousand dollars because the world catches on to you—you let escape the smallest smile. Such a small, rare smile! I loved seeing it. Anita, if I'd only had daughters of my own, perhaps you would have been spared.

I kept up with Charles and your family for as long as I could bear. The parents are back in Korea. The brother and the wife are in Texas with many children. Charles is married. After the settlement, the parents decided—please do smile at this—to give the bulk of my money to his church.

And now the end of the day is getting closer and I have my pills to take, or not to take, as I decide. The man who owns this house has been worried for me and has started to send in a nurse, a nosy black lady I very much like except when she nags me too much about the meds. She cooks me Haitian food, fried pork, which in these sentimental days of mine reads a bit like trayf, so I eat it with

gusto. It is spicy and soft and agrees with me. She is very
pretty, this nurse of mine, but I can never remember her
name. It is Agnes or Angela or something with a French
accent. I never can remember, but no matter.

She does not mind if I call her Anita.

This was the last of the numbered manuscript pages. Stapled underneath, Andy found this note:

I expect it will not surprise you, Andy, that I am dead now.

He had to read the line three times and still it read like a
joke. A terrible sort of practical joke.

How do I know that I am dead? Because poor Watson (a
young lawyer and a former student of mine—and incidentally
what does it say about the academic job market that biology
students now turn to law school?)—poor Watson was under
instructions not to send this mawkish piece of bullshit to you
until I was good and gone. And since you're reading this, ergo
sum, etcetera. I have been cremated, my ashes sprinkled
spitefully by my poor dear Watson (I presume) about and
around the Princeton biology department. Fuck 'em.

He read this again too. Dead? He wasn't dead. He was so
viscerally alive! Everything Rosenblum had said, had taught
him—his words—he was alive!

Dead! I promise you it's the truth.

Should he even keep reading this? He didn't need to keep reading this. Tomorrow would be another spring day. The world spinning. The lilacs blooming. The hawks circling. Hank Rosenblum, alive in Montauk.

As for the particulars — well, I died sometime after you applied for tenure, Andy, and I'm guessing sometime before the end of this summer. It's now July of 2011 and I'm feeling like shit, I don't mind saying. The end can't possibly be near enough. Congestive heart failure has me wheezing like a goddamn accordion, along with some obstructive lung problems that I knew were coming at me, but fuck it, my pipe was a comfort that sullen old age was never gonna be. So here I am, dying. Or here I'm not, since now I'm dead. I'm a ghost, Andy! But don't be scared.

Don't be scared. Andy took a walk around the room. Went to the sink in the bathroom and splashed water on his face.

So fine, you might be wondering why I'm sending you all this right now, why of all my former students and dear ones, you (and you alone, Andy — no sibling rivalries for you, my friend!) received this missive, and what I expect you to do about it now that it's in your care. Well, to answer the second and easier question first: nothing. You don't have to do anything with this little book of mine. These pages are the smoke and emissions from a dying car, an unquiet mind.

As for why you: well, of course I was always very fond of you, Andy. And though you might argue that I was very fond of all my students (untrue, but it makes me seem like a better professor if you say so) I also never quite got over the idea that I did poorly by you. I knew about your wife dying, Andy, and that you were alone with those two tiny daughters, and I never did anything about it. I could have used some of the few contacts I had left, maybe arranged a postdoc somewhere. Something, anyway, to have kept you somewhat whole and sane. The sort of thing that a friendly and interested mentor would have and should have done. But I was still grieving for Anita then, in the worst part of the grief, and I wasn't able to think about anybody but myself. I assume you know the feeling, Andy, but that doesn't make it excusable. As long as we're on this earth we should do right by other people. Especially those who have been good to us. You were a nice kid, a loveable kid, and you had a bright future ahead of you. And now you've ended up in that shithole of a college. Well. At least you're not a lawyer.

Anyway, Andy, I hope you can forgive me my absence. I would have reached out to you before I died, but as you can probably tell, I've been a bit feverish. And I was afraid, perhaps, that you would judge me unkindly.

My hope for you is that you have come to a happy place in your life. (How old are you now, anyway, kid? Could you be forty?) And of course you have an awful lot left of it.

Enjoy it all, my friend, and know that I always thought of you with much affection.

And that was all.

Andy put down the pages. There was nothing to do about the cold pained surprise throbbing in him—no, he had not known that Rosenblum was dead, and had enjoyed (perhaps too much) the elaborate imaginings of surprising the old man at home, reconnecting, drawing him out of his solitude.

But the man was dead. He probably should have figured it out, but he was never quite the student Rosenblum wanted him to be. He splashed more water on his face, so that if he was crying he could not really tell. Then he took a cigar—his first one in a while—and went outside in the drizzly cold to light it, sheltering his Zippo with his hand. He tried to enjoy the lashing of the cold air as he stood on his porch and looked toward where the sun would soon rise. Across the street sat a prefab house with aluminum siding turning greenish, neighbors he rarely saw. But they were alive. Weren't they alive? And would it matter to him if they weren't? Did it matter that Rosenblum was gone if he refused to believe he was gone? Could he still be alive in Andy's mind?

Louisa's ghost just behind him. No, dummy, that's not how death works.

Andy walked down the street, the cigar smoke trailing behind him like a dog, ignoring as best he could the drizzle and Louisa's ghost, trying to conjure up Rosenblum's ghost instead, so he could yell at him. It wasn't fair of him to make Andy feel, once again, like an ignorant rube. He drew in on his cigar. Rosenblum was the one who taught him to smoke cigars, in the rose garden behind the math building, where smoking was politely ignored. Rosenblum cutting and lighting the cigar for skinny Andy, Ohio's prodigal son. Rosenblum was undeniably fat, his large head rimmed by a halo of wiry hair, brown eyes that didn't twinkle so much as glitter, a sharp nose, lascivious lips. Porcine Hardy to Andy's nervous Laurel. "Jesus, Andy, try to look like you're enjoying it."

Andy coughed, felt like a fool, tried to look like he was enjoying it. After a while, he did enjoy it, and he and Rosenblum would meet frequently behind the math building whenever the weather was nice, and Rosenblum would expound, and Andy would smoke happily.

Now, Andy walked down Stanwick Street with his cheap cigar between his thumb and his forefinger, even though the walk couldn't possibly warm him up. He surveyed the neighbors' houses, Roberta Hayes who still had Saint Patrick's Day leprechauns on her chicken coops. Sheila's Ford in her driveway. Which was odd, because whenever it was rainy Sheila parked in her garage.

The Ford's windows were fogged. Why would the windows fog? He crossed the lawn toward her driveway, in a hurry. He wiped a clear space on her car window with the sleeve of his sweatshirt.

She was in the driver's seat, eyes closed, mouth halfway open and apparently mumbling something in her sleep. "Sheila," he said out loud; her lips kept moving but her eyes stayed closed.

"Sheila!" He banged on her window, and she stopped moving her lips. Her head was tilted back and a thin line of drool leaked from the corner of her mouth. She rubbed her nose, turned her head the other way. She wasn't wearing a coat. Where had she been at four in the morning with no coat? Why was she sleeping in the car? Should he wake her up? He almost certainly should wake her up. Was Jeremy okay?

Andy took a step backward. It was Sunday morning. Jeremy was at his dad's. And if it was odd that she should be sleeping in her car—well, it was odd too to be strolling in nothing but a worn-out sweatshirt in the frigid dawn. Smoking a cigar. Who was he to judge Sheila?

Still—she looked vulnerable there. She was certainly vulnerable there. But if he knocked on the window again, woke her up, she might have to tell him things she didn't want him to know. He'd leave her be. He stepped backward, away from her car, then hurried home, dropping his cigar in a frosty puddle as he ran.

SIXTEEN

The next day he took the girls—quiescent, agreeable—to school and then headed to the office. The semester was in full strut now, after spring break, and he had his midterm grades to take care of, and a meeting of the student advisory committee, and the accreditation committee, and although the NSF grant wasn't due until next week he still had to figure out how to make his numbers work. He still wanted a NanoDrop spectrophotometer and perhaps a new ultracentrifuge, although the truth was if he had this new equipment he would have to keep performing experiments, and for some reason the thought of this, of dosing more mice and then dissecting them in order to prove his ever more unprovable theory that alcoholics were resistant to behavioral changes—in order to prove that Oliver McGee should stay in jail—it suddenly seemed more than just pointless. It seemed cruel.

Should he have knocked on Sheila's window? Should he

have left her there? Yesterday afternoon, on the pretext of checking in about the third-grade science fair, he had knocked on her door. Her hair was damp, and she looked tired but clean. Her house smelled like chicken nuggets. She told him *he* looked tired, and he agreed that he was. He left then, in a hurry.

That evening Rachel had made them lunches—tuna salad with curry powder packed into Tupperware in the fridge. Andy took his now to the picnic table by the faculty parking lot even though it wasn't quite warm enough to start eating outside. The wind tousled his hair as he walked across the old weedy campus, and he wondered what he would do with himself if he didn't teach here anymore, if he didn't get tenure. He was still, after all, in the first half of his life. He was still in possession of a thick head of hair. His tie blew eastward. Andy sat down at the picnic table and considered what, exactly, he loved about what he did. Mostly at this point it was the steadiness of it.

If he left here he could take his daughters to Ohio, his own mother and the Mother of Presidents. Or he could convince his mother to move with him somewhere else, Hawaii, California. He could have that beach house in California. He could find a job doing anything else. He didn't have to stay here, under the gray windy skies of the New Jersey Pine Barrens. He didn't have to keep dissecting mice. He wasn't sure anymore what he wanted to prove.

As Rosenblum said, he was still a young man.

"Mister. Hey, Mister."

But it was nothing, the wind.

That first night as newlyweds in their first apartment to-gether in Philadelphia, seventeen years ago, a lifetime, Louisa asked him why his mother hadn't remarried.

"Really? You want to talk about my mother?" They were in bed, where they'd been all evening, eating fried chicken from a bucket, entirely naked and planning their futures.

"She's a nice woman, and she's good-looking," Lou said, picking a crispy bit of skin off a drumstick. Andy had never eaten in bed before he met Louisa, never spent entire hours naked (nudity was for showers and medical procedures), never kissed anyone after waking up and before brushing his teeth. Her work hours were odd, staggered—she'd have twelve-hour shifts for three days straight and then a week off—and Andy found himself unable to write his dissertation when she was home (oh, to be naked, eating fried chicken off dirty sheets, Louisa's tan back) and unable to work when she was away, either—he could only sleep or count the hours until she came home. Now he pressed his thigh against her calf, picked up her arm with the scar along the cephalic vein and kissed her there.

"No, really, why do you think that is?" she asked. "Has she just not recovered from your father's death?"

Andy shrugged. In the years since he'd lost his father, he'd never considered his mother remarrying. They were so much a set, his parents—yin and yang, salt and pepper—that for either of them to make a life with someone else would have felt nonsensical. And as soon as he died, she'd seemed to cut off the part of herself that might share a life with someone else. She'd sold the house in Shaker Heights, moved to a condo in Akron. Sold his father's car, donated his clothes. "I think she lost the taste for marriage to anyone else," he said. "A lot of widows do."

"But not widowers?"

"Widowers remarry," Andy said. "At least that's what I'm told."

"Would you? If I died?"

"Jesus."

"I'd want you to," she said. She leaned back across the bed, totally naked, smelling like vegetable oil and chicken. "If I die, I want you to remarry. She has to be uglier than me, of course, not as smart or funny or blah blah blah."

He was still holding her arm. "A pale imitation." He sucked on her finger.

"The palest. But still. You shouldn't be alone, Andy. It's not good for a person."

"I can't believe you actually want to talk about this."

"Seriously, Andy."

Was this a conversation they had really had? In bed, on their first night as a married couple? Or was this a conversation he wanted to remember, especially as the undergraduates were spilling out of their classes and tumbling across the quad, toward the cafeteria or the few shabby eating places on Main Street in Reed Township? He was sitting here by the faculty parking lot, shivering in the cold, because he did not want to see Melissa. He had not seen her or talked to her since the baptism, and almost certainly she'd come looking for him in his office.

He wanted to think about Louisa, reimagine the things she might have told him.

"Andy! Is that you? I thought that was you. I was looking for you at your office but you weren't there."

Found, but it was only Linda Schoenmeyer, puffy and out of breath as she walked across campus in the wind. She was wearing one of her huge shawls, and the tassels at the ends fluttered. Her face was pink. "Rosemary said I might be able to find you here. Do you mind if I sit? Tuna, is that what you're eating? Looks good."

Andy gestured for her to take the seat next to him, but she sat down opposite him and crossed her hands on the table. Linda wore rings on every finger: moonstones, topazes.

"Is something the matter?" Had he forgiven her for her brutality at Marty's party? He probably had. She couldn't help her behavior any more than he could help his own.

"One of your students—you know Lionel Shell, correct?"

"A bit," Andy said. "I think he's a fan of mine."

"I should say," Linda said. "Somehow he's managed to finagle getting credit two times for your course."

"Yes, well—" Andy hedged. How annoying the way Linda always made him feel he'd done something wrong. "He wrote two entirely different term papers, we had two different reading lists—"

"No, that's fine. It's just he's in my ornithology class this semester and I was wondering if he seemed, I don't know, all right to you. Mentally."

"I don't—I mean he's never been the most normal kid, I guess. He's eccentric."

"He's incredibly depressed, Andy. Or at least that's what I think is going on. I caught him crying outside my classroom twice, and when he bothers to come at all, he just sits there looking like his best friend died. It's disturbing. Sometimes he starts to shake. And then sometimes he takes these frantic notes—at least I thought they were notes, but when I asked to see what he was writing he refused to show me."

"He shakes?" Andy said.

"Shakes," Linda said. She shook her head, cast her eyes toward the picnic table so Andy could see the sparkly blue she wore on her lids. "I called him in for a conference, just to see what was going on. He said you were the only person on campus he felt like he could talk to."

"Me?"

"He also said a few things about existentialism I didn't really get." Linda blew out through her mouth. "I'm just wondering if you wanted to talk to the kid, maybe, or if I should get student services involved or what."

"His twin sister's an existentialist," Andy said. "That's what he told me."

"I see."

"He's very upset about Camus."

"Camus," Linda said. She allowed herself a small smile, then thought the better of it. "Well, I don't know much about that," she said. "Or anything else as far as philosophy goes, but if this student's going to blow then I think it's our responsibility to get him the help he needs. And since he said you were his close adviser—"

"Hardly," Andy said. "The kid doesn't even like me, as far as I know. He took my class twice just so he could fight with me about God."

"I'm just telling you what he told me, Andy. I asked him if there was anyone he thought he could talk to, and he said you were the only person who might understand."

"Okay," he said. "I'll get in touch with him."

"You sure?" Linda said. "I could put in a call to student services." She pulled her shawl around her shoulders, waited for Andy's nod. "By the way," here her voice turned coy, "it was very nice to meet your lady friend. I have to say I was surprised. Not at all what I expected. But you've been alone long enough."

A shot of cold stabbed at Andy's gut. Linda found out about Melissa?

"How long have you two been together, anyway?"

Andy found himself searching for how to phrase it, how to

explain himself, not that Linda seemed the least bit mad—only amused. Why was she amused? Wasn't it actionable behavior to become sexually involved with an undergraduate? And here he'd done it so stupidly, so casually, letting her become part of his life.

"Oh, don't tell me it's over already," Linda said, trying to gauge Andy's muttering. "That's really too bad. We all liked her so much."

Sheila. She meant Sheila.

"Well," Andy said. "We're just—" He waited for his tongue to recover his words. "It's still a casual thing."

"I see," Linda said. "Well, like I said, a very nice lady." She stood, heavily, hands on her knees. "Anyway, do me a favor and get in touch with Lionel Shell. I don't want any of our students offing themselves on my watch." And then she lumbered back toward campus, into the wind, her shawl blowing behind her like a sail.

DUTIFULLY, ANDY SENT off the e-mail to Lionel before he returned home for the evening: Just checking in, wanted to see how you were—which sounded much too chummy for his ears but he wasn't sure how else to phrase his concern. Then he got back in time for Rachel's Caesar salad and homework.

"You know, for a scientist you really don't know much about geology," said Belle, who had moved on from volcanoes

to a map of the striations of New Jersey bedrock. Her draw-
ings were spread out in front of them on the kitchen table. Behind them, sitting on the counter, Rachel was using his laptop
to type away in Google Chat, talking to someone he didn't
know about something his eyes weren't good enough to catch.

"I haven't studied geology since college, Belle," he said,
gently tugging on one of her braids for insubordination.

"Yeah, but you don't even know how to spell *aeolian*. I
mean, come on." She shook her head at him, left for the siren
call of the TV.

"Rachel, what are you writing?"

"Nothing."

"Did I give you permission to use that program?"

"I'm in public," she said. "What's your problem?"

Andy sighed, got a glass out of the cabinet. He needed to
steal his laptop back momentarily, see if Melissa had written
to him, try to figure out what to say back to her. He poured
himself some water, wished there was some junk food in the
house, something his daughter hadn't assiduously prepared.
Something with nitrates.

"So who were you writing to, anyway?"

"Lily Dreisinger," Rachel said.

"Why don't I know this Lily Dreisinger?"

"I don't know," Rachel said. "You've met her. She was at
the father-daughter dance."

All those glittery preteens, impossible to tell apart. Andy

leaned back against the counter. "You were writing to her quite enthusiastically."

"We're in a fight."

"You are? About what?"

"God," Rachel said.

"Seriously?"

"I told her about Belle's baptism, about how we believe in God now, and she said that we didn't believe in the real God because we don't belong to a church, and how we were probably still going to hell, and I was like, whatever, you're an idiot, and she was like I shouldn't pretend to be something I'm not just to fit in. We've been kind of fighting about this for a while. She's sort of really mean when it comes to this stuff."

"I see," Andy said. He sipped his water. His ripple effect.

"Is that what you think we were doing?" he asked. "Just trying to fit in by going to church?"

"No," she said. "That's what I told Lily, that it's not like everyone needs to do exactly what she does to be cool, or whatever. But she can be such a bitch."

"Rachel—"

"Sorry," she said, looking abashed. "I shouldn't say that."

"No," he said. "You shouldn't."

In the back of a cabinet, he found a small package of Oreos, which had probably been there for months. Did Oreos expire? He shook out several cookies, put them on a plate, sat down at the table across from his daughter. She looked at them for a second, weighing the various chemicals and sugars, and then gave in to being eleven and popped one in her mouth.

Andy ate one the way he did as a child, twisting off the top, licking off the cream.

"We need some milk," Rachel said.

"True," Andy said, but neither one got up to get any.

"So I have a question for you," Andy said, when they had reduced the number of Oreos on their plate by half. "Why do you think we really went to church? If it wasn't just because everybody else does?"

Rachel shook her head, wiped some chocolate crumbs off her mouth. "I think we were trying to be happy," she said.

"That's all?"

"What do you mean that's all?" Rachel said. "It's a big thing."

She twisted off the lid of an Oreo, mimicking Andy. "We were trying to be happy," she said again. "And I think we were."

SEVENTEEN

When he finally saw Melissa again three days later, she was the apologetic one. "Studying for finals," she said, throwing an arm around his neck, even though they were practically in public, in his office. "What a drag." Then she kissed him, and he almost gave himself whiplash twisting away. "What's wrong?"

"We're in my office," he said.

"So?" She moved some papers off his chair, sat down on it, slung a leg over the arm like she was posing for a men's magazine. Had he ever seen her sit like this, her legs splayed apart?

"Melissa," he said, gesturing with a hand to get her to sit up straight, but she didn't seem to understand. How would he feel if Rachel came into her professor's office (Rachel, only seven and a half years from college, ten years younger than Melissa) and sat right down and spread her legs like this? He would kill her, that's what he would do. He would ground her until the end of time.

"What, are you sick of me?" She batted her eyes at him the way she sometimes did, as though he should find her irresistible.

Andy grinned through his embarrassment, shook his head.

"So what's the problem?"

He sat down on his desk near her, and after a moment's thought took her warm pudgy hand. He had to do this. Did he have to do it here? Probably, unfortunately.

But before he could speak: "So I have the rest of my paper," she said.

"Your paper?"

"Jeez, fuzzy-head," she said, taking her hand away so she could smack him, playfully. "My independent study. You know, the reason I met you in the first place."

They were still doing her independent study? Suddenly the whole of the past nine months seemed to tunnel away from him. There had been moments he could remember—his trip to Florida, the baptism—but the day-to-day stuff, the research, the grades, the showering, the commuting, the soccer practices: had any of this even happened? He ran a hand through his hair to make sure it was still there.

"Are you okay?"

"I just—I've been sort of out of it lately," he said. Maybe he was wrong about Melissa. Maybe she really could understand him. This was how he felt after Lou died: unsure about everything, about who he was supposed to be and what he knew. Melissa was looking at him, concerned. "I've been having a hard time with my focus," he said.

"Are you sick?"

"I'm not sick."

"Because my uncle, for a long time, he had all these problems focusing and concentrating and then it turned out he had Lou Gehrig's disease." She smiled, abashed. "Not that I think you have Lou Gehrig's disease."

"Melissa, look, I'm not sure we should keep doing whatever we've been doing," he said, but she wasn't listening, or if she was she was going to pretend she wasn't. She was riffling through her backpack, retrieving a large white binder. Written on the cover, in marker: The Proof of God's Hand, an Independent Study, Written in Conjunction with Andrew Waite, PhD, by Melissa Anne Potter, April 15, 2012.

"Your independent study," he said, weakly.

"Do you like the title?"

He took it in his hands. It was heavy: the expensive brand of binder. He flipped it open, thirty pages, with a table of contents listing things like "The Human Eye" and "The Paradox of Nothing."

"But did we ever really work on intelligent design together?" he said. "I mean, did we really write this in conjunction?"

"Well, I guess we didn't really *write* it together," she said. She looked guilty. "I could change that title if you want. Maybe just 'written under the auspices' or something like that."

"No," Andy said. He put the binder down. "What I mean is that I can't remember us ever really talking about intelligent design together. I don't remember ever going through the facts of intelligent design, trying to pin them down and prove them."

"Are you serious?" Melissa said. "We talked about God forever. We went to church together!"

"Yes, but I don't think I—did you ever explain it to me?"

She looked at him, blank and worried.

"I just don't think I did a very good job of challenging you," he said.

"That's because you didn't want to challenge me. I convinced you of God's design," she said. "Or my books did. Or Pastor Cling. I shouldn't really take the credit," she said. "But we came to an understanding of what God's design is. We both did. You read the books!"

She was a wide girl with a wide-open face, open gray eyes framed in thin lashes. Her bushy hair in a ponytail, her cross resting comfortably beneath her clavicle. She had brought her legs back together and was now sitting primly, her hands nervously clenched on her lap. She was a good person, a sweet person, and he had failed her in more ways than he could count.

"I just don't even know if we ever properly defined intelligent design," Andy said.

"It's all here," she said. "In my paper. I defined my terms, of course I did." The space between her eyes wrinkled. "I don't understand what the problem is, Andy. We talked through all this stuff. Remember? We talked about images of God, and about the way God has a design for each of us, and we talked about vindictiveness and justice—"

That old decrepit testament.

"We talked about the way God is watching over each of us."

"Right, but in terms of the design of human beings—I just don't remember doing any adequate research into that with you. I don't remember doing any interrogation. If we had—if we had I don't think I'd be able to sign off on this paper, Melissa."

"Excuse me?"

"I'm sorry. But nothing we talked about convinced me that God, or an Intelligent Designer, specifically planned out the biological function of each living thing."

"You've got to be kidding me," she said. She sat back in her chair. "Where is this coming from? Are you mad because I bought your daughters those clothes?"

"What proof did you use? What scientific proof?"

"Are you mad about something else?"

"No, Melissa—I'm just trying to do my job. I didn't do a very good job by you, I'm afraid, and I'm trying to make it up to you now. I can't let you turn in this paper without ever directly interrogating you on the science behind it."

"The eye, remember?" Her cheeks were turning flushed. "We talked about the animal eye? About the way that the eye is so complex that there is no way it could have spontaneously appeared, because light-sensitive cells wouldn't evolve into the rods and cones necessary to the function of the eye, remember?"

"Why wouldn't they?" asked Andy, who had no recollection of this conversation.

"What do you mean?"

"I mean, in your paper—did you explain why this wouldn't happen? Why light cells wouldn't evolve into rods and cones?"

"Of course I did! Because they're too complicated. I quoted all those books you read. Those books you said you loved."

"Melissa, don't cry."

"I'm not crying—I just—" But she was crying; she wiped an eye with one of her soft wide arms. "I just don't understand why you're being like this all of the sudden. We went on this spiritual journey together this year and you're acting like it didn't happen."

The blue of my grandfather's eyes.

Melissa's eyes flooded again, and again she wiped at them dumbly with her arm. Andy wasn't sure how he had let this happen, how he had taken everything this undergraduate had to give and left her like this. How he had failed her. How grief never went away, only changed. Yet it always felt so much like fear.

"What about nothing?" Melissa sniffled.

"Nothing?"

"The paradox of nothing," she said. "That's another one of my major points, that physicists all agree that there is no such thing as nothing, but if there's no nothing, then where did we come from? We must have come from something. And that something is the higher power. Right? Back before the big bang, there was something. And something was God."

Andy thought of his mice, the mice that were supposed to be turned into drunks. He could not finish the grant based on what was *supposed* to happen; he could finish his grant based only on what really did happen. And what really did happen was that some of his mice were drinking and some of them weren't and he still had no idea why. There was no disputing it; he didn't know. He needed proof. That's what science was. Asking questions and figuring out the answers based on measurable facts.

"Where's your proof, Melissa?"

"Jesus, Andy, where's yours?"

"Melissa," he said, quietly, "it's *your* paper."

She squeezed her eyes shut for a moment, then opened them. "Does this mean I'm not going to get credit?"

"Look, of course I'll give you credit. You did write something for me."

"Yeah, but clearly it's not a paper you're going to accept. And I don't want you to give me credit out of mercy." She took a breath. "I mean I want you to do it because you believe in my project. I want to convince you. That's what I'm here to do. That's what I came to Exton Reed for. I'm convinced of it. I know it. I came here to show you the light."

"Me?"

"Lionel Shell challenged me, and I did it, I proved it. I got you. For a moment you believed in God."

Lionel Shell challenged her. "You took me on as a dare?"

"It wasn't a dare, exactly—"

"You took me on because—"

"Because I wanted to save your soul!" she said. "Because I knew you were a single dad and you had this miserable look on your face and Lionel told me that whenever he saw you, you looked like you'd just seen a ghost! And we agreed that it would be the right thing to do—the *Christian* thing to do—to try to get you to see the light of God's truth. And you saw it! Don't pretend you didn't!"

"Melissa—" Without thinking, he reached for her hand.

"Don't touch me!"

The air in his office was still. She looked glumly out the window. Outside, the sun was finally shining down on the campus, the former Exton Ladies' Institute of Reed Township gussied up in the sunshine. A few hardy groundskeepers were tending to the lilac beds that sprouted near the Student

Union, and the manurish funk of mulch wafted up to Andy's office.

"I just don't understand how you could have baptized Belle if you don't believe."

"I've been searching for something for a long time, Melissa. I was hoping God was it."

She sniffled again.

"But I don't believe that God created biological life on earth. I wanted to—or at least I wanted to hand God responsibility for that, for a lot of things—but I don't think I can. It still doesn't make sense to me."

"I don't understand you," Melissa said.

Andy couldn't figure out what else to say.

"You took advantage of me," she said.

"You were trying to take advantage of me."

"No," she said. "No. I was trying to *help* you. Maybe even to save you. And then you took advantage of my innocence."

"Is that really the way you see it?"

"You're such a disappointment."

"I'm sorry, Melissa."

They sat like that for a few more minutes, on the chairs in his ratty office, and Andy found his eyes drawn to the seagulls circling outside his window—they were so close to the ocean—and thinking about his mice downstairs, and how there were still so many things left to figure out. Which was his job as a scientist. Which was why, a million years ago, he had gone to the pond with his mother and collected paramecia. Why he had started to learn the world.

"Andy? You there?" Rosemary opened his door, saw he was with Melissa (busted again with Melissa!), made an apologetic murmur. Maybe he would pick some lilacs for Rosemary. She certainly worked hard enough, and he wasn't sure he ever really thanked her for everything, her discretion. "Some mail came in for you, I thought I'd drop it off."

She handed him a letter, a cancelled stamp in its corner.

"You can open that," Melissa said. "I'll go."

"No, stay," he said. It was his duty to finish this conversation. He would not let Melissa go before doing well by her, although he had no idea how to do well by her. Probably the right thing to do would have been to send her away the first time they'd met.

"I want to withdraw my study," she said. "I don't know if that's possible or not, but I'd like to try."

"Melissa, I'll pass you."

"I didn't come here to get passed," she said, quietly. "I came here to change minds. To change your mind. And you're telling me your mind will never be changed, so I don't see what the point is of me turning in this paper."

"Please," he said, "let me read it."

"I'd rather not," she said. She took the binder, stuck it back into her backpack. "I'll see Professor Schoenmeyer about withdrawing."

"That's not necessary."

She pressed her lips together. "I'm also going to have to tell her about the inappropriate relationship we had. I don't think it would be responsible of me to just let that go."

"I understand."

"You do?" she said. "You understand?"

"Yes." She was always going to be his out from this life, just not in the way she imagined.

Melissa looked like she wanted to say something, then shook her head, shaking it off. "Tell your girls I said hi," she said. Then she stood, humped her backpack onto her back, and galumphed toward the door. She was hunching again. He wondered if he would miss her, or if the girls would expect to see her again. He imagined they wouldn't. People drifted in and out of their lives all too easily.

He looked around the office, expecting to see Lou smirk at him. How he'd screwed it up this time without her. Hurt this girl, hurt someone who mattered to him. Probably lost his job too. "Lou, what you got for me?" But she wasn't in the office. Outside, the seagulls were circling, narrowing in on an errant package of French fries someone had left on the ground.

He wondered what Melissa would say in her letter to Linda; he wondered if he could rebut it. Or if he'd want to. Well, of course he'd want to. Suddenly a cold spring of panic in his chest. No job—no job! What would he do without his job? How would he take care of his girls? But at the same time he couldn't figure out if that feeling in his chest came from the fear that he might lose his job or the fear he might have to keep it.

EIGHTEEN

The fields behind the school were boggy and muddy; too much rain over the winter had left them full of mosquitoes, but both his girls' coaches were relentless, and they played into the evening on adjacent fields under April's draining sun. Andy marched back and forth between third-base lines, his shoes sucked in by the mud. The soccer moms were now softball moms, and a few dads were there too, shouting encouragement to their players, swing-batta-batta-swing. Kids in their Phillies jerseys, dads in their Phillies caps and cargo shorts.

Both girls crapped out after softball practice; here, Belle was the stronger player, but Rachel kept at it doggedly, even though she'd been marooned in right field as punishment for her terrible batting average. She swung like she was trying to strike an enemy.

"You have to be more patient," said Belle, who had only

recently graduated from an automatic pitch machine and was feeling sage. "You're swinging too early every time."

Rachel grunted. "Is it okay if we just get pizza or something? I don't really feel like cooking."

"Do I ask you to cook too much?'

"Ugh, don't go feeling all guilty, Dad, I just don't feel like doing it tonight." She sprawled out on the couch, and Belle collapsed on the love seat beside her; they were like two pooped golden retrievers, blondish and winded. They left nowhere for Andy to sit. He opted to go cross-legged on the floor, called Joe's, ordered a half-mushroom, half-plain. For a treat, a few cannolis.

When someone knocked twenty minutes later he thought it was the guy from Joe's and found a twenty before he opened the door.

Jeremy Humphreys. Such a slight kid. Eyes wide, mouth halfway open but unable to speak.

"Jeremy?"

Looking scared.

"Jeremy, what's wrong?"

"My mom's really sick," he said, in a rush. "I'm sorry to bother you but I don't know what to do."

Andy called out to the girls, hurried out of the house in his socks. "Sick how?"

"Throwing up, not making a lot of sense," Jeremy said. He

was a step ahead of Andy as they ran down Stanwick Street. The kid was pale and skinny, with Sheila's warm eyes and a smattering of freckles on his nose. Dirt on his clothes—he'd been at softball practice too, but Andy hadn't even noticed him.

"Should we call an ambulance?"

"She said not to, but I—I didn't know what to do. So I came to you."

"That's good, Jeremy. That's the right thing. She's conscious?"

"I think so. But she's really out of it."

"Okay, it'll be okay," Andy said, wondering where Jeremy's father was, how he could get in touch with the man if she had to go to the hospital. Also, he had never left his girls alone before, at least not while they were awake. But he remembered that only in passing, then put it out of his mind.

Inside the big old house, Jeremy grew tentative. "She's upstairs, in her bathroom, but she's not wearing any clothes. Or she wasn't. So I don't know—"

"Why don't you go up first, put a towel on her," Andy said, and followed Jeremy's narrow shoulders up the wide stairs and into Sheila's bedroom, where he had never been before. The room was darkened, the shades were drawn, but Andy saw an empty bottle of Citra, the extra-large bottle of white, in the wastepaper basket. And he could see the figure of Sheila's body on the floor of her bathroom, which was attached to her bedroom, and also darkened. "Jeremy, oh God, Jeremy, you didn't," she said. Her voice was clear, but there was a smell of vomit coming from the bathroom. "Jeremy."

The boy was crying.

"Oh, Jeremy, it's okay, honey. Oh, honey — " He could see the soles of Sheila's feet splayed out, and that she had pulled her son to her, and was holding him to her. Andy could hear him crying softly, the hacked-off cries of an embarrassed kid. He thought to himself that he should leave, but also he had promised Jeremy that he would make sure his mother was okay, so maybe he should do that. It was probably time for him to start doing that. He thought about that night two weeks ago, how she had mumbled in her sleep in her car. How he'd imagined, for the smallest moment, she'd been cursing him.

"Andy? Are you there?"

"I'm here."

"Thanks for coming," Sheila said. "I — give me a minute."

Jeremy emerged from the bathroom, looking tousled. He gave Andy an embarrassed shrug. "I don't think she wanted you to come."

"Well, I'll just talk to her for a minute, make sure she's fine," Andy said. "And then I'll be on my way."

Jeremy smiled, shrugged again, and sat down on the bed. He kept his eyes on Andy. "How was practice?" Andy asked.

Jeremy looked at him like that was the stupidest question

he'd ever heard. "It was fine." In the bathroom, running water, a toilet flushing, the spray of some kind of room freshener. The water running again, this time for a while. Should he leave?

"Just one more second, Andy."

When she came out, she was wearing a bathrobe and her brown hair was loose, unclipped. Her face was scrubbed pink. Her smile was weary, but it was there; she was smiling.

"Mom?"

"Why don't you go downstairs, honey."

"Are you okay?"

"I'm fine," she said. She kissed him on the head. "I just want to talk to Andy for a minute."

"You're going to be okay?"

"Honey, I promise," she said. "Do you want me to call Grandma to come over?"

"Can I play PlayStation?"

"Or there's pizza at my house, if you want," Andy said.

"No," Jeremy said. "No thanks." He walked out of the room; a few moments later they heard the reassuring bleep-bleep-crash of the PlayStation. First-person shooter. Jeremy, victorious.

"He won't leave me," Sheila said.

"He's a sweet kid," Andy said. What had Jeremy told Belle? One day they'd be brother and sister.

"I forgot I can't drink on my medication," Sheila said.

"I didn't know you were on something."

She lay down on the bed, on her back. She patted the bed for him to sit next to her. He lay down instead. They both studied the ceiling. This one, like the one downstairs, was plaster, and webbed with cracks. Decorative molding around the edges of the ceiling, and a fancy chandelier, painted white with lots of small crystals hanging down in the middle. This was almost certainly the oldest house on Stanwick Street, probably the home of a prosperous farmer or a glass magnate eighty years ago. And then hard times, and the surrounding property was subdivided into a few small cottages, a few midcentury brick homes, like Andy's modest one four houses away.

"Jeremy's dad is having another kid," Sheila said. "He told Jeremy about it last week."

"Oh God," he said.

"I know," Sheila said. Sheila's ex-husband served as sheriff in one of the neighboring towns. Handsome in a brutish way. Drove an American sports car.

"It was just—it was just the last thing. I just felt like it was the last thing I could handle, after everything else this year."

"What do you mean?"

Sheila coughed. Would she throw up? Did he need to bring her a bucket? He moved to stand, but she touched his shirt for a moment so he stayed.

Her breathing was heavy next to him, and from his peripheral vision it seemed like her eyes were closed.

She coughed again. There was a light sheen of sweat on her skin, her neck and where her bathrobe fell open at the chest. He wondered how long it had taken her to finish the whole bottle, and how much she had thrown up. He also wondered why he wasn't more dismayed at her. For a long time the idea of drunkenness of any sort repelled him—and drunkenness to the point of vomiting, and when your son was at practice!—but he wasn't appalled at Sheila at all. Instead he felt the odd sense of wanting to hold her.

"In AA meetings you talk about how long you've been sober, and every day feels like a triumph, even though it's not supposed to. You're supposed to be reminded that recovery is fragile and that you can slip up anytime. But that's never how it felt to me. I always felt like, here I am, five years and eight months sober, so look at me, I'm practically cured. Which I know is not how you're supposed to feel. But still, after five years—that's not just remission. I'm cured, right? And so every once in a while, I didn't tell anyone, I'd have a glass of wine. By myself, maybe during lunch, or on my day off I'd go to Philadelphia, to a bar or something. Just one glass. I was really good at only having one."

"So you haven't been sober?"

"Andy! I've been sober as a deacon! I mean I've never been drunk. I don't get drunk anymore. I just had that one glass every so often. Or sometimes two."

Which was nonsense, he'd seen her in the car, but he let it pass.

"Anyway, Thursday's my day off, and I drove by the liquor store on Route 84, and I thought, what the fuck, I don't feel like going to a bar in Philly, I don't feel like finding some sad New Jersey pub somewhere, I want to go home and sit outside in the grass and have myself a drink. Or several. I mean I knew when I bought that big bottle that maybe I'd have several, but that's not what I told myself. I told myself it would just be one glass, outside, because it's such a nice day. But also if I was going to start drinking again in a responsible way then it would be responsible, costwise, to just buy the big bottle." Downstairs, Jeremy shouted at his game.

"I could see how that might seem logical," Andy said.

"Please, it's bullshit. But that's what the alcoholic brain instructs you to do. Or at least *my* alcoholic brain."

People and mice. Mice and people. Andy felt he should confess to her the failure with his mice but he would wait, tell her later.

"Anyway, I forgot about the medication I'm on. Wellbutrin, it's like an antidepressant, but it's also supposed to help me stay sober. It makes you really, really sick if you drink too much. You can get away with one glass, maybe — but drink as much as I did and it really knocks you out. I've been out on my ass since three this afternoon."

"How much did you drink?"

"As much as was there," Sheila said. She put a hand on her head, was quiet for a while. "I think I got most of it out of my system, but I still feel like shit."

"Do you want anything?" Andy asked her. "I have some Aleve at home."

"No, I think just rest. I don't want to take anything else," she said. She was still sweating, but her sweat smelled faintly sweet and familiar. Could it be that Sheila's sweat smelled like lilacs? No—that would be silly, romantic. And he would have noticed before. She rubbed at her temple with her left hand. "I think I've ingested enough."

He looked at the patterns of cracks on her ceiling, tried to find some symmetry.

"Wellbutrin's pretty primitive, as far as medication for alcohol dependency goes," Andy said. "Within ten years, we'll see much more effective treatments."

"That's your research, right?"

"Well, other people develop the medicine. What I do is really nothing," Andy said.

"Ah," Sheila said. She sighed. The lilac smell again, which he realized was probably her room freshener; underneath was something more honest and acrid. "So have you unlocked any mysteries yet?"

"Just that things are more complicated than they seem," Andy said. "I thought I had some answers, but the mice just refused to behave the way I thought they would. I don't know. It's been a surprising failure."

"How many mice did you have to dissect to figure that out?"

He snickered. Next to him, Sheila sighed. He did not reach out for her hand or even let the side of his body casually touch hers but still he had that urge to take her in his arms.

"You really hurt me, Andy," she said. "I don't know any other way to say it."

He wanted to pretend that he didn't know what she was talking about, but that would be impossible. He had hurt Melissa and he had hurt Sheila, and the fact that he'd never meant to hurt anyone—the fact that he'd been so hurt himself—it was no excuse.

"I'm sorry."

"You were seeing that student, weren't you? Your babysitter?"

He didn't want her to think of him as the kind of person who dated students. He thought back to September, the lobsters, how she used to seem like she admired him. "I got a little overinvolved," he said. "I regret that."

Even though she didn't move, her body seemed to recoil from his. "What happened?"

"I ended things," he said. "She's threatening to tell the chair."

"So you might not get tenure?"

"Maybe."

"And then what?"

"I really don't know."

Sheila laughed, a bitter little bark. "That's a pretty big punishment."

"I deserve it."

"I suppose," she said. "It's not nice to take advantage of students, Andy. I'm sure you knew that."

"She talked to me about God," he said. "She told me things I really wanted to hear."

"And this is how you repay her?"

He didn't say anything. Sheila put the heels of her hands in her eyes, rubbed. He didn't know why he was still lying next to her but it seemed penitential to be prostrate. Or was that something Melissa would say? Rosenblum? Louisa?

"I'm sorry I hurt you, Sheila. You didn't deserve it."

"No," she said. "I didn't." Rosenblum, Louisa, Melissa, Joyce McGee, but the only voice in his head was his own. How could he have left her in the car like that? She could have frozen. She could have been attacked. And that was the crime she didn't even know about. Should he tell her? He moved his mouth, trying to think of what to say, trying to think if this was how he was supposed to come clean. But the words wouldn't come.

"Do you want me to invite Jeremy over for some foosball? That way you could sleep for a while, if you wanted."

"You don't have to."

"No, I want to," he said. "Please, let me help."

"I don't know if he'll want to go."

She didn't say anything else, and Andy waited a few moments before realizing that she was asleep. Conscious, though — when he poked her she said, "Hmmmm?" —but exhausted, which made sense. Lots of depressants in her system. She could probably sleep through until morning, when she'd wake up with a splitting headache.

"Sheila," he said. "Sheila, I've done so much I regret." She didn't answer. He felt fairly certain she was sleeping.

"Jeremy," he said, finding the kid alone in the glow of the television. He was firing rapidly at some masked gunmen on the screen, his little hands moving with unnerving speed. "Listen, the girls are at home with some pizza, and I was thinking of taking everyone out for ice cream tonight. Curley's just opened up again for the season. It'd be great if you came along."

"How's my mom?" he asked, still shooting.

"I think she just needs some rest," he said, then added, tentatively, "stomach bug." He wanted to protect Sheila, just like Jeremy did.

"Yeah, some kids at my school had that," he said. He put down his weapon, wiped his sweaty hands on his sweatpants. "We should leave her a note."

"Of course," Andy said.

They left the note for her on the big dining room table,

where a school year ago he had eaten Sheila's seafood stew, a gesture he had never entirely thanked her for. He would start making up for that now.

"What's your favorite flavor?"

"I like vanilla-chocolate twist," Jeremy said, as they walked back down Stanwick Street. "And maybe we can bring home mint chocolate chip for my mom."

"Does she like that?"

"It's her favorite," Jeremy said.

"I'll remember that," said Andy, who would.

NINETEEN

Then there's the question of what to do with laboratory mice when you don't need them anymore. Feed them to the owls? Let them run free? Treat them like lobsters and take them down to the shores of the Atlantic, let them scamper into the dunes? But he imagined his poor alcoholics without their ethanol, and their delirium tremens, and of course it was irresponsible to introduce laboratory mice into the natural environment, their immune systems were so shot—but maybe they'd still figure out how to breed. Maybe they'd give rise to a whole new subspecies of alcohol-crazed house mice! When future teenagers were accused of raiding the liquor cabinet, they could legitimately say, wasn't me, we must have an alcoholic mouse infestation. Evolution gone awry, like science fiction. Andy rubbed his arms in his chilly basement laboratory. It wouldn't do. So he sat down at the lab table, opened up his laptop, and methodically erased, page by page, his NSF grant.

He would never have gotten almost half a million dollars and he didn't need it for this garbage, anyway.

The mice could go to researchers up at Rutgers, or at Princeton, he thought. Or maybe he could just dose them all into a gentle slumber, or dose them to death and ask the tech to burn their carcasses. Or he could let them live out their natural life spans, years and years of running around their same bleak cages. Years and years of feeding and cleaning up after these poor patented mice. He could make their care the responsibility of some dedicated undergraduates. Animal Husbandry 101. An independent study.

Well, it was an idea.

He'd solve this one later. For now, his plans during the upcoming weeks of waiting to hear about tenure: the great pleasure of dreaming of a new future, somewhere beyond this patch of New Jersey.

As his reward for giving up, he extracted Rosenblum's manuscript from his briefcase. Another thing he was going to do this summer was edit this thing, get it into some sort of shape for publication—surely some journal somewhere would want it. Maybe he could go to Montauk, get some of the work done there. Evidently there were motels along the ocean, and he and the girls could go to the beach, maybe try a little fishing. Fish! Another thing he could study. Or maybe just hand Rachel some bluefish fillets and see what she could come up with. And when they returned from the beach, sunburned and sandy, they would get in the car and drive inland, house to house, and Andy would find where Rosenblum used to live and he would tell his girls about his old friend.

He thumped the pile of papers up and down on his lab table, then returned them to his briefcase, from which another, smaller letter slipped out. What was this again? Rosemary, right, the other day, Melissa, there is no God, Melissa walking out, the end. The letter without a return address.

Dear Professor Waite:

I am writing this letter and mailing it from my home in Delaware where I've been coming on weekends. It has been easier to be here for many reasons which you'll soon understand. I've also wanted to see my sister I mentioned she's a student at community college here and she still lives at home. She's my twin sister, I think I mentioned. She and I talk a lot about ideas about God and the point of it all.

On the bus to Delaware I've been rereading a lot of the texts you gave us in class like Darwin and Dawkins and Rosenblum. I started to become interested in a lot of the things they said and thinking about them in as scientific a way as I can. What I've decided after doing this reading and talking to my sister is that they might very well be right. What I mean is the more I read, the harder it is to keep my faith in God as the Father and Creator of all things. As you know I have been a devout <u>Christian Believer</u> my entire life and so this loss of faith has been very traumatic for me. I have had a hard time keeping up with my studies and have been wondering a lot about what the point is of everything if there is no God be-hind everything.

I have also taken special note of the Anita Lim story, which is the story of your friend Rosenblum, which I'm sure you know. I find this story quite interesting because Anita Lim found faith where I have lost mine, and yet both of us seem to have been driven to despair by the change in our beliefs. I do not know much about Ms. Lim but her story feels very heartbreaking to me and <u>yet I do understand</u> why she felt she had no choice but to do the terrible thing she did. And also in a world without God it seems to me that it is maybe less terrible because <u>nobody will judge you on the other side</u>.

Anyway, Professor, I feel that I wanted to share these real-izations with you, as you have been kind enough to entertain my delusions all these years and also ask after me and my health. I am not going to come to your office to bother you anymore but if you would like to find me I have been spend-ing time on campus in the classroom where you taught There Is No God. It is not as crowded there as it is in the library so nobody will bother me or find me.

<u>In closing I would like to say that you were right, and I am sorry.</u>

Sincerely,
Lionel Shell

Andy sighed, stuck the letter back in his briefcase. What a pain in the ass that kid was. Linda was right—they probably should refer him to mental health, although mental health's credibility had been shot for a few years now, ever since that kid jumped to his death from the top of Carruthers. When was that, 2006? A while ago, anyway, and the kid had a drug problem, but he'd been in mental health counseling for a while before then and they never noted any suicidal tendencies. They hadn't even put him on antidepressants. And then that gruesome death.

Still, there'd been some turnover in mental health since then, and at least they were a decent first stop. Andy wondered if he knew anyone over there.

What had Rosenblum advised him? To be good to other people? In a way that he hadn't been to Melissa, hadn't been to Sheila, hadn't been to Oliver. Well, maybe it was time to try something new, try reaching out to Lionel, who was clearly depressed and probably needed the kind of help an older, professorial type could provide.

Andy took out the letter again. *I have taken special note of the Anita Lim story. Both of us seem to have been driven to despair by the change in our beliefs. In a world without God, nobody will judge you on the other side. You were right, and I am sorry.*

Rosenblum's death had taken him by surprise. He was so blind sometimes.

For the second time in two days Andy found himself racing out of a room with his heart in his mouth, only this time he had the icy feeling he was too late.

Should he take the elevator? No, no time, he kept running, imagining the plumbing pipes crisscrossing the classroom's ceiling, and how Anita hanged herself from a pipe of the very same kind. Up two flights, three. What would he say to Lionel's parents? His twin sister? I had the suicide note in my bag for a day and a half before I made the time to read it?

But was it a suicide note? *Nobody will judge you on the other side.* Too horrible, keep running.

I'm sorry.

The door to Scientific Hall 501 was stuck and impossible to open; had Lionel jammed it? Andy was sweating, his face wet from sweat or panic or some combination. He had left his briefcase in his lab and with it the building's master key. He was reduced to banging the door back and forth in its jamb and screaming Lionel's name. Would someone hear him downstairs? Would someone magically appear with a key? He imagined Lionel's small body hanging from one of the sturdy ceiling pipes. Oh God, no. No. That poor fragile body. The sweater-vest, the glasses, the hopeful, scornful face. What would happen next? He wouldn't touch the body, he would run downstairs and call—who? Nina? Linda? The dean? The police? He'd call the police. Maybe that's what he should do right now, call the police.

Lionel!

He banged the door back and forth more ferociously, thought: please please please.

And then, the door opened. "Sorry," said Lionel, very much alive. Earbuds around his neck. "My music was turned up."

Lionel. A sweaty T-shirt. No sweater-vest. "And I was busy reading too." Andy thought he might fall over from exertion. He wanted to punch the kid in the smug face.

"You're here," was all he said.

"Thanks for coming," Lionel said. "Are you crying?"

Andy wiped his face again. Soaking, he was soaking.

Lionel opened the door wider. "Come on in," he said, and invited Andy into Scientific Hall 501 as if it were his own room. In fact, he had made it like his own, spreading out his books on the table, drawing the blinds. He had his computer open—a beat-up laptop, much like Andy's—and a stack of notebooks.

"You set me up," Andy said.

Lionel looked at him, confused.

"That was a manipulative note."

"It was?"

"And Melissa Potter," he said. "Sending her to try to change my mind."

"I didn't send her," Lionel said. "I just made a suggestion. The rest was her. And it was in the spirit of love." He took off his glasses, the kind that changed color in the sun, and wiped them on the corner of his T-shirt. "You want some water or something? It gets hot up here, I always keep a few bottles."

Andy sagged in the corner of the room. Above him, the web of pipes gurgled. "What are you doing here?"

"Mostly reading," he said. "*The Origin of Species, The Selfish Gene,* stuff you gave us and also some secondary sources."

"You're kidding."

"*The Will of DNA,* that's a good one," he said. Early Rosenblum.

"Why here?"

"I told you, it's quiet," Lionel said. "And I know I won't bump into any of my Campus Crusade peeps up here. I'm not really ready to come out to them yet."

"Come out?"

"As a bright. That's Dawkins's word for *atheist.*"

"You're an atheist?"

"I prefer *bright,*" Lionel said.

"You're kidding," Andy said again.

"You did a good job, Professor," Lionel said. "You presented good materials, you explained to us the way evolution works. And I mean, like you said, the thing is—the majesty of the world, the way the world works, is so profound, you don't really need to make it extra profound by layering in the supernatural on top of it."

"Is that so?" Andy said. His heart was slowing back down to its normal pace, but still that urge to punch Lionel in his smug little mouth.

"You can look at only one thing," the kid said. "Like take the owl, right? An owl has serrated wingtips which silence airflow around them, so they can hunt in total silence. And their facial structures, their flat faces, help channel sounds into their ears so they can hear their prey. And their brains contain auditory maps, in a way—so all they need to do is hear a faint sound and they can pinpoint where it's located to a degree."

"Interesting," said Andy, feeling sweat collect at the base of his spine.

"I've been reading Schoenmeyer. Your colleague. She's a really good ornithologist," Lionel said. "Did you know that barn owls are the most widely distributed species on earth? It's no wonder, really. I mean they're such incredible hunters."

Andy bent his head forward, rubbed his damp hair. He'd shower later. Tonight: a shower, a quiet evening with his girls. Next week he'd grade. And he would take them to Montauk this summer, before camp started.

"You taught me a lot about wonder," Lionel said.

Andy lifted his head.

"It's like—" Lionel said, "it's like the thing about God is that he pretty much gives you all the answers. You can wonder about God and God's spirit and what God wants for us, but it's a pretty narrow focus. Right? But in nature, in the world, there are so many mysteries, so many things we don't know—but these are things we can find the answers to, if we want! We don't have to study ambiguous ancient texts or, I don't know, wait until we die. We just have to study."

Andy was still sagging. "I'm surprised to hear you say this."

Lionel shrugged. "I'm not an existentialist, by the way. I read Camus too and I don't agree with his analysis of the pointlessness of existence. I mean, he thought the big question was whether or not to kill yourself! Can you imagine? You only get, what, a few decades on this earth—can you imagine wanting to turn out the lights early?"

Andy pushed back his chair.

"I think I might go to graduate school, actually."

"Grad school."

"I mean, I don't know if my grades are good enough but what I'd really like to do is follow your path and go to Princeton. I have this dream—I mean, I get that Anita Lim was a once-in-a-lifetime genius, but evidently she left all her data somewhere and I'm wondering if I can pick it up and maybe keep it going."

"You're not serious."

"Why not?" Lionel smiled shyly. "Like I said, Professor Waite, you've really been an inspiration to me."

"Well, I'm . . ." What to say? "I suppose I'm pleased, Lionel."

The kid nodded.

"So I guess I should let you get back to work?"

"Do you mind if I check in with you over the summer? I'm going to start putting together my grad school applications, and I could use your help. You know, if you're going to be my mentor."

"Oh, Lionel," Andy said. "I'm not going to be your mentor."

"Why not?" Lionel said, his voice heading upward. "I hope I haven't put you off over the years, Professor Waite. I've just been on a journey, you know? And you've been such an instrumental part of that—"

"Lionel, I doubt that I'll be back on campus next semester, and even if I were, I don't think I'm in an appropriate position to be anyone's mentor."

Lionel's eyebrows shot northward. "What do you mean you won't come back? We *need* you here, Professor Waite! You're the only link we have to rational atheist thought! Without you—"

"I just think—I think I'm going to head in other directions. See some of the country. Spend time with my girls."

"What, is it tenure? You'll get tenure!" Andy didn't know if he should be flattered or worried by the craziness in Lionel's voice. "I'll write to people! We'll figure things out! We *need* you, Professor Waite! Without you—who will lead us brights here on campus? Who will be our voice?"

"You're your own voice, Lionel. You always have been."

"No. No! I'm a reflection of yours! And I've realized that religion is a failed idea, just as you've been teaching! Religion is a failed idea, and if we don't spread the word soon then our whole world will be endangered! Just like you said! How can you just walk away from what you've been teaching all these years?"

Andy stood. He needed to collect his briefcase, put away his mice, go back home. "It's not a failed idea, Lionel. You should know it's more powerful than that."

"Are you serious, Professor?"

He nodded, walked toward the exit. "Listen, Lionel, wherever you head next, don't forget you needed God once and you might again."

"I can't believe you just said that," the kid squeaked. "Are you some sort of traitor? You sound like a traitor."

"I'm sorry, Lionel," Andy said, and then he closed the door.

He was unsurprised then to see Louisa standing at the other end of the hall, almost out of sight. She was walking away. He called her name; she didn't stop.

"Louisa," he said again.

She kept walking, but just as she was about to disappear from view, she looked at him, and she was smiling.

EPILOGUE:
SUMMER BREAK

The day after he turned in his final grades, Andy woke up, as had once been his routine, at five thirty. He hadn't realized how this organizing principle of his life had disappeared, but it had—he hadn't been writing his letters, and he missed them.

Down the hall, the girls slept deeply in their own beds. Now that Belle was baptized, she said she felt safer at night, wasn't scared to sleep by herself. Evidently Madeline had told her that if you were baptized, then when you died you went to heaven, no questions asked. "So nothing bad can ever really happen to me, right? I mean, if worst case I go to heaven—"

"Belle, don't talk about that."

"Yeah, but I mean if like worst, worst case—"

"Belle, stop it," Rachel said. "We're not interested in the hereafter." They had been eating Rachel's eggplant parmigiana, and Andy wondered where she had learned the word *hereafter*.

At a quarter of six he was in front of his laptop on the kitchen table. "Dear Oliver" he wrote. For some reason he felt that now they were on a first-name basis.

> It has come to my attention that your sentence has been extended another two years, and I know that the next two years will seem agonizing to you. I have visited Okeechobee Prison only as far as the hearing room, and even that place is difficult to spend much time in. I can only imagine how much you must want to leave.

Andy stretched his hands, cracked his knuckles. Continued.

> Your mother has brought it to my attention that, while in prison, you earned a bachelor's degree from the University of Florida in the arts. If I remember correctly, Oliver, you were a fine artist before your incarceration, and your teachers said that you were especially good at drawing.
>
> Through my contacts at various research journals and textbook companies, I know that, periodically, assignments come up for medical illustrators. If that kind of work seems appealing to you, then once you are released I would be happy to put you in touch with the right people.

Andy struggled with the next paragraph. Should he apologize for his role in Oliver's parole case? Should he apologize for even offering to help? For the awkwardness? The forced-seeming nature of the gesture?

I wish you the best as you get through the next two years of your sentence. If you see your mother, please tell her I wish her well too.

Sincerely yours,
Andy Waite

He pressed "print." It had taken him an hour and a half to write these few paragraphs, but he was happy with them. For the first time, he addressed the letter to Oliver, put a stamp on the envelope, and stuck it in his mailbox to await the postman.

Then he went back inside to wake up his girls.

ACKNOWLEDGMENTS

I couldn't have written this book without the generous help of the following friends, family members, and institutions:

Julie Herbstman and her colleagues at Columbia's Mailman School of Public Health, along with Steve Moffett and Joe Martin of Rutgers-Camden's Biology Department, explained their research, let me tour their labs, and fact-checked my science. The nurses and pediatricians of the Englewood Hospital NICU, who took such loving care of my son, provided comfort and inspiration. My high school buddy, the pastor Richard J. Lee, gave me insights into life at the Bethany Well church. James Brust provided the college motto. Lauren Butcher at New Jersey's Raptor Trust and the biologist Erik Charych shared their enormous expertise. The writers Carmen Adamucci, Elisa Albert, John Biguenet, Kelly Braffet, Lise Funderburg, Kate Kelly, Owen King, Stephen King, Binnie

Kirshenbaum, Rolf Potts, and Lisa Zeidner offered all the right support at the right times. The Moriuchi, Colletto, and Ferner families provided crucial reinforcement on the home front. The books of Richard Dawkins, Daniel Dennett, Francis Collins, and of course Charles Darwin brought me knowledge and pleasure.

I am endlessly lucky to have Jerry and Adele Grodstein, Elliot and Mychi Grodstein, and Jessie, Iain, Owen, and Natalie Kennedy as my shoulders to lean on. And where would I be without Kathy Pories and the amazing people of Algonquin Books? Where would I be without my dearest Julie Barer? No place good, that's for sure.

And finally, for their love and their patience, and for bringing me such joy, I dedicate this book to Ben and Nathaniel Freeman.

WITHDRAWN